CASTING

Also by Jane Barry

THE CAVENDISH FACE
THE CONSCIENCE OF THE KING

CASTING
JANE
BARRY

BANTAM PRESS

LONDON · NEW YORK · TORONTO · SYDNEY · AUCKLAND

TRANSWORLD PUBLISHERS LTD
61–63 Uxbridge Road, London W5 5SA

TRANSWORLD PUBLISHERS (AUSTRALIA) PTY LTD
15–23 Helles Avenue, Moorebank, NSW 2170

TRANSWORLD PUBLISHERS (NZ) LTD
Cnr Moselle and Waipareira Aves,
Henderson, Auckland

Published 1991 by Bantam Press
a division of Transworld Publishers Ltd
Copyright © Jane Barry 1991

British Library Cataloguing in Publication Data
Barry, Jane
Casting
I. Title
823.914

ISBN 0–593–02035–9

Typeset in 12/13 pt Bembo
by Photoprint, Torquay, South Devon

Printed in Great Britain
by Mackays of Chatham, PLC, Chatham, Kent

To my Mother

CASTING

CHAPTER

ONE

VIVACIOUS BLONDE (35) slim, chic, very attractive, seeks . . .

Come on. Be honest.

ATTRACTIVE BLONDE (38) slim, petite, likes Mozart and Ian McEwan, Fassbinder and fish and chips, seeks good-looking, intelligent, unattached man for . . .

I said, be honest . . .

TIRED, DEPRESSED BLONDE (out of a bottle, roots need attention) knocking on 41 and not particularly well-preserved, sick of watching married men searching for their socks under her bed in the small hours, sick of snatched meetings and sad weekends, sick to the back molars of being second best, seeks man, any man so long as he's unattached and will stick around till morning for a cuddle . . .

Hold on a moment.

Of course, when I say any man, I don't mean a man whose beer gut strains the credibility of his fourth shirt button. I don't mean a jogger or a computer freak or a football fanatic or a man whose idea of virility is to carve up his fellow drivers in his Porsche – style company racer –

I'm not that tired and depressed, and I'm having my roots fixed tomorrow morning. What I mean is . . . please, fate, send me a man who is just a little like Alex. But without the trouble and strife.

As the level in the Gordon's bottle dropped, my mother was wont to recall how she fell out of love with my father. This had happened in the sixth week of their marriage. My mother had been preparing supper in the kitchen and my father had come up behind her with, as she thought, amorous intent. She had turned to reciprocate, but my father, instead, had seized a raw herring from the draining-board and thrust it in her face. Staring at the glazed eye not an inch from her own, at the fishmonger's wound dripping a watery red, my mother, or so she averred, had felt love void itself like air from a puncture. Too late, all those years afterwards, for me to suggest it was my father's idea of a joke – while generally held outside his immediate family to be a good sort, he was scarcely renowned for the dazzle of his repartee – herring had never again been served in our household, and a war had broken out whose hostilities, despite my mediations as unwilling third party, were only ended once and for all by his death.

'It's perfectly simple, darling heart,' said Gilda, helping herself to another glass of my Rioja. 'You can put it all down to a basic design fault.'

Jamie-Beth tittered expectantly. I, with half my mind on my answering machine, resolutely barren of messages when we had returned from the theatre (still no word from The Virgin after eight and a half days), blinked at her uncomprehendingly. 'Put what down?'

'Men, darling. It's a design fault.'

Gilda would not tell you her age if you threatened to extract every one of her Dior-enamelled nails, but she used to be an actress and is still very beautiful – auburn hair like

the tendrils of an abundant vine, perfect oval face above a
swan's neck, and long, long legs that silence restaurants
and bring taxis screeching obligingly to the kerb. Yet all
this male adulation counts for nothing with Gilda, who
is happily divorced and cohabits with little Miss Iowa,
Jamie-Beth, also an actress, though aspiring and – perhaps
because of her penchant for unshaved legs and eight-hole
Doc Martens – currently 'resting' behind the counter of a
feminist bookshop in Islington.

'The pecker, darling heart, the one-eyed trouser snake,
the weapon, King Priapus. Just think what a vastly
superior place the world would be, if only the male
privates were better packaged. Consider why women are
so sensible – their naughty bits are elegantly stowed away,
safe from mishap, leaving their minds free to contemplate
more important issues. Men, on the other hand, are constantly worried the hanging tackle is going to get caught
in the machinery and fail to function – or, worse still, get
chopped off. It's an obsession with them. So they take to
prevarication and dog-sniff-dog routines in meetings, they
drink pint after pint of lukewarm lager to prove they're
intacto in public urinals, they surround themselves with
encouraging objects – cricket bats and golf clubs, cars like
fibre-glass condoms, Kalashnikov rifles and cruise mis-
siles. If I were God, I'd simply modify the design so the
whole works was retractable like a radio aerial, and could
pop out ready for action only when needed. Then there'd
be no more bureaucracy, no more football hooligans, no
more war, and we could all enjoy the simple business of
living. But I'm afraid my application for Creator of the
Universe seems to have got lost in the post yet again. And
that, darling heart, leaves only one logical solution . . .'

I could, of course, see precisely where Gilda was
tending. I had, though I would not for the world admit it
to her, once, on the Hilary-Everest principle, gone to bed
with a woman. It had all been perfectly amicable, but I had
been left with a sense of things unfinished, like coming

11

to the end of a jigsaw only to find pieces unaccountably missing. A shame, really. I enjoy the company of my own sex, and in many ways Gilda's solution would have been so much easier.

'Don't get carried away,' I said, laughing. 'True, my life needs sorting out. But it's really not that much of a problem.'

Jamie-Beth leaned forward with missionary fervour. 'Oh, but it is a problem, Dee. I know you won't mind me speaking frankly, but your attitude is one *big* problem. See, your self-image is negatively defined by the traditionalist oppression of gender stereotypes, limiting the parameters of your psychosexual experience and damaging your potential for self-realization as a unique human being.'

'Ah,' I said.

'Like you don't exist unless you got some man dominating you like a goddam mind terrorist.'

'Men do have their occasional uses,' I said.

'But you know how to put up shelves,' said Gilda sweetly. 'I've observed your wizardry with the sander and the power drill.'

'For getting fucked, read fucked-up,' said Jamie-Beth.

(Eight and three-quarter days, and no message from The Virgin. True, I'd told him to go away, but perhaps I hadn't anticipated his taking me this literally. No chance of phoning him at this hour, of course. He'd be at home with his wife, watching something anodyne on television, mind empty, not missing me, not even thinking about me.)

'I've nothing against men as a species,' I said. 'It's married men. And the fact that when you reach my age that's all there is available.'

'I know, darling. But to advertise, as if you were looking for a second-hand washing-machine or a clapped-out Ford Cortina? Second-hand and clapped-out is what you'll get.'

'You never can tell,' I said.

Gilda snorted. 'When all the time the answer is right

12

under your nose? You run a casting studio. Every day we casting directors deluge your portals with male creatures of all shapes and sizes. Tomorrow morning, look carefully at what's hanging around your coffee machine and you'll probably find something to suit.'

I laughed, rising to replenish her glass. (If I got up early I could phone The Virgin in his office, before his secretary arrived to fob me off or he got locked into a meeting. I'd phone and tell him I hadn't meant it about him going away, hadn't meant one word of it.)

I did not, of course, get into The Casting Couch early next morning. It was ten o'clock before, nursing a hangover, I crawled up the stairs to the first floor, to find the reception area next to my office crammed with waiters.

They did, indeed, come in all shapes and sizes. There were Greek waiters, Chinese waiters, obese waiters, lissom waiters, seedy waiters in gravy-stained tailcoats, natty waiters in aubergine bell-hop jackets, waiters with toupees and waiters with grog-blossom noses, even one or two who were waiters from the waist up only, whose jeans or Bermuda shorts proclaimed that their metamorphosis from out-of-work Australian models had been hampered by the need to finish a game of squash.

The board on the door of Studio One announced that Zig Zigeuner of Maestro Movies was casting a cola commercial and that the casting director was Rodney Peacock. Pressed on all sides by bow-ties, Rodney's assistant, the perpetually harassed Zoë, was handing out scripts; in one corner a Levantine waiter with a gold tooth was already mouthing 'Sí, señor!' with appropriate facial contortions, while an imposing maître d' was working out his motivation with a copy of the Sun as an improvised tray. I felt sorry for them all. Zig cares nothing for Stanislavsky, is unmoved by fragile egos and arduous journeys undertaken by public transport from obscure outposts of the Home Counties. His casting technique is legendary: he once

13

auditioned sixty aspirant Supermen in around one and a half hours and ever since then has been striving to break his own record.

Bearing in mind Gilda's advice, I cast my eye over the crowd round the coffee machine. But a few over-heard snatches of conversation were enough to assure me that this was a classic Rodney Peacock casting session and that, should my glance single out an Adonis from the Viva Zapata moustaches, his eyes, far from locking with mine in fatal recognition, would be questing for a nicely-muscled eighteen year old with a thirty-four-inch inside leg. Struggling for my own paper-cupful of stewed black coffee, I forged my way to the reception desk.

Samantha looked up from inspection of her 22 carat engagement solitaire. 'No messages, Dee,' she said with a sigh of pure pleasure.

I swear Samantha files my messages, or takes them home to Penge to line her trousseau drawer.

'Are you sure no one's called?' I said.

She batted four layers of Fabulash at me. 'Only a Mr Jello, twice, for Zig Zigeuner. Nobody loves you this morning, Dee.'

The yellow pad for telephone messages was, I noticed, wedged between the pages of a hefty paperback entitled *Realms of Desire*. On the cover a couple in Ruritanian costume embraced before a turreted edifice reminiscent of Dracula's castle, while the blurb screamed: 'He ruled a kingdom, but their passion ruled his heart!' My hand went casually for the tantalizing sliver of yellow paper. Samantha's hand, too, shot out protectively.

'Careful, Dee. You'll lose my place!'

We stood frozen for an instant, both grasping the book, our eyes engaged, hers reflecting injured innocence, mine paranoia. Then the switchboard buzzed.

I swear that she held on deliberately after breathing 'Hullo, Casting Couch?' into the receiver, that she levelled her eyes with mine again on purpose to make my stomach

14

lurch, before discarding her telephone voice and giggling: 'Oh Wayne, lover, it's you!'

'I'll be in my office,' I said, attempting to stalk off, colliding instead with a gaggle of waiters and distributing my coffee generously over all of us.

Mopped down and seated behind my desk with fresh coffee and a cigarette, I reminded myself why I was not going to phone The Virgin, why the only pleasure in receiving messages from him would have been to ignore them. There are many things a woman deluded by love will put up with, but having her lover remember it is his wedding anniversary seconds away from the point of climax is not one of them.

Yet I had loved The Virgin. Oh, not as much as I had loved Alex. But I had loved him all the same. Not that I had anticipated being remotely attracted to him. He is short, while I prefer tall men; he has sandy hair which usually looks as if someone has been chewing it; there are often ink smudges about his nose and he habitually wears a half-startled, half-puzzled expression, like a squirrel that has forgotten where its acorns are buried. Although he is creative director of his own small advertising agency in Greek Street, and is undoubtedly brilliant at writing witty lines for dog food and disposable nappies, his hold upon the practical details of life, from the wearing of matching socks to the whereabouts of his car keys, is tenuous. Yet, though I have often suspected a craftiness in such broadscale incompetence, there is something beguiling about it too, something endearing even in his cowardice, and in the incapacity to tell convincing lies which had propelled him into blurting out to his wife that he was in love with me, thus precipitating his three months' stay in my flat.

To my surprise, I had enjoyed living with him, had even enjoyed the business of making sure he had clean underpants and enough functional buttons to hold his shirt together. Unlike Alex, competent, incisive Alex, he

15

did not monopolize my time or try to direct my life. He had his own preoccupations, his own needs for space and silence. His lop-sided view of the world made me, too, shift my perspectives; his habit of seizing issues and worrying them like an anxious terrier – anything from Nicaragua to the relative merits of Joyce and Proust (anything, so long as it had no direct bearing on day-to-day living) – induced in me an unaccustomed tranquillity, as if he were generously agonizing for both of us.

But then, of course, his wife had begun divorce proceedings and had threatened to annex half his shares in the agency. After a heartrending fortnight, he had slunk back to the marital home, and for three months I had refused to see him. Finally and against my better judgement, we had made a furtive meeting in a pub in Covent Garden and had agreed upon a clandestine affair – the sort of civilized diversion both of us had believed we had embarked upon before our emotions had hijacked us. But how can you simply put love back in its box? And how can a man who finds the fly buttons on his 501s an insuperable administrative problem be expected suddenly to command the Swiss-watch efficiency required for organizing an affair?

Yet I missed him. And, worse still, he had made me realize what, apart from his love, I was missing. I was tired of uncomfortable contortions on carpets and sofas, I yearned for the missionary position in a nice conventional bed. I was tired of feeling lascivious to order, of rotating my underwear to the dictates of my diary, of always looking just the right degree bright and cheerful and never saying what I truly felt. I longed to crawl home to a frozen dinner for two in front of the television, to no make-up and a shabby dressing-gown, to snoring and bedsocks, and biscuit crumbs in the sheets. Besides, I was forty. My strike rate, even before The Virgin, had begun to falter. There was a limit to how long I could expect to go on racketing around London pretending to be a twenty-two year-old.

16

Hence the advertisement. I reached for my laser-lock, matt leather, executive high-flier briefcase (repository of my make-up, Dutch cap and a month's unpaid bills) and extracted the latest edition of *Bright Lights*. As I was fumbling for the Lonely Hearts pages, the phone rang.

'Hi babe!' breathed a honeyed voice.

I stopped shaking and slopping my coffee, and managed neatly to field the framed photograph of my cat Mabel as it clattered from the edge of my desk.

'Hi,' I said, trying not to sound disappointed. It was The Scorpion.

I had embarked upon The Scorpion four months ago as a means of laying off some of my hurt about The Virgin. After all, I reasoned, if The Virgin could be with someone else six nights a week I, too, could be permitted an infidelity here and there. The Scorpion runs an art gallery in Neal Street and I had met him at a private view. His suits are Jean-Paul Gaultier, his watch Cartier, his car a Porsche, and even the bags under his eyes are probably by Vuitton. He has a wife and three children in Holland Park, and sex with him is like being in bed with the entire Royal Shakespeare Company. Nevertheless, after a brief interchange of synthetic endearments, I wrote him in my diary for the following Monday.

When I put the phone down I was aware that my head was throbbing and that my hangover had reached the green and slimy stage. Now that all was up with The Virgin, there seemed little point in retaining the services of The Scorpion; I had made the date in my diary as if by some Pavlovian response. But then so many of my responses were conditioned by prolonged exposure to married men. The Virgin and The Scorpion, nicknamed by their star signs, for instance, for the sake of discretion. Before them there had been the Crustacean, The Dart-Player, The Ramrod, The Fish Tank, even The Terrible Twins.

I noticed there was cigarette ash in my coffee. Suddenly I felt like crying.

The train had stopped at a station. Not Adlestrop – no idyll of meadowsweet and birdsong, but stained red brick, I remember, and dusty macadam.

'I think I'll get a paper,' said my father.

'Oh no you don't!' said my mother. 'Remember the performance last time.'

'What performance?'

'The performance,' said my mother, glancing at me, then sending him one of those hard, unfathomable looks that were the currency of grown-ups.

'Have a heart, Kitty.'

'Please, Gerald. It's me that has to cope with it. It's me that gets the comments and the disapproving stares.'

'All the same,' said my father, 'I'd like to stretch my legs a bit.'

He rose and, letting out the leather window strap, bent to unlatch the carriage door. Then I understood.

'No, Dada, no. No, no, no, no!'

But the door had slammed behind him, he was on the platform, already disappearing from view.

The panic rose hotly inside me. He had got off the train and now it would go without him. 'No!' I screamed. 'No, no, no, no, no!' The train would go without him and we should be left in this smelly brown railway carriage alone. My heart was pounding, the horror of it filled me until I felt I should explode. I flung myself at the carriage door but my mother dragged me back, making me scream the harder.

'Dada! Dada! Da-da!'

'He'll only be gone a minute. He'll be back in a minute, you'll see.'

A minute? I could not endure this pain a meaningless, limitless minute. He had abandoned us. The train would

18

leave him on the platform and we should never see him again. As if to confirm it, our carriage lurched and there was a sudden hiss of steam. I threw back my head in a howl. My mother pulled me on to her lap and stroked my hair and thrust my toy attaché case at me. I howled and howled. My eyes were shut tight, the tears oozing out painfully between my eyelids. My mouth was full of tears and snot.

'He'll be back, Deedee. Anyway, he can always catch a later train. Don't cry, sweetheart, it'll be all right.'

A whistle shrilled. The train juddered and began slowly and heavily to move. My howling turned to a gargle, I started to retch.

Suddenly there was the thud of running feet and the carriage door flew open. My mother paused in the act of swabbing my face with her handkerchief. I was dimly aware of my father, out of breath and clutching a newspaper.

My mother was silent while he settled into the seat opposite. Pressed against her, I could feel her body stiffen. I continued to sob and sniff and retch, for I was beyond stopping.

'Now look what you've done,' she said.

My father did not look at us, but rustled his paper defensively.

'A child of three! How do you expect a three year old to understand?'

A pause.

'Well, do something. Don't hide behind that bloody paper. Stop her crying! You're her father.'

My father bent forward and tousled my hair clumsily, using a phrase, culled from some Light Programme comedian, which he was irritatingly to employ in similar circumstances for the rest of his life. 'Dinna fash yourself, Deedee. Dinna fash yourself.'

I let out a renewed wailing.

'I've had just about enough!' said my mother.

19

'Stop crying, Deirdre,' said my father. 'Don't be a silly cry-baby.'

'I'm packing my bags when we get home,' said my mother. 'I'm leaving you.'

My father looked as if he wanted to hit me, but that would not have been in keeping with his being a good sort. 'Stop crying!' he said desperately. 'You'll go to bed early, young lady. And have your sweet ration stopped for a week. Can't you see you've upset your mother!'

Running The Casting Couch was not arduous. This had been my design when I had sold my shares in my production company and had gone into partnership with Ambrose Glass to set it up. The idea was that once it was profitable I should be free one or two days a week to paint in my studio at the flat, to prepare for the exhibition I was always promising myself. The Casting Couch was now making money, all three floors of it – indeed Ambrose and I were considering leasing further premises. But I had few finished canvases to show, indeed I had not picked up a brush for weeks. Sometimes I wondered what I did all day. Oh, there were the camera operators and the boys in the edit suites to look after, stock to order, the rent review to be considered, casting directors to be propitiated with lunches and theatre visits. But the sum total scarcely constituted a full-time job.

I thought once again of Gilda's advice. Upstairs on the third floor they were casting extras for the next Alex Power feature, to be shot on location in Scotland. I must stop moping, take myself in hand. I reached for *Bright Lights* and stared again at the Lonely Hearts columns. I fetched another cup of coffee. I lit a cigarette. I adjusted the position of Mabel on my desk. At last there were only thirty minutes left before lunchtime, nothing for it but to begin. After all, I could not consign the wretched thing with its giveaway address to the office mail and Samantha's scrutiny. I would post it on my way to meet Ambrose at the Groucho Club; and then I could reward myself with a long and leisurely lunch and later, perhaps, a spot of shopping. I had managed, with supreme self-control, I remembered, not to buy one single item of clothing in the last ten days.

I had finished my final draft of the advertisement and was working out on my calculator what damage it would inflict upon my overburdened credit card, when the phone rang. Cursing, I grabbed the receiver and snarled 'Dee!' into it.

A faint gibbering came back over the line.

'Who is it?' I snapped.

'Dee, it's me. Me, Dee.'

'Oh,' I said, subsiding limply into my chair.

'Are you OK?'

'I – I'm busy. Really busy.'

'Me too.'

'Up to my eyeballs.'

'Same here. Up to my eyeballs in Meaty Doggi-Chunx.'

'Yuk,' I said, nevertheless letting slip a nervous giggle.

'Thing is – I mean, I know you said – I know I ought to – but, well – thing is, are you free for lunch?'

'I can't see you.'

'Oh. Right. Of course. I understand. It's just that – oh, Dee love, we need to talk.'

(He's had a change of heart, he realizes he's made a ridiculous mistake, he's told his wife the game is up, he's . . .)

'I can't see you because I have a business lunch with Ambrose.'

'Oh. Right. Well, what about tomorrow?'

(Change of heart? He's no more had a change of heart than Atilla the Hun converted to pacifism. Tell him you're going on a three month sabbatical to Uzbekistan, tell him to drop dead, run himself over with his own car, garotte himself with that hideous scarf She gave him for Christmas.)

21

'I miss you, Dee.'

(Go on, then. Tell him.)

'I'm not free tomorrow . . . but I could do Friday.'

(Oh, Dee Devlin, you wimp!)

'Then Friday it is. I mean it, Dee, I miss you badly.'

'And I miss you too.'

'One o' clock, L'Escargot, upstairs?'

(Uzbekistan! It's still not too late.)

'Yes. Yes, that sounds wonderful.'

After I had carefully inscribed 'Virgin, L'Escargot' in the appropriate space in my diary, I discovered that my hangover had disappeared and that my lethargy had been miraculously replaced with a sudden dynamism. I applied this to refurbishing my make-up and spraying myself liberally with Mitsouko. As I grabbed my handbag to leave for lunch the completed advertisement form caught my eye. I read it through, made to crumple it into a ball. Then common sense reasserted itself. It took two seconds to address and seal the envelope.

Samantha was deep in *Realms of Desire* as I passed through reception and, if I looked as furtive as I felt, she was oblivious.

TWO

DEAR ANGELA ADVISES: I'm having an affair with a married man eleven years older than myself who promises to leave his wife. He says he loves me and swears that, sexually, his marriage is over. But every time I press him to name the day we can be together he makes excuses. What shall I do?

P.S. Do not ask me to give him up as I love him and cannot live without him.

ANGELA ADVISES: This man is using you, lovey. Like all men, especially the married kind, he is only after *one thing*.

If he is experiencing problems with the sexual side of marriage, suggest that he write in for my helpful pamphlet, 'Bed and Bored? You Married Her, You're Stuck with Her, So Stop Whinging And Get On With It'.

Meanwhile, try to forget him. Take up macramé classes or enter a religious order.

Remember, if you continue to listen to his lies you will only *end up hurt*.

Alex is a Libran; but he never went down in my diary as anything other than Alex. I was twenty-nine when I went to bed with him, we were together on and off for six years, and he was my first married man.

Alex Power. Tall, charming, manipulative, hooligan Alex. He was still directing commercials then, still struggling to get the backing to shoot a feature. He had a wife, a son of eighteen, a daughter of sixteen, and a mistress of ten years' standing; and even now I believe that what happened between us came about initially quite by accident.

Certainly, during the six months I had been his producer, I had not been aware of any sexual tension between us. Oh, I found Alex attractive – but so, apparently, did half the women in Soho. And true, I had reached that stage in my current entanglement (with Hamish, my last single man) where I could no longer feel compassion for his adenoids or feign enthusiasm for the *Ring Cycle*. But Alex had never indicated the slightest stirring of lust.

Alex's wife was seven years older than him and was called Dido. She favoured ethnic robes of droopy cheesecloth, baked her own bread and lectured on Medieval English at London University. Alex's mistress was forty (his own age) and was called Diana. She wrote freelance for a fashion magazine, preferred Joseph and Dorothy Bis, and rarely ventured into the kitchen except to slice cucumbers for a face mask. Alex called them both Di, thus presumably saving himself embarrassment in moments of abandon or absent-mindedness. (For telephone purposes in the office, they were coded Di I and Di II.) Diana was married to an international oil executive who, when not conveniently inspecting oil wells, was equally conveniently kept till all hours at his office having meetings about them. On the rare occasions when he was not out of the country or in a meeting, the ill-assorted foursome would dine together at each other's houses. At other times, when Alex was genuinely away on a shoot, Di I and Di II would get together for a convivial evening swapping the gossip on *prêt-à-porter* and *Sir Gawain and The Green Knight*. They all seemed perfectly comfortable with this arrangement, as

24

if by common consent they had taken in the feral beast, infidelity, and tamed it into a nice domestic pussycat. Should the creature occasionally growl or tear flesh it was not apparent to me. And, besides, if I suspected Alex's eye of lighting on anyone, it was upon his twenty-three-year-old PA, Sophie.

Who knows what went through his head that evening in Poland Street? Perhaps the Dis had sensed a warning about Sophie and had been manoeuvring to distract him. Perhaps it had occurred to him that, uttered in the heat of the moment, Dee sounded closer to Di. Perhaps he expected to find a different person in the store cupboard and, having mustered his forces, simply went into action regardless. After all, it was logical to assume that, when the meeting ran late and both Sophie and I excused ourselves briefly, his PA would be the one to organize refreshments. He wasn't to know that when I came back from the lavatory Sophie was still trying to phone her boy-friend to say she'd been held up. So I was the one who went to the store cupboard to fetch the wine.

The store cupboard was a small box-room off the corridor that led from the offices at the front of the building, past the kitchen and lavatory, to the large meeting room-cum-studio at the back. Through some mystery of thermodynamics unfathomable to our architect, it formed a conduit for the ventilation system of the trattoria below so that, winter or summer, the air was heavy with a sour, ketchupy smell, like a packed tube train in August. Into this miasma, whenever desk-space threatened to disappear in the front office, Stanley the gofer would tumble stray film cans and video tapes. A model Zeppelin from a forgotten shoot, three crates of budgie seed (ditto), a collection of box files and cardboard packing cases and an exercise bicycle, nine days' wonder from the time Alex's vanity had invented an incipient paunch, completed the obstacle course through to the wine racks at the rear.

25

The meeting, convened to discuss a cake-mix commercial, had extended well beyond its useful length because the advertising agency had brought along a creative expert from the client's Chicago office, with a rule book specifying the precise angles from which Granny Garfunkel's Gourmet Gateaux could be shot. I had watched Alex nodding and smiling, but my expert's eye had detected the growing tetchiness beneath the charm. Now, standing before the wine racks, inhaling second-hand lasagne, I hesitated as to the best course of action – the St Estephe, which would soothe Alex, or the Bulgarian biddy rouge, stocked precisely because its interesting bouquet and arresting overtones were calculated to drive the most hardened palate out into the night in search of the antidote. I was still hesitating when I heard the door open, then swiftly close.

Alex stood between the Zeppelin and the exercise bicycle. I expected a burst of imprecaution about international cake-mix gurus, but instead an uncharacteristic, irresolute, haunted look crossed his face. Then, like a runner setting off on a marathon, he lunged across the yard and a half between us, seized me by the waist, thrust his lips upon mine and inserted his tongue between my teeth.

Partly from shock, it took me some moments to break free.

'I love you,' he said.

I gaped.

He made use of my open mouth for a fresh onslaught. This time, it took rather longer for me to disentangle myself. Somehow, almost without my noticing it, he had managed to separate my sweater from my skirt and unfasten my bra.

'Alex!' I said.

'I'm in love with you. I love you. I can't stand it any longer.'

'But, Alex . . .'

'I've got a vast erection.'

'I know,' I said. 'But, Alex –'

'I've had it for over an hour. There's that maniac in there drivelling on about air-to-fluid ratios in pre-mixed icing and there's me imagining you stretched stark naked on the table, your breasts piped with chocolate, your navel filled with whipped cream and cherries, and me licking it off you, very, very slowly. I'm in bloody agony.'

'But, Alex . . .!'

Twelve and a half hard, sinewy stone of Alex Power propelled me into a mountain of empty cardboard boxes. His left hand moved upwards beneath my dangling bra, his right wormed its way inside my waistband. I endeavoured to cross my legs to conceal the fact that I was disconcertingly wet.

'No, Alex! Back to Granny Garfunkel.'

'May she drown in a vat of her own mixture!'

'Back to our client.'

'May he be choked with his high-velocity icing nozzle!'

'Oh, Alex . . .'

'Oh, Dee. Oh, Jesus, Dee!'

A cardboard box fell, ricocheting off Alex's head. The Zeppelin broke free from its moorings and began thudding erratically against the ceiling. We lurched towards the exercise bike, mouths locked, hands feverish. He managed to haul himself across the saddle and began to drag me after him, hiking my skirt up beneath my breasts in the process. The bike, despite its stabilizers, teetered. I felt his hand tugging at my tights and suddenly recollected myself. In the same moment, my feet, which had unconsciously connected with the pedals, began to spin, first forwards, then backwards, before violently disconnecting themselves again. He clutched at me to save me from falling. I pushed him away. He lurched sideways, catching a flying pedal on the shin. I fell back painfully against the handlebars. The bike itself heaved and began to topple, striking a glancing blow to a tower of film cans. In slow motion, the tower seemed to sag, sway, right itself, then crumble

27

majestically, hurling cans resoundingly about us like a peal of church bells.

We crouched in the rubble for some moments, listening for voices, for the clatter of Stanley's or Sophie's running feet. But the meeting must still have been deep in the intricacies of cake slicing and crumb control. The only sound was the gentle thud, thud of the Zeppelin as it bounced aimlessly from wall to ceiling.

'Ow!' said Alex.

'Serves you right,' I said. 'Attempting rape in the middle of a Granny Garfunkel meeting.'

'Well, when may I attempt it?'

'Not at all,' I said. 'We work together, I'm your producer, it would be totally unprofessional. And anyway – anyway, you're married.'

Silently and separately we disentangled ourselves from the bicycle and began setting our clothes to rights.

I was still struggling with the hook and eye of my bra when he came towards me. He has thick, dark, unruly hair and a habit of pushing it back from his forehead which makes him, for a split second, look deceptively boyish and vulnerable. He did this now and smiled. Alex Power's smile is his most formidable weapon.

'You know, Di was only remarking the other day what a mercy it is that I've got myself a producer with a functional brain at last.'

'Oh,' I said. 'Thank you. Which Di?'

'Both,' he said.

He put his arms around me and his hands upon mine and carefully fastened my bra.

'I love you,' he said.

I stared up at him in disbelief. He kissed me, rather gently. Above the wafts of garlic, I smelled the warmth of his skin at the base of his neck, clean and sweet, and I had a sudden image of myself, mesmerized, like a rabbit frozen in the headlights of his Range Rover.

★ ★ ★

28

I capitulated six days later on a recce in Weymouth. Afterwards I was conscience-stricken. Even now, I have rules
about married men, and one of them is to avoid those whose
wives I know and like. Dido was an intelligent, pleasant,
motherly person whose gravest defect was to smear lipstick
on her front teeth, who had indeed been nothing but kind to
me. It comforted me when Alex reassured me that they had
ceased to share a bed after their daughter, Suzie, had been
born; but it was not my moral sense that was comforted.
And when, six weeks after my fall from grace, Dido invited
me to the country for the weekend, I was aghast.

'I can't, Alex. I can't sit there eating her food and smiling
at her and watching her put herself out for me. I should feel
a two-faced creep. And supposing she can tell. Supposing
she realizes something's going on?'

'What is she to think if you turn down all her invitations
and suddenly stop speaking to her? Besides, I miss you
over the weekends something rotten.'

'Well . . . well, if I go, we mustn't . . . nothing must
happen.'

'Our chastity, my darling Dee, will put to shame a
whole convent of Carmelite nuns.'

And, if you discount a small skirmish in the outhouses
and our taking the scenic route to collect the Sunday
papers, he kept his word. But I felt a creep, all the
same.

Then there was Diana. In truth, I did not much care for
Diana. She had a way of inspecting you from the height of
her immaculately powdered nose which conveyed that she
had observed the wrinkles in your tights and the poorly
camouflaged zit on your chin and was unimpressed.
Besides, she was married herself and was thus betraying
two people whereas I, at least, was only betraying one
(Hamish had survived the onslaught of Alex a mere three
weeks). Nevertheless Alex and Diana had been together
for years.

'It's a habit,' Alex said. 'We're both bored with it.

Anyway, Di's never been quite sure about this sex business. On the one hand she says it's the best exercise for her thigh muscles. On the other, it makes a terrible mess of her hair.'

Bored or not, Diana was quick to detect what Dido seemed blissfully to ignore. She took to turning up unexpectedly in the office and to having sudden career crises on which Alex alone could advise. He seemed to treat her outbursts with tolerance. He said he was slowly but surely easing himself away, but did not want to inflict gratuitous hurt. I strove to be sympathetic and to control my jealousy. Oddly, relations between the two Dis seemed markedly to cool during this period. There were no more cosy foursomes, no more grass widows' evenings. Diana announced she was getting a divorce. There was a spate of phone calls, which Alex seemed too busy to take. Then silence. A month or two later she called to say she had accepted a job on American *Vogue*. Alex took her out for a farewell dinner and reported the next morning that she was enthusiastic about starting life afresh in New York. Somehow, Diana's departure eased my conscience about Dido. I told myself I was simply maintaining the status quo. There had always been Dis I and II. Now all that had changed was a vowel sound.

But there were other aspects of my relationship with Alex that worried me. In a way, he was almost too good to be true. Though his reputation even at that stage was high, he was the easiest director I have ever worked with. Despite his alcoholic Irish parents and childhood kleptomania which, he once confessed, had brought him within a whisker of approved school, he appeared to have grown into an enviable accommodation with the world: crews would put themselves out for Alex, sweating over difficult camera movements in cramped conditions; props men would rush willingly into the wilds to find wax fruit or a stuffed boar's head; in a business where bitching is

30

endemic, there was usually much bantering and laughter on Alex's shoots.

He was successful, he was charming, he was unquestionably kind – when Stanley's cocaine habit swallowed up his bank balance and his capacity for work, the company paid for him to spend time in a clinic and Alex went personally to Plaistow to reassure his mother – for a man who loved to talk, he was a patient and sympathetic listener.

And then there was his dominating physical presence; wild hair, dark face grooved and battered by heaven knew what past excesses of Celtic debauchery; six-foot-three frame, spare and hard-muscled, suggesting the whiplash energy of the dedicated athlete (although Alex's most usual exercise was opening claret bottles): there was about Alex Power, despite his sensitivity and kindness, an aura of carefully restrained violence, a sense of something primitive only recently and painstakingly civilized, which enhanced the charm with an undercurrent of danger. In the street, women with manes of hair and cover-girl faces would fling themselves, squealing, at him as though they were greeting him after an absence of years; at parties they would lurk vivaciously in his orbit, or sometimes even favour me with drunken confessions, in the hopes that I, as his producer, might exert influence on their behalf.

Why, then, should successful, attractive Alex Power, out of all the women in the world, choose me? Certainly I try my best with what I've got, struggle valiantly with my impossibly fine hair, endeavour to ignore my crooked nose, battle with whatever exercises are currently in vogue for keeping my recalcitrant stomach in check; but I am never going to make the front cover of *Elle*. In those first weeks, when Alex said he loved me, I was still dogged by the suspicion that, worse than an accident, it was some perverse practical joke. I felt vulnerable, immobilized, the rabbit once more. I resolved to wrench my eyes from the dazzle and bolt.

I did not, of course. Within a month I could not watch

31

him push his hair from his eyes without an unsettling in my stomach, could not see him leave a room without feeling a light had gone out. We made love obsessively, on the office floor, in restaurant lavatories, in empty studio dressing-rooms, in the bushes of a roundabout somewhere in Milton Keynes. And it was exciting, the deception, the intrigue, the secret signs, the laughter every time we put discretion at risk. Not that Alex was particularly discreet. He seemed unembarrassed to be caught with his hand up my skirt or mine pressed to his fly. He demanded that we spend every possible minute together and work, with its long hours and frequent locations, provided a convenient alibi (was convenience, perhaps, a factor in his choosing me?).

Oh, too-good-to-be-true Alex Power was not without his faults. He was ridiculously jealous and completely unashamed of it. When poor, forgotten Hamish wrote me a letter of reconciliation, which I, unthinking, tore up and left in the waste-paper basket, he dredged it out and jigsaw-puzzled the pieces together, and pretended not to understand why I was outraged. He was, as Jamie-Beth would say, a sexual terrorist; and he could be serpentine when it came to getting his own way. But I no longer cared – I was now crazily, hopelessly addicted. Of course I hated waking up alone, hated the empty weekends. But, come Monday, there would be Alex, the smell of his skin, the ridge of muscle at the base of his vertebrae, the warmth of his body as it fitted protectively around mine. And, when we were not making love, we talked, until I felt we knew everything there was to know about each other. I began, unavoidably, to wonder where it would end. After all, to the single girl, the words 'I love you' suggest a certain logical progression.

On shoots we had taken to pretending to fly back a day earlier than the crew, checking into a different hotel so that we could spend the night together. One evening we sat over coffee and Soberanos in the chrome and smoked-glass

32

twilight of a restaurant in Marbella (Alex had a curious penchant for dark restaurants – the more your eyes strained to discern what was on your plate the better he liked it; I used to think it was a manifestation of the romantic in him). My leg was pressed between his, his hand rested on mine. 'I do love you, darling Dee,' he said.

'And I love you, Alex.'

'I wish . . .'

'Yes?'

'I can't stand being apart from you. I can't stand wondering what you're doing, who you're with, what you're thinking. I want to be with you – live with you.'

My hand, lifting my brandy glass, faltered. 'But – Dido . . . ?'

He sighed. 'I owe Di a lot. I was an uncouth Paddy from the bogs of Mayo when I met her. I'd never had a home in the proper sense of the word. If it wasn't for Di, I'd still be propping up bars and getting into fights.'

'We can't hurt her,' I said.

He studied my face for a moment, then sighed again. 'All the same, I'll have to tell her. We can't go on for ever like this, you and I.'

'But Alex, we already have so much –'

'You do want us to live together, don't you, darling?'

'I want it, Alex. But I don't have the right. You've got a family to think of. And you and Di have been married for twenty years.'

'I'll have to break it to her. The only question is when? It wouldn't be fair at the moment. She's in the middle of marking exam papers. And Suzie's got her mock A levels coming up.' He twined his fingers with mine and smiled. Under the table our knees edged closer. 'Bless you, darling. Thank God you're so understanding.'

'But you understood, Dee. You told me you understood.'

At my shoulder a waiter mumbled.

'Darling, he's trying to ask if you're having the steak *au*

33

poivre. Oui, au poivre pour madame. You know it wouldn't be fair.'

Distractedly I shifted my elbows to accommodate the plate. We were in the darkest restaurant Alex could find in Cannes, at the end of a choc-ice shoot. 'Fair? It's not a situation that encourages fair play. Someone's bound to be hurt.'

'*Oui, monsieur, à la tartare pour moi. Oui, melangez, s'il vous plait.* Dee, Tom's going to Sydney for a year. And Suzie's revising for her A levels.'

'She's always revising for something. Last year it was mocks.'

'Well, it's the real thing now and it's important.'

'It's always important. Next year it'll be university. Followed by three years for her degree. Then, knowing my luck, she'll decide to do a Masters or a Ph.D. And we'll still be scuttling furtively down hotel corridors in the dead of night when I've got false teeth and you need a walking frame.'

'Dee, don't cry. *Monsieur, une autre bouteille de Calon-Segur,s'il vous plait.* Please, Dee, you can't cry here.'

'Why not? It's dark enough. Perhaps that's why you like dark restaurants, Alex. When you decide to have a row, people can't see me crying.'

'I don't want a row, Dee. It's the last thing I want. And I can't stand it when you cry.'

The waiter came with Alex's steak tartare and slowly and solemnly mixed the ingredients, like a chemist making up a poultice. The *sommelier* came and showed Alex the claret bottle, and uncorked it, and waited reverently for Alex to pronounce his verdict.

I blew my nose in my table napkin. 'Oh Alex, I'm sorry. I'm sorry for being such a cow. It's just that I love you and I want us to live together. And you've been promising to break it to Di for nearly a year.'

He put down his wine glass. The lock of hair had fallen over his forehead, but his attempt to push it back

34

was half-hearted. He stared for a moment at the squab of raw meat on his plate. 'Oh Dee, my love. I have a family to think of. And I've been married to Di for twenty years.'

Our first Christmas together. I've always hated turkey – it reminds me of Christmas dinner with my parents, the three of us watching television fixedly in the hope of avoiding a quarrel. Besides, there's no point in a giant bird and all the trimmings when there are only two of you. I'd served oysters and wild duck and out-of-season strawberries from Harrods. Alex had provided Pol Roger and a 1961 Latour. We had made love and opened our presents and then I had put the duck in the oven and we had made love again. And now we were sitting at the table toying with the last of the claret. It was sepulchrally quiet, as London is on Christmas Day. Alex was staring out into the empty street. I was watching the lights of my tiny tree wink on and off, on and off.

I thought of his clothes hanging in my spare-room wardrobe and of the shirts piled neatly in his suitcase although there was an empty chest of drawers, shirts he unpacked to wear and then, each time they were washed and ironed, meticulously packed again.

I knew he had gone away, knew he was sitting at the big refectory table in his kitchen in the country, with Tom back from his stint on the sheep farm, and Suzie recovering from a failed exam, and Dido, her face crimson from cooking, her smile a lipsticky blur. I knew there would be a giant tree in the sitting-room, and under it the wrapping from a great many presents. I knew there would be goose, with Dido's own special fruit stuffing. I watched Alex carefully sharpen his favourite carving knife. I saw how he rescued Dido from the burdened serving dish, and pulled back her chair, and helped her out of her cardigan, saving a droopy sleeve from the gravy boat . . .

35

Alex shifted in his chair. 'What are you thinking, Dee?' he said.

'That I love you.'

He looked at me. He smiled like someone receiving confirmation that his bank account is overdrawn. 'Come on,' he said, getting up. 'Let's go for a walk. I need to stretch my legs.'

You get used to celebrating birthdays on the nearest convenient day. You evolve a technique of present-buying, nothing personal, no shirts or fountain pens, but books, records, something any friend might give. This year it was a book on Hockney, fly-leaf carefully blank – you learn to avoid inscriptions, even in code.

The mussels, the *boeuf bourguignon* and the syllabub had all been a success, but the cake was a disaster. I had never baked a cake before and had taken it out of the oven half-way through to see how it was coming on. Dido would not have done that, Dido would not have needed to stay up half the previous night sculpting sponge, cutting the crater in the middle into a hole in a vain attempt to make it look part of the design, as if a cake like a giant Polo mint was just what I had intended. The icing, too, had proved a problem, dribbling into a small lake at the centre, leaving patches of alopecia on the top and sides. Nevertheless, I had painstakingly piped 'Happy Birthday Alex' round the circumference and, failing forty-three candles, had stuck in haphazardly as many as would fit.

I lit them now and struggled from the kitchen, flames lurching dangerously, a stray gob of mysteriously-still-moist icing falling upon my shoe. Alex was sitting with his back to me, leafing through the Hockney. With my offering hidden behind the door, I groped for the light switch.

'You're optimistic,' he said, out of the darkness. 'In the *Sun* this morning it says the average male has sex 2.4 times a month. Which means, in the last four hours – Good God, what's that?'

36

'Guess,' I said, wobbling towards him.

'It's an edible frisbee, it's a contraceptive device for a female Sumo wrestler –'

'Close,' I said.

' . . . it's the most beautiful bloody birthday cake I've ever seen.'

I put it down in front of him. We both began to laugh.

'Granny Garfunkel!' he said.

'Slicing technology and crumb control.'

'That wretched exercise bike.'

'You had lipstick on your neck. Like a vampire bite. All through the rest of the meeting.'

'I wanted you so badly. Oh God, I wanted you.'

'You have to blow the candles out,' I said. 'Alex, why are you crying?'

'Because you baked me a birthday cake.'

'Oh, come now, Alex –'

'Because I love working with you and being with you and making love to you. Because you're my greatest friend. Because, tottering in with your appalling, funny cake, you looked like a naughty eleven year old. Oh Dee, my darling, come here.'

I blew out the candles myself and we sat in the darkness with our arms around each other, rocking gently backwards and forwards.

'I'm a bastard,' he said. 'I live with you and then I leave you. But I can't stand it when we're apart. Oh darling Dee, will you let me come back and be your lodger again?'

'But, Alex, did you see the buckets in the back bedroom?'

'Buckets? I spotted a chamber pot, two mixing bowls and something that looked like an elephant's foot.'

'And then you said it was coming on to rain. I thought he'd have apoplexy.'

' "Just a few slates off the roof. Nothing that can't be fixed." '

'Mr Thirkettle. "But please call me Roger." '

'Roger, Roger, the DIY bodger.'

'It's a wonderful house, though.'

'Wonderful, darling. All the original stained glass –'

'– and the original ceiling mouldings.'

'And that huge front bedroom for you to use as a studio. I could have a dark-room if I ever get round to taking stills again.'

'I wonder what we'll do with three garden sheds?'

'And a bricked-up room in the basement, doubtless concealing a strangled parlour maid.'

'There was a funny smell.'

'That was probably the mushrooms.'

'Mushrooms?'

'Just a *soupçon* of dry rot. But, as Roger the Bodger says, nothing that can't be fixed.'

We were dining in the darkest restaurant in Broadstairs, at the end of a cornflakes shoot. It was an Olde English establishment, glum with fibre-glass armour and distressed oak panelling as plastic as the flowers. Alex's pâté looked like Play-Doh, my melon had the texture of polystyrene. But we couldn't have cared less.

'Oh Alex, it's a wonderful house. How long till we exchange contracts?'

'The surveyor's report should be ready when we get back to London.'

Ungluing a vinyl cherry from my melon, I paused. 'Alex – it will pass the survey, won't it?'

'No question, my darling. There are one or two problems. But, as Roger the Bodger says –'

'– nothing that can't be fixed!'

I picked up the telephone. The voice at the other end said: 'You're in bed with another man.'

If you are going to complicate your life install an answering machine. Avoid a bedroom extension. Never just pick up the phone, even if it rings three times, angrily, in the space of seven minutes.

'It's him,' said the man in the bed. 'It's him, isn't it?'

Frantically, I mouthed: 'No, of course not.' Then, into the receiver, I said: 'I beg your pardon!'

'I knew it,' said Alex. 'I had a premonition.'

'Where are you?' I said.

'I'm in a restaurant.'

'You're supposed to be in Venice, on holiday with Dido.'

'I'm in Venice on holiday with Dido, in a restaurant. And you're in bed with another man.'

'It *is* him,' said the man in the bed (whose name was Robert). 'It's Alex.'

'Shush!' I said, panicking.

'There you are. You're talking to someone.'

'To the cat,' I said.

'Who is he? I'll break his legs, I'll fucking garotte him!'

'Well. Clint Eastwood happened to drop in, said he had a free evening. And then Paul Newman called –'

'Don't try to be smart, Dee.'

The man in the bed was struggling into his underpants.

'Smart!' I screamed. 'You're the one who thrives on deceit and intrigue. You're the one who wants to spend his life with me one minute and leaves me the next. Five years we've been playing your sordid little games. And I'm sick of them. I'm sick to death of all the lies and excuses, Dido's menopause, Suzie's unsuitable boy-friends, the dream houses that always fail surveys –'

'I'm being torn apart, Dee.'

'*You're* being torn apart?'

'I'm catching the next flight back to London.'

'You can catch bubonic plague for all I care. I don't care what you do, Alex Power! And what I do is none of your business!'

I slammed the phone down. I was distantly aware of the man in the bed hovering, fully clothed in the doorway. I did not look up as he crept away.

★ ★ ★

39

We were in the Virgin Islands, at the end of a tinned pineapple chunks shoot. Alex had booked us into an American honeymooners' hotel, five hundred acres of carefully-manicured subtropical foliage with blocks of ethnically-thatched love nests disposed discreetly amongst the vegetation. To reach the restaurant we had travelled by camouflaged bus in a crush of dazed couples fingering brand-new rings and staring into each other's eyes. Now, at a moonlight cook-out on the beach, we ate crayfish and drank Red Stripe by the flame of a guttering candle. On the shore a steel band played, a brazier flickered. It was, according to the brochure, the perfect setting for romance.

Despite the dress rules, which prescribed jackets and cocktail frocks, the air slapped you across the face like a warm flannel. I flicked a mosquito from my arm and felt another stab my ankle. I was thinking of Alex's imminent departure for Los Angeles. He had been locked in discussion about his feature for months, meetings I had no part in, although he told me much of the detail when he came home. But now the money had been found, the script agreed, a shooting schedule finalized. He would be away, he said, for six months, during which time it was assumed I should run the Poland Street company and fly out on visits. After all, there was no job for me on the production.

I peered at Alex through the gloom. He was far away, as he had often been recently, pondering some intricacy of his script.

'What are you thinking?' I said.

He jerked himself back with an effort, pushed his hair from his forehead, favoured me with The Smile. 'I was thinking,' he lied, 'how much I love you. And you?'

'I was thinking about that house on Clapham Common. We could go and look round it over the weekend.'

'Ah,' he said. 'I'm sorry. I forgot to tell you. I promised to go down to the country.'

'But you can't. Not this weekend.'

'I'm sorry, my darling. I promised Di.'

'But Alex, it's my birthday on Saturday.'

'Oh, my darling Dee – I'm mortified. I'll make it up to you when I get back.'

'I spent my last birthday on my own – nursing root-canal fillings, as I recall. And the birthday before that –'

'Dee, I've said I'll make it up to you.'

'Why must you go this weekend? Why go at all? I thought you'd sorted out everything about the divorce.'

'Di's not very well. And she's worried sick about Suzie. She's announced she's engaged to a Hare Krishna monk.'

'Oh, for heaven's sake –'

'Dee, Suzie's my daughter.'

'Suzie's twenty-two years old. She could marry Rasputin and you couldn't do a thing about it.'

'She's my daughter and I'm a lousy father to her. You've never had children –'

'No, Alex, I've never had children. I'm thirty-five on Saturday and I've never had children.'

'Now please, Dee, don't let's start on that one. I'm going to the country this weekend and I can't get out of it, even if I want to. When you're in a more reasonable frame of mind I'm sure you'll understand.'

I stared at him. I thought of his silences and evasions. Suddenly everything seemed blindingly clear.

'Alex, you have asked Dido for a divorce?'

'Dee, darling –'

'You have asked her, haven't you, Alex?'

'Dee, please, not now –'

'Don't lie to me, Alex. Just this once, don't lie.'

'I have tried, truly, my darling. It's simply a question of finding the right moment.'

'The right moment? Oh yes, of course.'

'You know she's having a difficult time with the change of life.'

41

'Don't I just! She can't wait for the next hot flush to phone you up and recount the details.'

'Don't be heartless, Dee. It's not like you to be heartless.'

'No. It's like me to be brainless. And everybody's fool. So just for the benefit of my addled brain, let's spell things out. Although you say you want a divorce, you have never actually mentioned this fact to your wife.'

'Be reasonable, Dee –'

'You never intended to mention it.'

'I've told you, I need to find the right moment.'

'And when is that, Alex? When Mars is in conjunction with Jupiter and Venus is in your eighth solar house?'

'Oh, for Christ's sake –'

'Do you, or do you not intend to divorce Dido?'

'Don't hector me, Dee.'

'I am not hectoring you.'

'And don't shout.'

'I am not shouting!'

'And please, don't start crying. You can't cry here.'

'Why not, may I ask? In the last six years you've made me cry in restaurants all over the world. Other people choose places to eat for the chef or the wine list, but you – you choose them nice and dark for Dee to cry in. So what's wrong with this one? The moon's behind a cloud, the candle's at its last gasp. I could have an hysterical seizure and no one would be any the wiser. Of course, I'd question the paper table-napkins – damask or linen are so much more substantial if you're planning a really satisfying weep. But, all in all, in my Good Crying Guide, I'd give this place four stars. It's the perfect ambience for a complete nervous breakdown.'

'Dee, what are you doing?'

'Searching in my bag for the key. I'm going back to our purpose-built honeymoon haven to pack my suitcase!'

Sobbing, I queued for the return bus to our bungalow. Entwined couples disentangled themselves briefly to stare. As I fumbled with the key, I heard squeals and giggles

42

from the shuttered rooms on either side of ours. Even in the undergrowth things seemed to sigh and squirm. Somewhere inside my head, a voice asked how I should get a car to the airport at this hour, let alone catch a plane, but I was too angry to listen. I flung my suitcase on the bed, pulled out drawers, tore open the wardrobe. I strode purposefully towards the bathroom. There, neatly positioned on the threshold, was a dead bat.

Stifling a scream, I staggered backwards. Behind me, through the thin block-board wall, the giggles changed, took on a throaty quality, transformed themselves into moans. I stared at the bat, at its leathery wings, its gaping jaws, its fur already seething with grateful insect life. And, as I stood there looking at it, the sounds from beyond the bathroom wall changed too, swelling to the same throaty wail. I stood, immobilized, caught between the two waves of sound undulating towards their separate crescendos, the two conflicting rhythms building, accelerating. I stared at the corpse on the bathroom threshold. Volleys of sound bounced all around me, criss-crossing, ricocheting from walls and ceiling, belabouring me like rifle fire.

'Jesus!' said Alex, from the doorway.

I pointed, speechless, at the bat.

As he sprayed it with insecticide the bathroom wall achieved the climacteric with a tearing groan. As he wrapped the cadaver carefully in lavatory paper the bedroom wall followed suit with a series of high-pitched shrieks. There were some sighs, the crash of a bedhead against block-board, the gurgle of bath water suddenly running out.

'You must give it to the hotel management,' said Alex, returning empty-handed from the night air. 'Few establishments run to stereo.'

I smiled wanly.

He put his hands on my shoulders. He looked, I noticed, exhausted, haggard. 'Alex Power Rodent Operatives Inc.

at your service. That bat put up one hell of a fight, ma'am, but I guess he's given you all the trouble he's gonna give.'

'Oh Alex,' I said.

He took my hand and led me gently over to the bed. Then he put his arms around me, pressing me to his chest, cradling my head in the crook of his neck. I smelled his warm, sweet smell and felt the pulse at the base of his throat. I subsided against him, drained.

'Darling Dee,' he said, stroking my hair. 'I'm sorry.'

'I'm sorry, too,' I said.

'I'll talk to Di. I'll talk to her this weekend. I promise.'

'And that will be an end to it? No more weekends?'

'Dee, my darling, I want you to be happy. But you must understand. I can't just cut Di out of my life. She's not very good at managing on her own.'

'And I am?'

'Please, darling. Understand. She's looked after me, supported me when I started with nothing as a photographer's assistant, she's always been incredibly loyal –'

'And I'm not?'

'For twenty years she's been my greatest friend –'

'You told me I was your greatest friend.'

'Shush, Dee. Keep your voice down. I thought we'd agreed not to quarrel. Let's take a hint from our neighbours and go to bed.'

I sprang away from him. 'One dead bat and you think everything will suddenly be moonlight and roses. One dead bat, and you think stupid old Dee will lie back and open her legs and six years of treachery and games-playing will just be forgotten. Tell me, Alex, what will Dido do while you're in Los Angeles, since she's so bad at managing on her own? Or have you promised to take her with you?'

'Stop this, Dee! And keep your voice down!'

'Is that why she's given up her lectureship? So she can go with you to LA?'

44

'She's taking a sabbatical year to write a book.'

'She's taking a year off to go with you to LA.'

'I'm going for six months. On my own.'

'You've never been anywhere on your own, Alex Power. You're not happy unless you have at least two women running in circles round you like demented hamsters.'

'You've worked with me for seven years. You know what a challenge this film is –'

'Is Dido going to spend time with you in LA?'

'She can come and stay if she wants to. So can you.'

'Dido is going to spend time with you, Dido is going to live with you in LA.'

'You're twisting my words, Dee.'

'I don't need to, Alex. Everything that comes out of your mouth is as twisted as a stick of barley sugar. Twists are not an optional extra. Twists are built into the design.'

'For Christ's sake, can we please stop this? I've told you I can't cut Dido off. If she wants to visit me in LA, she can visit me. She is, after all, the mother of my children –'

I stared at him blindly. In the mechanism of my brain an alien hand seemed to throw a switch.

'Oh yes! Bully for Dido! She's lucky she met you before the pill came along, and the duty to swallow it like a responsible grown-up. But then Dido doesn't care for all that sort of thing, does she? Her idea of sexual fulfilment is a close textual analysis of the *Canterbury Tales*. Darling Di, the perfect wife and mother! So what's poor Alex to do while Di sits at home with her legs crossed, knitting lampshades? How will poor Alex get his end away? He'll find some sucker, won't he? And he'll promise her everlasting love and a house and babies – babies tomorrow, never babies today. And she'll believe him, won't she, Alex? Oh yes. But all the time, once you've had your oats, your hump, your bang, once you've chewed me up and spat me out, you'll be planning to

45

crawl back to the ample bosom of The Perfect Wife and Mother, back to the woman who can't tell lipstick from toothpaste, who's made the menopause last longer than *War and Peace –*'

He hit me then. I bounced backwards off the flat of his hand into the chest of drawers, striking my left cheekbone on one corner as I fell. I remained spread-eagled, face pressed to the floor, for some moments. Then, slowly, I levered myself up by my elbows.

He was staring down at me. His face was grey, the skin seemed to hang on it like a baggy stocking.

'I've hurt you,' he said. 'Oh God, Dee, I've hurt you.'

'No more than usual. No more than you've hurt me every day for the past six years.'

An odd look crumpled his face, as if he were about to sneeze. Then, mumbling something, he made for the door.

Too late, I flung myself after him. 'Oh Alex, come back! I love you, I'm sorry! I'm so sorry . . .'

From the bedroom wall there came suddenly an irate, insistent hammering. I fled whimpering to the bathroom. Even before I had crossed the threshold the hammering began there too, setting the bathroom cabinet ajudder. I put my head back and let out a long animal howl, then leaned against the basin until the noises subsided.

I surveyed my reflection in the mirror. An unknown face stared back at me, a face swollen and shiny from crying, crimson between grey runnels of mascara. There was blood pouring from a gash on the left cheek, while on the right the imprint of a palm stretched towards the bridge of the nose, promising at least one black eye. The nostrils streamed mucus, the mouth was stretched as if it were snarling. A mad, hateful, ugly face.

We were lunching in Los Angeles at Richard Nixon's favourite restaurant when Alex told me his divorce had come through. He was still supervising the final edit of his feature, I had flown out to shoot an instant coffee commercial with Bert Goldoni, the director I had joined forces with when I had left Poland Street to start my own company.

We were on the main course when Alex casually mentioned receiving his divorce papers. It was so dark we had borrowed the wine waiter's torch to read the menu. I said 'Oh yes,' or 'Oh, have you?' or something like that, and went on eating my clams.

CHAPTER

THREE

I had resolved to take myself in hand and was rummaging through caked brushes and solidified acrylic tubes in preparation for a day off, painting, the next day.

My studio doubles as a spare-room, although most of the floor space is taken up by my easel and the bed has all but vanished beneath a welter of hardboard off-cuts and paint-stiffened rags. The french windows opening on to the balcony overlooking Battersea Park let in a long shaft of midsummer evening sun, which lighted cruelly upon the ultramarine stain squatting spider-like in the middle of the carpet, and upon the pall of dust which had settled over filthy jam jars and discarded sketches and the multi-coloured impasto of my palette. Mabel played hide-and-seek behind stacked canvases or chased balls of crumpled paper, pausing every so often to look up at me gleefully.

The painting I had been working on before the advent of The Virgin, a six foot by four foot sheet of hardboard, was propped, face inwards, against the mantelpiece. I manoeuvred it over to the easel and sat back to look at it. I had based it on a photograph I had taken in Madrid, which, together with my preliminary drawings, was pinned to a corkboard on the far wall. In the photograph, three figures sat on a bench beneath a statue, a fat woman in a sunhat, a middle-aged man and a younger girl; the fat woman and the man had their heads turned to the right and were laughing (at a dog, out of shot, chasing pigeons), while the girl, though sitting close to them, was separate, her eyes gazing ahead, towards the camera. In my painting, I had ignored the background detail, substituting a pale yellow wash which revealed the tooth of the hardboard, and had begun to build up the figures in ochres, umbers and siennas, cropping them above the waist, shadowing the woman's face with her hat brim and turning the man fractionally further in towards her. Only the girl remained as she was in the photograph, contained, isolated, her shoulders hunched, her pale face with its luminous eyes staring bleakly outwards. The intention had been to convey a sense of complicity, the woman mysterious (perhaps promising, perhaps withholding), the man attentive, even supplicating, the girl with her wistful stare somehow drawn in, covertly involved despite her apparent separateness. Yet, as I surveyed my effort now, the man and the woman looked as solid and homely as their originals and the girl, on whom I had done the most work, merely dyspeptic.

I thought of my advertisement, which had duly appeared in *Bright Lights* that morning. I imagined tall, good-looking unattached men eagerly ringing it in red pentel. I imagined tall, good-looking unattached men, their red pentels passing remorselessly over it, pausing instead three advertisements down, at 'Sporty Female, 25'. I chipped disconsolately at a rock-hard crust of paint with my palette knife; and was relieved when the doorbell rang, heralding my neighbour from the second floor, on her weekly visit to borrow a cup of gin.

Chrissie is a divorce lawyer, a partner in a large City firm of solicitors. She is thirty-five and, like me, lives

49

alone and, though she is good company, always impeccably dressed, and attractive in a clean, coolly-efficient way, confines her social life to dinner parties and trips to the opera with girl-friends, never, to my knowledge, having dallied romantically with a man in the three years she has occupied the flat below me.

I fetched bottles and glasses while she cleared herself a space to sit down.

'Oh,' she said, sipping her drink, 'isn't Mabel *sweet*!'

Mabel, who had been scrimmaging inside a large brown paper bag, obligingly popped her head out to give Chrissie a taking look. Mabel is a smoke tortoise-shell Persian, descended from illustrious, trophy-winning ancestors. Sitting, she looks like an exotic owl, standing, like a miniature yak, and rolling on the rug with her legs in the air, remarkably like what you might find if you emptied out the Hoover bag. Mabel's heredity, while it has over-endowed her with fur, has been somewhat stingy in the provision of brain cells. Nevertheless, she has enough low cunning to detect flattery. Instantly, she was up on Chrissie's lap, fixing her with round, blank, golden eyes, and kneading her skirt with her paws.

Chrissie, on my asking how work was, embarked upon a maze of a story that seemed to involve one of her senior partners, two secretaries, a parking space and a potted plant.

'. . . but he never did admit he was in the wrong,' she ended. 'That would have completely destroyed his machismo.'

'Men!' we both exclaimed reflectively.

'Mind you,' I said, still thinking of the advertisement, 'it's probably time I lived with one again.'

'Really?' said Chrissie, tickling Mabel behind the ears, apparently unconcerned about the gobs of dribble percolating the crisp linen of her skirt. 'I should have thought you'd have been put off. After the last one.'

'The Virgin?' I endeavoured to remove any trace of

50

nostalgia from my voice. 'Well, you know all that stuff –
about one rotten apple, et cetera . . .'

'I shouldn't have thought you had any room for a man,
either. I saw you from my window, getting out of a taxi
with carrier bags again. Your wardrobes must be on the
point of explosion.'

'I've been the model of self-restraint. No serious shopping for nearly three weeks. Not until today. Anyway,
don't you miss it yourself – having a man around?'

Chrissie edged her face around Mabel's tail, which was
feather-dusting her nose. 'Not really.'

'I suppose it's your work. All those embattled couples
every day demanding to have the Le Creuset casseroles cut
in half, and the hi-fi and the family goldfish.'

'No. I just prefer living on my own.'

'But isn't it a bit sterile?'

'Selfish, perhaps. It's all about territory. Mabel understands. If I want to have the armchairs at a precise
ninety-degree angle with the coffee table, there's no one
to interfere.'

I remembered that The Virgin, although he had arrived
with only one small suitcase, had possessed a habit of
leaving little piles of things, political pamphlets, stacks
of small change, all over the flat like droppings, so that
I had been obliged to work quite hard on myself to resist
clearing them up.

'If I want to have a bath at four in the morning, or play
nothing but Mahler's Fifth for a week, or live on a diet of
kippers and muesli, I can. I just shut my front door and
get on with it.'

'Exquisite though a combination of muesli and kippers
might be,' I said, 'don't you ever get lonely?'

'I think you can often feel lonelier when you're with
other people.'

'But even so,' I said carefully, 'haven't you ever wished
you lived with someone?'

Chrissie took a long gulp of her gin. 'Oh, but I did,'

51

she said. 'Before I lived here. He moved in with my best friend while I was away on a case in Bournemouth. I simply couldn't risk being hurt like that again. Not ever.'

'Ah,' I said softly.

'Quite frankly, Dee,' Chrissie said, 'I think you're a lot better off with Mabel.'

'Thing is,' said The Virgin, 'you listen, Dee. You listen and you really understand.'

I had, in fact, drifted off during his polemic on the South American rain forests, had been wondering why, whether it is the negotiation of a multi-million pound merger or the simple fixing of an assignation, men always leave business till the coffee. I pulled myself up abruptly and smiled.

It had been in my mind this morning to cancel. But, on reaching the office, I had attributed my pessimism to what I was wearing – my suit, pulled on in a sleepy blur, now seemed to shriek 'last year's' from every seam, as well as exaggerating my hips, foreshortening my legs and being quite out of balance with my shoes. I had rushed out hurriedly to one of my favourite shops, just off Great Marlborough Street, and had soon found the remedy; a loose cinnamon linen jacket and cinnamon trousers with a tiny cream motif.

True, the new ensemble needed different earrings and a cream silk shirt (exactly the shirt I had hanging in my wardrobe, as a matter of fact, but – could one ever have too many silk shirts?). However, the belt I was wearing would do, and my shoes now worked to perfection.

On the way to my favourite shirt shop I passed the shop that had interesting earrings. In the interesting earring shop I also bought a hat, coarse straw with the brim pinned up, sou'wester style (ideal for concealing my ever-tiresome roots). In the shirt shop I remembered that, alas, I was wearing a black bra (but could one ever have too many bras?). On the way back from Marks & Spencer

52

I saw an irresistible pair of shoes (much more stylish with the hat than the pair I had on).

It was nearly lunchtime when I staggered back to the office and, looking at my five carrier bags, I was consumed with guilt. But, after all, shopping gave me a buzz of adrenalin, shopping helped me think. Hadn't I, somewhere on the way from the shirt shop to Marks & Spencer, found the answer to the trio beneath the statue, discovered a way completely to rework the painting? Twirling in the long mirror of the Ladies, I felt my heart lift. The hat was splendid, the shoes a masterstroke – what a shame I hadn't gone all out and bought a new belt. Hurrying down Old Compton Street, turning into Greek Street towards L'Escargot, I caught my reflection, satisfyingly, in plate glass windows. And now, sitting upstairs, across the table from The Virgin, basking in the additional warmth of Kir and white wine, I was all at once in better spirits than I had been for days.

The Virgin, who never noticed other people's clothes, seemed, by contrast, crestfallen. A Band-Aid slanted across his left eyebrow. He was, I had observed, wearing one yellow sock and one red.

'You listen,' he was saying. 'Rosemary never listens. You can see her eyes go blank the moment I start talking, like shutters coming down.'

I knew better by now than to offer any comment on the idiosyncrasies of wives.

'She wasn't even pleased that I'd remembered our anniversary.'

'Well, you were rather late,' I said.

'I told her I'd got caught by a client, had to take him to the Café Pelican. And anyway, I bought her a present.'

'At ten-thirty?'

'The all-night garage shop at that roundabout near your place. But I might as well not have bothered. You'd have thought I'd insulted her, the way she behaved.'

'What on earth did you give her?'

53

'The Portable Tummy Trainer. You know, one of those whajamacallits with a pull-up bar and foot pedals. "Takes inches off the tummy in just minutes a day." Compact little gadget, even fits in a briefcase. She threw it at me.'

'She didn't?'

'Well, there's not a great selection at your local all-night garage. And she's always going on about needing more exercise. She can be most unreasonable at times, my wife. She's a very jealous woman. Did I tell you she once attacked me with –'

'An upholstery mallet? Yes,' I said, 'you did. Is that where you got the cut? From the Tummy Trainer?'

He fingered the Band-Aid. 'Oh no,' he said. 'She's been on a course in Manchester all this week. Back tomorrow.'

My heart lurched. A whole week of freedom, and he had not told me, had simply let it slip away.

'Of course, she's been phoning me every evening, making sure I'm not up to anything. And after the anniversary episode I've had to keep a low profile. Thing is, though, she's left me with The Dog.'

'Ah,' I said.

After The Virgin's advertising agency had gained the Meaty Doggi-Chunx account, it had been deemed politic for him to acquire one of man's best friends, and he had duly become the owner of a Dobermann. But it soon grew abundantly clear that, even as a puppy, the animal was confused about its role in life. Far from being the sleek, macho accessory, the five stone of snarling muscle that would enhance The Virgin's creative credibility, The Dog is, not to put too fine a point on it, a wimp. The Dog won't cross busy roads or climb stairs, but has to be carried in his owner's arms. The Dog suffers from agoraphobia, psychosomatic in-growing toe-nails, a fixation with his doggy blanket and a delicate digestive system which requires boiled rice and specially-cooked prawn omelettes. Inevitably, The Dog is violently allergic to Meaty Doggi-Chunx.

54

'I've had to bring him into the office all week,' said The Virgin. 'He's been sick three times, twice in my briefcase. And yesterday he tried to bite the Doggi-Chunx client.'

'Good heavens,' I said. 'Is this the dog who faints at the sight of postmen, the dog I last saw held at bay behind a filing cabinet by a visiting Yorkie?'

'The client was wearing a purple tie. That's the only thing that seems to get The Dog going. Makes him see red, purple.'

'So all will be well so long as your burglars remember to dress in shades of violet. But what about your eye?' I said. 'I didn't think mauve was your colour?'

The Virgin bent pathetically over his wine glass. 'Oh, Dee. Don't laugh,' he said. 'I'm in the most terrible trouble.'

'Trouble?' I said.

'It's all The Dog's fault.'

'Poor Dog.'

'I've broken the antique Chinese whajamacallit Rosemary's Auntie Irene gave us as a wedding present.'

'Oh dear,' I said.

'Thing is, when I got back from the pub last night – and I'd had no more than a couple of pints –'

'Of course,' I said.

'Well, there seemed to be quite a lot of mess – washing-up and stuff. So I thought I'd better do some clearing up. I thought I'd start with where The Dog had been sick on the spare-room duvet. So I went upstairs and got the duvet cover and went into the kitchen to put it into the washing-machine. But the washing-machine was full of water –'

'Oh dear,' I said.

'It came gushing at me like Niagara Falls. So I stepped back, and I must have skidded in it. Anyway, I grabbed hold of the handle of the fridge – the deep freeze bit – to save myself. And, would you believe, the whole lot toppled over. The lights went out and I think I got an electric shock –'

55

'Oh no,' I said.

'Well, that sent me staggering back into the dresser, with all these jars – flour and sugar and stuff. So there I was, in pitch darkness and three inches of water, covered with flour and frozen peas, still tingling from God knows how many hundred volts going through me – she could have come back, Rosemary, and found my corpse marinated in orange juice, then she'd be sorry – so anyway, I thought the most sensible thing was to go down to the cellar and mend the fuse –'

'Quite right,' I said.

'But I wasn't to know, was I, that The wretched Dog was cowering in fear at the top of the cellar steps? And that's how I split my eyebrow open.'

'So your kitchen looks like a war zone. And the antique whajamacallit was one of the casualties.'

'The fruit bowl. Oh no, that was in the bathroom.'

'Oh?' I said.

'You see, after I mended the fuse I could tell I was bleeding from somewhere. So I went upstairs to get a plaster, looked in the bathroom mirror, felt rather faint suddenly, sat down on the bathroom stool – and sat in the fruit bowl.'

'I suppose if I asked why . . . ?'

'I was soaking some socks.'

'Oh, my love,' I said. 'You are a complete and utter klutz.'

The Virgin favoured me with his agitated squirrel look. 'But what about the fruit bowl? Rosemary will –'

'Batter you with the upholstery mallet? What's it look like, this Chinese antiquity?'

He fished a nibbled pentel out of his pocket and drew a picture of it on the tablecloth, complete with arrows and annotations.

'Rice,' I said. 'Those opaque things that look like pieces of tooth are rice grains. Chinese rice porcelain. It's not antique. You can buy one just like it in any shop in Gerrard Street.'

'I can?'

'You can buy one after we've finished lunch. Rosemary will never know the difference.'

'Oh, Dee.' He beamed at me, a relieved squirrel, eyes suddenly bright, the spikes of his chewed hair sticking up like fur. 'Oh Dee, you are wonderful. I knew you'd have the answer. Shall we try a glass of Beaune de Venise?'

We sat, sipping the sweet wine, smiling fuzzily at each other. His eyes drifted to my hat. 'Oh, Dee, you look so beautiful today. You've done something different with your hair.'

'You are a klutz,' I said.

'I wish I didn't fancy you so much. We could be such good friends. Do you . . . ?'

'Yes?' I said.

'Would you – do you think you could forgive me enough to have dinner with me next week?'

'I thought you were fresh out of late passes?'

'I'll get one. Next Wednesday. Oh, Dee, just dinner . . .'

'I'll think about it,' I said.

But as we were descending the stairs to the street and his arm crept around my waist, my body seemed to melt quite naturally into his. And when, at parting, he kissed me expansively upon the lips, I found no difficulty in responding.

'All right,' I said. 'Wednesday. Just dinner.'

Dear Vivacious Blonde,

Re your advert in *Bright Lights* for a tall, slim, attractive, unattached man, I am quite tall (5' 6"), quite slim and quite attractive. I am sorry about the photo, it is not a very good one, I have been on a diet since it was taken and I am having my front teeth capped.

I am single since my wife ran off with her aerobics instructor last year. My interests are hiking, train spotting, watching TV and many more. My address may put you off as your advert says London only, but the part of Birmingham I live in is very nice, almost like the country, and there is a very good Intercity service.

I expect you will get lots of replies and put this letter to the bottom of your pile but I am happy to wait till you work your way down to me. Please write or phone . . .

PS Do not be put off by the paper, I have been meaning to get some proper note paper in.

PPS Also I prefer to write in felt tip, but did not have one to hand.

PPPS Please keep the photo, it really does not look like me at all.

Hi there, Vivacious Blonde!

So you're looking for a tall, attractive, unattached man? Your search is over!

I am all of the above plus a whole lot more you never dreamed of. No photo, I'm afraid, but if you write me a letter enclosing a photo of yourself, maybe we could get together some time.

Or, if we find we can't get the magic going, I have plenty of unattached friends who are just crazy for vivacious blondes . . .

Dear Friend,

You may wonder why I am answering such a personal message as your advert with a photocopied reply, but I have taken the liberty as it is the most efficient way to let you know my details and requirements.

I am close on fifty, divorced with grown-up children and am the managing director of a business manufacturing disposable toothbrushes.

I am genuine, sincere, humorous, well-balanced, reliable, energetic, confident, manly, attractive and economically-viable.

My interests include the arts, music, films, museums, wining, dining, the countryside, travel, historic buildings, computer sciences, military uniforms, astronomy, entymology, numismatics, campanology and meeting people.

I am fit in mind and body and am interested in all sports including football, softball, baseball, handball, volleyball, cricket, tennis, squash, badminton, motor racing, cycling, boxing, sailing and darts, as well as exercising by swimming, jogging, weight-training, wind-surfing, mountain climbing, Yoga, judo, hang gliding and walking.

My ideal life companion should be able to share all my interests, and in addition have an appreciation of the disposable toothbrush market. She should be positive, cheerful, domesticated, well-organized, dependable, feminine, intelligent, caring, healthy, a good cook and of child-bearing age, as well as being active, outgoing and sporty . . .

Mrs Hopkins had said we should all take home the comb cases we had made that afternoon as presents for our mothers. Even then, walking from the Evanses, three doors away (where I stayed after school till my parents returned from work), I suspected it was a lost cause. My mother possessed a comb, most people had combs, but I had never met anyone who kept theirs in a case. Besides, the colours were all wrong – bright green felt, sewn down the sides with purple blanket stitch and decorated with a scarlet cross-stitch border. I couldn't imagine my mother greeting it with any more enthusiasm than she had shown for the crayon drawings I had brought home three weeks ago, or the bright blue scarf with yellow horseshoes my father had given her for her birthday. I imagined my mother, her face held up to be kissed, her lips pursed and her cheek turned a little away, as if she were steeling herself for an inoculation. I walked down the alley that divided our house from next door's and in at the back, through the kitchen.

Their voices came from the dining-room.

'Well, you'll have to go on your own,' my mother was saying. 'I can't go. How can I?'

'You could wear that blue dress you wore to the Mayhews,' said my father.

'It's not blue, it's turquoise. And for your information it's five years old. It's going under the arms – quite apart from having stains down the front where you slopped whisky all over it.'

'I think you look very nice in blue,' said my father.

I edged myself into the doorway. My father stood by the sideboard with his back to me. My mother was over at the table, her hands full of cutlery from where she had begun to lay for supper.

'It's all right for you, Gerald. You're a man. You can go to your cricket bunfights and nobody notices your dinner-jacket looks as if you were demobbed in it. You don't have to put up with Avril Mayhew peering down her nose as if you were something the cat dragged in. Just tell me – when did I last have a new dress? When did I last even have my hair done?'

'Have a heart, Kitty,' said my father. 'You know things are a bit tight this month.'

I inched myself across the threshold, clearing my throat. 'Ma –'

'You don't care, do you? You've never cared. Other men pay their wives compliments, other men like to show off their wives. But you – you don't care if I go around looking like a bag of washing. You don't even notice!'

My mother paused, her voice drowned in tears, the knives and forks clutched painfully to her aproned stomach.

With determination I stepped forward. 'Ma,' I said, holding out the comb case.

Both turned. Both stared for a second or two at me and at my peace offering.

'Ah, Deedee,' said my father brightly. 'Why don't you run down to the shed and put some linseed oil on that bat of yours. You've just time before supper.'

The shed was down a concrete path, past a wilting bed of marigolds and the raggedy lawn my mother complained my father never mowed. The shed had a double door like a stable, and I sometimes amused myself by opening the top and leaning out over the lower half, pawing the ground and neighing. Inside, amongst the garden tools and creosote cans, was the hamster's cage on a shelf. And beneath the shelf, propped against a flower pot containing the bottle of linseed oil and the rag torn from one of my father's old vests, was the cricket bat. My father had bought it as a surprise for Easter. It had a black rubber grip and on the face, burnt into the wood beneath the maker's name, was a signature that read 'Peter May'.

My father liked all forms of sport, would happily tune the wireless in to anything from athletics to boxing. But his main preoccupations were rugger and cricket. Every Saturday, ever since I could remember, my mother had packed us sandwiches and hard-boiled eggs in grease-proof paper and we had set out for the afternoon. My mother never accompanied us, for although she was often lying on the sofa listening to the wireless when we returned, she had established Saturday as her busy day. In the winter, I would sit freezing on a mackintosh sheet beside the touchline while, above me, red-faced men screamed, 'Knock-on!' or 'Off-side!' or 'Kick for touch, you silly bugger!' In the summer the mackintosh sheet was often abandoned as we huddled against the rain in the pavilion, while the red-faced men, in measured tones, talked knowingly of 'Short square leg' and 'Silly mid-on' and 'googlies'. Of the two, I probably liked the cricket least – or hated it more – the warm orange squash from a soggy straw, the midges, the interminable pauses where white-clad figures seemed to saunter aimlessly about the field, the sheer, incomprehensible inactivity of it.

61

Sometimes I managed to sneak along a story book in my blazer pocket and would contrive to read a few pages while my father was engaged in intricate discussion of the bowling or the outfield. But mostly, I escaped into my own thoughts.

Nevertheless, my father persisted. When we visited my cousins in Bromley, who had a large garden, we even played cricket, but this usually ended, quite literally, in tears. One of us was always hit by a ball, or run out by a grown-up – the grown-ups seemed to enjoy making up the rules as they went along. Last time my cousin Patrick had cried on being declared by my father to be LBW first ball, although Patrick was eleven and not permitted anything so babyish. And, as for me – well, I never knew when to run or when to stay, could not hit the safest throw or hold the simplest catch. This puzzled my father profoundly, as if my inability defied some natural law like the earth being round or hot air rising. And so he had bought the cricket bat.

Now, on sunny evenings, we would go down the road to the park and I would sit with my new bat on the lumpy grass, watching while he knocked in a set of stumps and then solemnly paced away from them, pacing, counting, marking the other end of the wicket with his tobacco pouch. This done, he would position me in front of the stumps, crouching over me, bending my arms and legs and torturing my fingers into the correct grip, his hands on my hands swinging the bat backwards and forwards. At last, when he was finally satisfied that all that could be done in that department had been done, he would take a hard rubber ball from his pocket and walk very purpose-fully away from the tobacco pouch. He would walk for ever, it seemed, polishing the ball on the seat of his grey flannel trousers, as if he were deliberately waiting for the moment I stopped concentrating. And then, of course, he would be upon me, pounding towards the tobacco pouch, his arm raised, hurling the ball. Sometimes I would duck, sometimes I would attempt a feeble fly-swat at it, sometimes I would just stand there, blinking, frozen with terror. I never hit it; and it would go hurtling off towards a group of women walking their dogs, or into the rough grass; and I would have to chase after it, hunt it down and bring it back, so the whole sequence could begin over again.

After a while, as a variation, my father would take the bat and I the ball, and I would go hobbling off beyond the tobacco pouch while he dug himself into his crease and took up his stance (knees bent because of the smallness of the bat), shoulder high, tongue clenched between his teeth, as was his habit when he was concentrating. And I would stagger up to the mark and throw, underarm, as hard as I could; and he would call, 'Wide!'; and I would limp away to rescue our ball from the jubilant dogs. We would go on in this way till my bedtime saved us, whereupon he would tuck the stumps under his arm, and start for home in great, invigorated strides, while I trailed behind, my head pounding, the soles of my feet burning.

'Don't worry, Deedee,' he would say, as I struggled to catch him. 'You'll soon get the hang of it. You'll soon be up to your cousin Patrick.'

I felt a sympathetic sting in my eyes.

'Bat needs plenty of linseed oil to keep the willow supple. Do it regularly. Like cleaning Hamlet's cage. It's a good bat, with Peter May's autograph on it. Captain of England. Now there's something to live up to.'

I stared at the bat with Peter May's name on it, the bat that needed regular linseed oil. The shed was pungent with the smell of the hamster cage, sodden sawdust and rotting cabbage rising up to overwhelm the other, subtler shed smells of binder twine and earth and methylated spirit. In the far corner, blade hidden behind the rusty lawn mower, was the axe my father

63

had bought to cut down the blighted apple tree. I reached for it, weighed it experimentally in my grip, imagined the shiny steel pitting satisfyingly into the willow, imagined the honey-smooth surface splitting, splintering, shards flying, till all that was left of the oil-guzzling monster and its taunting signature was an unrecognizable heap of chips and dust. But no, it would mean early to bed and no sweets for weeks, and more raised voices carrying from the dining-room as I lay sleepless, unable not to hear.

I replaced the axe and turned my attention to Hamlet, who was nowhere to be seen, curled up in his ball of hay. I opened the door of the cage, prodded his wilted heap of dandelion leaves temptingly, jiggled his water bowl. Finally I prodded the hay itself and was rewarded by angry black eyes and a pair of yellow teeth, which offered themselves to my finger before appearing reluctantly to have second thoughts. I fumbled in my pocket for the comb case, inspecting it for a moment. Then I thrust it in through the cage door. I watched as Hamlet pattered here and there over the green felt, his nose whiffling distrustfully, until at last he seized one corner between his teeth and, dragging the whole clumsily beneath him, trailing sunflower seeds and droppings, made off with it into the depths of his hay.

I turned towards the open top half of the door with its view of the house. Dispiritedly, I contemplated being a Palomino or an Arab stallion. After a while, my father appeared on the back step.

'Deedee! Time for your supper.'

I unlatched the bottom door and ran up the path.

'Your mother's not very well, so I'm cook for the night. Heinz spaghetti do you? And a nice fried egg?'

I nodded mutely.

'Come on, Deedee, dinna fash yourself. I've got a present for you. A surprise.'

My heart lifted. I imagined a hairslide with pearlized

blue swallows on it, a Yo-Yo, a glass cat with its back arched and the tips of its tail and ears a glowing red. I followed my father into the kitchen.

'I couldn't give it to you last night. When I got back from what your mother terms my cricketing bunfight, you were fast asleep. But here it is now. Something pretty special for my special girl.'

He pointed at the kitchen table. On it lay a folded piece of white card with a blue cord threaded through it and a tassel. I picked it up. 'Grapefruit or Brown Windsor Soup. Roast Beef with Yorkshire Pudding, Fillet of Dover Sole . . .'

'There, Deedee. What do you think of that?'

Scrawled across the bottom of the menu in blue fountain-pen ink was the inscription: 'To Deirdre, with best wishes. Peter May'.

Dear Vivacious Blonde,

As I sit at my typewriter at 2 a.m. I apologize in advance for wasting your time. Oh, I'm tall all right – five eleven – and slim, in fact I could do with an inch or two round my hips to balance my shoulders, which are rather wide and tend to make me self-conscious. I hope I'm fairly attractive – I certainly feel happier with my body now than I have done for years. And I'm unattached. So what's the problem, I hear you asking?

Well, dear Vivacious Blonde, I'm afraid I'm not male. I'm a tall, slim, attractive, feminine transsexual. Also 38, also blonde and, on a good day, fairly vivacious. And I'd love to write to, or even meet up with, a woman like you to talk to as a friend.

Oh, I realize you won't want to dish out your address to some loony in lingerie who's had the nerve to write like this. But if you phone me, perhaps we could chat and maybe, who knows, arrange to meet on neutral territory. Please phone, I'd love to talk to you about anything from films to frocks and the joys of being feminine.

Meanwhile, I hope your doormat is littered with letters from gorgeous unattached males.

Yours,

Ann (Smith)

FOUR

It was, for once, a proper summer's day. By ten o'clock the sun glared from a cloudless sky. In Brewer Street the freshly laid tar from yesterday's roadworks was already beginning to melt, in Berwick Street gusts of decay rose from the detritus between the fruit and vegetables stalls. As I reached D'Arblay Street and climbed the stairs to The Casting Couch, my armpits were trickling and my upper lip was damp. On the threshold of the outer office, I paused to blink. Sitting on chairs around the walls, reading newspapers or fanning themselves with their beards, were twenty or so Father Christmases, complete with hoods, belts and boots.

I made my way to the coffee machine. Samantha was on the phone to Wayne, inspecting her baby-pink nails as she talked, watching with fascination the glints of sunlight refracted in her solitaire. I waited. On the desk a new novel lay open, cover upwards. *The Wanton Waves*. 'They were cruising in smooth waters but there was fire down below.' Idly, I picked it up and read:

His eyes were shadowed by the peak of his officer's cap, his manly jaw was set, his mouth a hard, grim line. Suddenly she gasped as he seized her roughly, bruising her flesh with cruel kisses that melted her to the very core of her being . . .

I had met Wayne once, a plump, moon-faced, mild-mannered boy in a Lacoste sweatshirt and builder's-cleavage jeans. I wondered if he knew what he was getting himself into.

Samantha came off the phone with a replete sigh. She prinked her hair. 'Only a Mr Jingo calling for Zig Zigeuner. No messages for you, Dee,' she sang.

Gilda was using my telephone, perched elegantly on a corner of my desk, legs crossed, one Manolo Blahnik high heel dangling. I thumped my briefcase down and began reorganizing my hair.

'Petra's left Jonathan,' Gilda announced. 'Sent him home to his wife. But she's making sure she keeps the flat he was buying her.'

'Oh,' I said neutrally.

'You're too scrupulous, Dee. If you had flats for all your married men, you could start a property company.'

'Thanks,' I said.

'How's it going, anyway – the quest for Mr Single?'

I directed my eyes towards the outer office. 'So much for your notions about the talent round my coffee machine.'

'The job lot of Santas? Zig's casting a ginger-wine commercial. Got to be on air in October, so we can shop even earlier for Christmas. But *Bright Lights* – are you reeling from the avalanche of eligible replies?'

'There are one or two possibilities,' I said.

Gilda applied her gold Dunhill to her cigarette, the very thrust of her chin and arch of her eyebrows radiating a noble restraint in the swallowing of her 'I told you sos'. Then, all at once her face lit up.

'You're crazy, Dee. Know what we should do? Darling heart, we should hold a casting session!'

'*I'm* crazy?' I said.

'Seriously, Dee. You have all the facilities here. If I were

68

to round up thirty of the best-looking actors and models in town, ascertain by devious cross-questioning of their agents that they're unattached and available –'

'Gilda –' I said.

'We'd put them on film, of course, so you wouldn't have to make any on-the-spot decisions. You could take the tape home and mull them over at leisure.'

'Gilda – !' I said.

'We'll only need a couple of hours if we use the Zig Zigeuner technique. "Stand on your mark. Turn to the right. Now to the left. Drop your trousers. Thank you for coming." We could open a couple of bottles of champagne and ask that nice Thai place to send some food over, make a bit of a party of it. My dear, it's a brilliant idea. Don't you think it's staggeringly, startlingly brilliant?'

'Oh, Gilda,' I said, shaking my head and laughing. 'You are quite mad!'

'Mad?' she said, exhaling smoke, affronted. 'I think I've just demonstrated I'm a genius. Seriously, darling heart, don't you see? It's the instant answer to all your problems.'

'I may not have problems,' I said, reflectively. 'It looks as though The Virgin may be on his way back.'

In one sharp movement, Gilda precipitated herself from the desk and into both shoes. 'Dee Devlin, I despair, I truly do. Here am I, offering against my common sense, against my principles, my every inclination –'

'It's very kind of you, Gilda –'

'Here am I, undertaking to apply my finely-tuned brain to your quest for a single man. And what do you do?'

'But Gilda, I'm still very fond of The Virgin.'

'The Virgin,' growled Gilda, stubbing out her cigarette viciously, 'is not single. In fact, darling heart, I wouldn't rate his qualifications on either count.'

★ ★ ★

69

'Oh, Dee, my love,' said The Virgin, 'you're not going to be difficult, are you?'

'Difficult? Just dinner, you said. Dinner last Wednesday, as I recall.'

Against the tide of after-work drinkers that washed the bar of The French, we had managed to secure a table in the corner. The Virgin twisted his pastis glass, avoiding my glance.

'You were fine about it last week on the phone. You said today would suit you better.'

'That,' I said, 'was before I found out about dinner.'

'Thing is, I'd forgotten Wednesday was Rosemary's Tai Chi evening. I was on a three-line whip to baby-sit The Dog.'

'Bloody Dog!' I said.

'Oh Dee, you're one of the few people who's got a soft spot for The Dog. It's something I love about you.'

I was aware of his bright squirrel eyes lifted towards me, pleading. One corner of his shirt collar flapped like a butterfly wing against his jaw, giving him a lop-sided, wounded look.

I sighed. 'All right. So explain about dinner. Explain why we have to be at my flat by seven-thirty.'

'I've told Rosemary I'm in a video edit, till midnight.'

'So?'

'She's bound to phone and check.'

'And if you're at my flat she'll be out of luck, won't she?'

'Well, thing is' – his nose twitched, the wing of his collar beat a tattoo against his jawbone – 'thing is, Dee, I've given her your number.'

'You what?' I said.

'She says she's fed up with me phoning to say I'm in a meeting when she can hear the pub sound effects in the background. She says if I'm going to tell lies it's about time I learnt to be convincing.'

'She's going to be highly convinced when she phones and gets my answering machine.'

'You could turn your machine off.'

'And then what?'

'You pick up the phone and say you're Visionary Video.'

'She'll know I'm not.'

'You could do one of your voices. Your Samantha impersonation.'

I weighted my voice with breath, then let the tone rise out of it, soaring to a peak before plummeting suddenly, like an erratic cardiogram. 'Hullo, Casting Couch. Good after-noo-oon!'

'That's it, Dee. Perfect. Then you tell Rosemary to hold on while you put her through to me.' He beamed. 'There you are, you see. Simple.'

'It strikes me,' I said, 'if you were just to phone Rosemary yourself that would be a whole lot simpler.'

'Oh no, Dee. You don't understand. She's a very jealous woman, my wife. If I phone her I might not be at Visionary Video at all. I might be anywhere. I could be at your flat, for instance, making violent love to you.'

'Don't push your luck, sunshine,' I said. 'Just dinner – remember, that was what you promised.'

'Well, if you're hungry we could stop by that Indian near your place and pick up a takeaway.'

With gentle perseverance I have trained The Virgin to discard his shoes and socks before stripping off his trousers and underpants. He removed them now, and began to kiss me.

'Spicy Poppadoms,' he murmured.

'Chicken Tikka,' I said, my hands sliding down to his shirt buttons.

'Chicken Tikka,' he agreed, unfastening my bra. 'And oh – oh, Shami Kebab.'

'Prawn Pathia,' I whispered.

'Rogan Gosht,' he sighed.

'Pilau Rice.'

'Bhindi. And Brinjal.'

'And mmmm' – I said, unbuckling his belt – 'a Paratha. A stuffed Paratha.'

'Oh shit. A stuffed Paratha. Oh shit, oh yes.'

'And Cucumber Raita. Mmmm. Mmmm. Lovely, creamy Cucumber Raita.'

'Oh, oh, yes please, Dee. Oh yes, yes . . .'

I paused with my hand inside his underpants. 'You don't think we should wait, do you, till Rosemary phones?'

He raised his lips from my nipple. 'Oh my love, if we wait things will get cold.'

The phone rang. The Virgin, forgetting that he was hobbled by his Levis, staggered and fell backwards on to the bed. Kicking aside my skirt, I raced for the studio.

'Hullo, Visionary Video,' I gasped.

On the other end of the line there was a bemused silence.

'Visionary Video. May I help you, caller?'

'You've got the wrong number,' said a voice.

'Mother –' I said.

'You've got the wrong number. This is my daughter's number and I've been dialling it for years. If she's moved she would have told me. Though, mind you, with all the messages I leave and never get an answer, I suppose I wouldn't know from one day to the next –'

'Mother,' I said. 'Mother, it's me.'

'Then why are you pretending to be a video machine?'

'Mother, I –'

'I worry about you, Deirdre. I've called you five times this week and you're always out. And now you're pretending to be a video recorder.'

'Mother, is this urgent?'

'Not urgent, exactly, no. But I was talking to Mrs Thing yesterday – you know who I mean, Mrs Thing at Number Five – and she was telling me her daughter's been involved in a very nasty mugging, so I thought I'd better call to make sure you're all right –'

'Mother, I'm fine –'

'The terrible things you see on TV nowadays. Sex

72

fiends and terrorist bombs and gangs of streamers on the underground –'

'Steamers, Mother.'

'I worry, Deedee. I phone and you're not at home. I think of my baby girl alone in the streets of London after dark . . .'

'Mother, I'm forty years old. I haven't been raped, mugged, or sold off to the White Slave trade. I've told you, I'm fine, AOK, top-hole, absolutely one hundred per cent fine.'

'Well, there's no need to take that tone. What kind of tone is that to take to your mother?'

'I'm sorry. It's just that I'm rather busy at the moment.'

'A mother can't help but worry, you know. It's the cross she bears from the moment she leaves the labour ward.'

'That's sweet of you, Mother. But please – can I call you back?'

The Virgin has slender hips and pale, smooth skin, lightly freckled on his back, shoulders and upper arms. Naked, he looks like a sixteen-year-old boy. I kissed his nipples in turn and ran my tongue down his chest, round and past his navel. I took his prick in my mouth.

'Mmmm,' I said.

'Lime Pickle,' he moaned. 'Tarka Dahl.'

'Mmmm,' I said. 'Mmmm. Mmmmmm.'

The phone rang. I flung myself off the bed, charged down the hall to the studio, grabbed the receiver.

'Visionary Video.'

'You can keep up this silly joke all night, but it doesn't fool me, Deirdre. I'm not senile yet.'

'Mother, I said I'd call you back.'

'But you didn't say when.'

'You only phoned ten minutes ago.'

'Well, I don't want to be sitting here long past my bedtime. You know, I'm not as young as I used to be –'

'Mother, are you plastered?'

73

'On one medicinal gin, dear? I've just taken out my teeth to be more comfortable.'

'Mother. Please. I'm very busy.'

'And that's another thing that worries me, Deedee. You modern career girls, working morning, noon and night. Executive stress can be very unpleasant, you know. There was a TV programme only the other day – they said stress can confuse your hormones, make you grow facial hair –'

'Mother, I've got a friend round.'

'Well, that's nice, dear. Is she anyone I know?'

'We're in the middle of – we're having a spot of Indian takeaway.'

'Why didn't you tell me? I don't want to interrupt your dinner. I wouldn't have phoned if I knew I was interrupting anything.'

I caught one hip on the door knob as I careered through the studio door. I lurched towards the telephone receiver, groaning and clutching my side.

'Hullo – aaargh! – Visionary Video.'

'Deedee sweetheart, I know I'm interrupting and I know you said you'd call me, but I was thinking about that curry you mentioned –'

'Mother! Please!'

'I hope it isn't curried eggs. Or anything with chicken in it. Because you know all these scares about salmonella poisoning. Old Thing – you know, that nice one with the bow-tie and poppy eyes – was only saying on yesterday's nine o'clock news that last year sixty-four people died –'

'Mother, I'll call you. Tomorrow. I promise. Please!'

'I told you,' said The Virgin, emerging from my pubic hair. 'I told you we'd soon get everything heated up again.'

'Salmonella,' I murmured.

'You what?' he said.

74

'You get salmonella poisoning. From reheated food.'

'Salmonella Biryani,' he whispered, putting his hand where his mouth had been, pressing his erection against my pelvis. 'Salmonella Masala, Salmonella Bahji. Oh Jeez, put yourself on top of me. Salmonella Vindaloo!'

We rolled over and I came up astride him. His fingers closed around my nipples. I widened my legs and guided him into me, gasping as he entered, feeling him slide up inside me, butter-smooth. I clenched my muscles.

The phone rang.

I shut my eyes and began to rock very slowly backwards and forwards.

The phone continued to ring.

I rocked. It rang. I felt him start to wilt.

I hurled myself across the hall and snatched up the receiver.

'Mother, for Christ's sake!' I screamed.

There was an ominous silence at the other end of the line. 'Is that Visionary Video?' said an unfamiliar female voice.

'You've got the wrong number,' I said, panicking and slamming down the receiver.

I stood, stark naked, trembling, staring at the telephone as if it were a dangerous object. It seemed to return my stare, all ten round eyes of its old-fashioned dial glazed with venom. I backed away from it and returned to the bedroom. The Virgin was lying propped on one elbow with a questioning air. And I had scarcely launched myself on to the bed, had barely lifted both feet from the carpet when, shrilly, the ringing began again.

'She's had a lot of trouble getting through,' he said. 'Apparently the line's either been engaged or she's got the wrong number. She had to go through the operator in the end.'

He sounded almost accusing. I reached across to the bedside table for a cigarette. 'I hope she was impressed by my Oscar-winning performance. Though it was somewhat over-rehearsed.'

'Thing is, she's worried about The Dog. He won't eat the tuna risotto she made him, won't play with his catnip mouse, can't even work up interest in his doggy blanket. She says he just crouches in his basket, shivering.'

'Perhaps he's been frightened by a spider or duffed up by a gang of neighbourhood toms.'

'She says his eyes have this pathetic, tormented look.'

'Why doesn't she phone the vet?'

'She's not speaking to the vet. Apparently he told her The Dog has a personality problem, suggested we try a pet therapist. Rosemary thinks he's implying The Dog is the casualty of a dysfunctional family. She says if I came home more often –'

The phone began to ring.

We both remained for some moments frozen, listening. His squirrel eyes darted apprehensively, his nose quivered.

I sighed. 'You take it. Tell her they've switched the calls through. Or, if it happens to be my mother, say I've emigrated to Uttar Pradesh.'

He scurried away. Cradling my cigarette in the ashtray, I began to search amongst our strewn clothing for my bra. By the time he returned I was fully dressed and stroking Mabel, who had emerged from her retreat in the airing cupboard. Pulling her to me, I buried my face in her earth-coloured fur.

'She says The Dog's having a heart attack. She says I always leave her to cope on her own.'

I stood up, but did not turn round.

'Thing is, Dee, I think I'll have to go.'

'Yes,' I said slowly. 'I think you'll have to go.'

A PSYCHIATRIST SPEAKS

DEAR VICTIM: Your letter indicates that you are locked

in a masochistic behaviour pattern from which you will find it hard to escape.

I cannot tell whether your friend's dog truly suffered a cardiac infarction, as this is not my province. However, once a victim, always a victim. Your low self-image, product of your childhood failure to satisfy your father's expectations on the cricket field, conditions you unerringly to form relationships with complete shits. Your compulsive attraction to married men, who must inevitably reject you, helps you confirm, through this rejection, your own perception of your negligible worth. A tricky one, since we are dealing here with patterns established from infancy, involving defective identification and projection and an overdeveloped super-ego.

However, this is nothing that twenty years of intensive psychotherapy will not solve. Alternatively, have you considered killing yourself?

All nineteen stone of Ambrose Glass, my partner, was squeezed into his favourite chair in the Groucho Club. Ambrose has a very small face for a very large man, with a *retroussé* nose and a perfect rosebud mouth above his dewlaps, so that, watching his eyes working, you imagine a slighter person somewhere inside the folds of blubber, manipulating them like the man inside a pantomime horse. He was dressed, as is his wont during summer, like an extra in a film about Havana or leper colonies in Mozambique, in a crumpled linen suit, with a battered Panama on his knees, cradled gingerly, crown upwards, as if it contained birds' eggs.

There was a stranger with him whom I took, from his carefully casual designer jacket, to be one of Ambrose's ever-changing circle of acolytes, although as I drew closer I observed he must be in his thirties, rather older than Ambrose generally liked them. The stranger stood up and Ambrose, grunting, put aside the birds' eggs and heaved

77

upon the arms of his chair, levitating his customary inch before subsiding with a groan.

'Deirdre, my darling. Mel Jago. He's waiting for Zig.'

'Who seems, as usual, to have thrown away his schedule,' said the stranger, consulting his watch. 'See you, Ambrose. I'd better be off.'

He nodded to me and patted Ambrose on the shoulder. 'Nice boy,' said Ambrose, watching the stranger's narrow hips and long legs receding through the swing doors. 'Very talented. Nice boy. Which is more' – here he fixed me with a beady blue eye – 'than can be said for that creature you were seen with on Tuesday in The French. I thought you'd given him the push.'

I essayed a laugh. 'Are you spying on me, Ambrose?'

'Dear girl. Sergei saw you. Would have said hullo, but you appeared to be having something of a tiff. We both agreed we couldn't understand what a beautiful girl like you could see in a man who apparently chews his own hair.'

'You, Sergei, Gilda. You're all impossible.'

'Your friends merely have your best interests at heart.'

'Then you'll be pleased to know it's over. Definitely, this time. Definitely, absolutely over.'

He patted my knee. 'So that's why you look so woebegone. Like a wilted marigold. Poor Deirdre. It really is time you stopped all this skirmishing and settled for the delights of connubial bliss.'

'Like you and Sergei?' Ambrose and Sergei have bickered devotedly for twenty-three years. If Sergei decides he likes Rothko, Ambrose will immediately announce his dedication to Annibale Carracce; if Ambrose discovers Messiaen, Sergei will be in for a baroque phase; if Sergei confesses a partiality for *moules marinières*, Ambrose will proceed to catalogue the relatives, friends and acquaintances who have been brought within inches of death by shellfish poisoning. Once, when Sergei, forgetting he was crossing a two-way street, was knocked unconscious by

78

a van, Ambrose, arriving at the hospital, had jammed his bulk into the green plastic bedside chair and refused to be moved for two days. But, almost the moment Sergei could talk, they were quarrelling about the pyjamas Ambrose had packed and whether black grapes had more flavour than white.

'My saintly disposition is Sergei's good fortune. But a girl like you, Deirdre, amusing, intelligent, attractive – there must be a man somewhere who's just dying to snap you up.'

I laughed. 'I'm past my sell-by date, Ambrose. And anyway, name me one heterosexual man over forty of your acquaintance who's still available.'

Ambrose mopped his brow with a frayed silk foulard, considering. 'There's Sergei's bank manager. A recent widower, five-bedroomed house, golf club membership. Oh, I'll admit he's close to retirement and has a glass eye, but he possesses hidden depths. The other evening, over one of Sergei's ghastly *cuisine minceur* concoctions, he confessed he's always been an anarchist in his spare time.'

'Thanks, Ambrose, but I couldn't take the excitement.'

'The trouble with you, dear girl, you're too pernick-ety. A sexagenarian, one-eyed, weekend anarchist may not sound like love's young dream. But just think of the overdraft facilities.'

Edward Thistlethwaite, 42, six foot, eleven stone three, brown hair, hazel eyes, backward-slanting fountain-pen writing, an address in Fulham. Divorced, no children, working in publishing – he'd answered my advertisement, he said, because he'd only recently returned from a long spell abroad and hadn't yet met any women of his own age in London. He hadn't sent a photograph – his letter implied that keeping a stock of snapshots of oneself was an unacceptable vanity – but he'd sounded pleasant over the phone, and he'd said he'd be carrying a copy of *Bright Lights*. I, in a sudden dither about which clothes would

79

suit such an assignation – sexy, casual, efficient? – had said I would wear black.

Oh, it's true that most of the items in my wardrobe that aren't shades of cream or brown are a nice, safe black, but somehow, when I hurtled home early to change, this didn't make my problem any easier. I had an idea that people in publishing dressed rather formally, but would he find a tailored suit threatening? Would trousers mark me weird, a tight skirt seem too much of an overture? Everything I tried on made me look either like the Wicked Witch of Endor or a shop assistant. I wished I had not allowed guilt to triumph this morning, and had simply bought something new.

It occurred to me, gazing despairingly at the mountain of clothes on my bed, that I had been hurled backwards through time to my first teenage date. Hadn't I spent two hours last night touching up my roots, hadn't I woken this morning to find, at an age when acne should have been a distant memory, a zit lowering volcanically in the middle of my chin? And now, by the time I had disguised it with another layer of make-up, I was, unless I had exceptional luck with taxis, going to be late. I reminded myself that my enjoyment of teenage parties had usually been in inverse proportion to the time I had spent getting ready. Determinedly, I settled upon a short, full skirt, a linen bellhop jacket and a cream cowl-necked shirt, topping them off at the last minute with my straw sou'wester to counter the salesgirl effect. (Oh, I knew he would be looking for blond hair, but I could always sweep the hat off at the crucial moment.)

Edward Thistlethwaite, 42, six foot, hazel eyes. Despite strenuous efforts on the part of my common sense, I could not entirely banish an image straight from one of Samantha's novels, the quizzical eyebrows, the hard, square jaw, the hazel eyes clouded with a tenderness that belied the arrogant curl of his lip . . . After some toing and froing on the phone, I had suggested a cocktail bar in

80

St James's I had only visited once or twice, but recalled as being relatively empty in the early evening. When I arrived my legs were shaking.

Inevitably the bar was more crowded than I had remembered, and every woman I spotted amongst the grey business suits seemed to be wearing black. I hovered by the coat check, trying to home in on my target. There were three men with visible copies of *Bright Lights*, but one, alas, could be discounted straight away as, though tall and good-looking, he could be no more than twenty-five and had his arm round the waist of a glamorous redhead. Of the other two, neither resembled the heroes of *Wanton Waves* or *Realms of Desire*. I began to realize what latitude a simple passport description allowed. Colour of hair did not indicate quantity, weight did not specify how it was distributed, and a man's height can be hard to determine when he is sitting down.

I pretended to fumble in my handbag, stalling for time. Edward Thistlethwaite Number One sat sideways on a bar stool, his copy of *Bright Lights* ostentatiously displayed beside his glass of bottled lager. Though his suit hung upon his narrow shoulders and his knees jutted bonily, his waistband stretched to accommodate a water-melon bulge, and what remained of his hair, while, yes, it was brownish, ran in a strip across the back of his skull like badly-applied lampshade braid. He had a beaky nose and a hanging lower lip which somehow suggested adenoids and halitosis, and he wore rimless spectacles – wouldn't he have mentioned glasses, wouldn't they have been the most obvious thing to mention?

Edward Thistlethwaite Number Two sat at a table not far away from the coat check, reading his *Bright Lights,* so that until he glanced up at the clock I had an imperfect view of his face. A tanned, crumpled face, heavily pouched under the eyes – not handsome exactly, but at least devoid of any glaring deformity. He had hair, too, in acceptable quantities, slicked back from his forehead, the brown streaked with

81

silver. He wore a pale grey flannel suit and took occasional sips from a dry Martini; and, now that I examined him, now that I considered the shape of his head and the way that, when he peered at the clock, his brow crinkled like corrugated cardboard, was there not something world-weary yet debonair about him, something that vaguely suggested Edward of Wallis Simpson fame?

I hovered indecisively between them, Edward One with his monk's tonsure and stooped shoulders, Edward Two with his corrugated brow. Edward the Confessor or Edward VIII? Both were on their own and obviously waiting for someone. I could scarcely decide the question by going up and scrutinizing the colour of their eyes. I would take off my hat and slowly stroll the length of the room. Then, if neither responded, I should have to approach each one directly. Knowing my luck, I could put money on the outcome.

My legs were jelly. Shouldering my handbag, I took a step forward, lifted my hand to my hat. 'Hi babe!' said a familiar voice.

I whirled round. Beneath sleek black hair, six thousand pounds of Harley Street dentistry flashed at me like a Sabbatier knife. But I had chosen this bar because no one frequented it. And now, of all people, here was The Scorpion. I stared up at him, frozen with panic. He planted a moist kiss full on my lips.

'Hey, Dee baby. Great! Fantastic to see you! What are you doing here?'

I was aware of stuttering, of flushing beet-red like a small child caught with her hand in the biscuit tin. 'I'm meeting a friend.'

'Great! Fantastic! Anyone I know?'

Why had I said that? Why had I said friend? A friend is not generally someone whose identity you have to enquire after with the possibility of drawing a blank. A friend, too, when you encounter a lover, is preferably female, otherwise you have explanations to make. Why hadn't I said client, casting director, someone I might easily never have met before? Why did this reincarnated adolescent Dee Devlin possess so little presence of mind?

'I – um – er, well – I'm not sure . . .'

Perhaps if I were to whip off my hat now the real Edward would connect me with my telephone description and rise to greet me. But supposing it was Edward the Confessor? The very idea of implying to The Scorpion that this man with his seedy suit and adenoidal stare was even a distant acquaintance of mine filled me, unworthily, with shame.

'So she's not shown yet?' said the Scorpion, mistaking my wavering glance. 'Hey, then you can join Marcus and me for a glass of shampoo. I've just sold him a hundred thou of Patrick Procter and he's just sold me the new 911 Carrera 4 Porsche. I guess you could say we're both on a high.'

I considered The Scorpion with his Cartier watch and his St Laurent tie and his cream suit which, though undoubtedly also appropriately labelled, made him look like an ice-cream vendor. I wished he would be summoned by his mobile phone to one of his interminable transatlantic negotiations. Alternatively, I wished he would simply implode. Yes, he could save me from Edward the Confessor? But what about Edward VIII?

'Hey, come on, baby. Truly, it's amazing to see you. I've been meaning to call. Wow, what a night that was, last time! Wow, didn't you and me pull out all the stops!'

I considered The Scorpion. I took a decision. If Edward the Confessor responded I could simply stare through him as though he wasn't there. I snatched off my hat.

Was it my imagination that both Edwards looked up intently, both rose a fraction in their seats? Then, to my horror, The Scorpion, propelling me forward, cupped my left buttock with a proprietorial hand. By the time I could shake him off, both pairs of eyes were firmly elsewhere.

'Hey there, Marcus, this is the gorgeous Dee Devlin,'

said The Scorpion, moving his hand to my shoulder to give that, too, the squeeze of ownership. 'Isn't she gorgeous, doesn't she look sensational tonight?'

Marcus rose, red-faced and swaying, to extend a clammy hand. Though this table was directly opposite Edward VIII's and close to the bar, the only way I could command a view of both was to take Marcus's place. In desperation, stumbling over his feet, I wormed my way in beside him, grabbed the chair and sat down. Neither he nor The Scorpion seemed put out by my rudeness; they appeared to view my feverish desire to sit between them in the light of flattery. I realized, though The Scorpion held it better, both were already very drunk.

A waiter was summoned for a third champagne glass, the usual pleasantries were exchanged, then the conversation returned to cars and art prices and I was able to take stock. Up at the bar, The Confessor was draining his lager glass; opposite, Edward VIII, while on a second Martini, had cast aside *Bright Lights* to gaze round the room. How had I, a forty-year-old grown-up, managed to get myself in this pickle? We had arranged to meet at seven-thirty and the clock now registered five past eight. Still, both The Scorpion and Marcus had wives, there was only a dribble of champagne left in the bottle, they would be bound to take their leave any minute now. Left alone, I could resolve the situation. I would be forceful and direct, as I should have been the moment I entered. I should simply go up to both of them and ask their names. Oh I hoped, I hoped it was Edward VIII. I tried training my will upon him, compelling him to catch my eye. But, just as his gaze drifted towards me, The Scorpion snaked his arm round the back of my seat. I readjusted myself, even shifted my chair, but too late. Edward VIII was once again staring blankly at the clock.

Then a miracle happened. Up at the bar, Edward the Confessor took a note from his wallet, gathered up his *Bright Lights* and briefcase, and struggled from his stool.

84

The field was clear. The Scorpion and Marcus would leave and all I need do was walk up to Edward VIII and sit down. He had nice hands, I decided, square and tanned, with clean pink nails. And why had I thought him ordinary? There was a gentle, good-humoured look to his pouchy face, something beyond his resemblance to his namesake that made him no, not just attractive, but definitely handsome. I should simply go up to him and he would wave away my apologies with a charming smile. And, years later, we should joke about the confusion of our first date, about how a combination of fate and my foolishness had nearly prevented our ever meeting . . .

But no, The Scorpion was ordering more champagne. Again Edward VIII looked round, alerted no doubt by The Scorpion's mid-Atlantic loudness, again he looked away. I ground my teeth with frustration. There was a book of matches beside the ashtray. Perhaps if I used the flap to write a note, gave it to the waiter – no, took it over myself, pretending to go to the Ladies, dropping it surreptitiously beside his Martini as I passed . . . 'Dear Edward. Help! Please rescue me immediately. Love Dee.' The Scorpion and Marcus were now deep into property prices. Neither would notice if I scribbled furtively. I delved in my bag for a pen.

But then Marcus pushed his chair back, Marcus, staggering, announced he was off to the lavatory. I cast aside the match book in despair.

'Hey, baby doll,' said The Scorpion, slinking his hand back around my shoulders, 'looks like your friend isn't going to show.'

'I – I think perhaps –' Whatever ingenious phrases I had been about to deploy were suddenly erased by the sight of Edward VIII in conversation with the waiter, proffering a credit card.

'My wife thinks I'm having dinner with Marcus. But Marcus has a hot date with a foxy brunette . . .'

He leaned further forward, shifting his hand to my

85

knee. I was aware of Edward VIII staring across at us as he waited for his card.

'What say you and me take in San Lorenzo if they're not fully booked? Or maybe we could go back to your place and you could fix us bacon and eggs and we could make beautiful music together . . .'

He was edging his hand beneath my skirt now. I grabbed it, trying to push it away.

'What say we go back to your place and you put on that lacy basque of yours with the tight, tight bones and the black suspenders? Come on, how about it, little baby?'

His hand thrust against mine, scratching my bare thigh. We tussled openly. I could feel Edward VIII staring with distaste.

'Stop it!' I hissed. 'Stop it, this minute!'

'But Dee, baby doll –'

'Stop it or I'll empty the ice bucket over you.'

His hand fell away. Simultaneously, Edward VIII rose from his table and went purposefully to the bar counter for his credit card.

I surveyed The Scorpion. I hated his Cartier watch and his Rossi Brothers suit and his smile like a refrigerator sale-room. I hated his shiny black hair and his phoney mid-Atlantic accent. I could not understand what mental aberration, what hysteria over The Virgin had so confounded my judgement that I had ever permitted The Scorpion to touch me. I felt nauseated at the very thought.

'You're gross!' I said, gathering up my hat and bag.

'But Dee, baby, we make such beautiful melodies –'

'Nonsense,' I said, scraping back my chair. 'The only sounds you and I have ever made have been undiluted musak.'

As I tore through the bar I thought I glimpsed grey flannel shoulders just beyond the coat check. I would explain, I would apologize, we should smooth it over somehow, find another bar, begin the whole evening again. I reached the street door and burst into the fresh air, glancing around me frantically. He was about ten yards up the street, flagging down a taxi. I filled my lungs to shout, then stopped in my tracks.

Supposing he were not Edward Thistlethwaite? Supposing he had just been whiling away an hour before a dinner engagement and had brought along *Bright Lights* as a diversion? Supposing both he and Edward the Confessor had dropped into the bar quite innocently, and the real Edward Thistlethwaite had simply never turned up. I should not have the nerve to phone and find out, and one thing was certain, whichever the scenario – Edward Thistlethwaite was not about to make contact with me.

I watched him bend to give instructions to the taxi driver, watched him climb inside and close the door. As the cab drew away from the kerb I could see him relax, stretching one pale grey arm along the back window ledge.

Another 'For Hire' taxi appeared. I hailed it wearily.

CHAPTER

FIVE

Alastair, 44, five foot ten, fairish curly hair, a teacher, immaculate brown-ink italic (it was this last which had fascinated me, laid out as fastidiously as a party invitation, so that even the postscript about his Chinese birth year, marching neatly across the bottom of the page, described a perfect ninety degrees to continue up the right-hand margin). A vegetarian – hence our assignation in a whole-food bar in Hampstead.

We shook hands formally. He had a long thin nose tipped by two ridges of gristle which became pronouncedly white when he sniffed. He sniffed now.

'Are you, by any chance, wearing perfume?'

'Poison,' I said.

'It certainly is. I have an allergy to all types of perfume. It brings on acute rhinitis.'

The gristle twitched threateningly. I backed away. We agreed to move to a table next to the open door. His eyes began to water nonetheless. The gristly ridges whitened like knucklebones.

'Oh dear,' he said, 'you'll have to excuse me. I have hypersensitive sinuses. My sneezing fits usually last a full fifteen minutes.' He fished out a packet of Kleenex.

He closed his eyes and, with his thumb and forefinger, compressed the bridge of his nose.

I cast a glance at the self-service counter with its surgical salad utensils, its metallic trays displaying their contents like spare parts for transplantation behind a screen of sterile glass. 'I tell you what,' I said. 'You choose me something to eat, while I go to the Ladies and wash.'

When I returned his eyes were red-rimmed, but he seemed otherwise to have staved off the worst. A filled plate was set in my place, and a glass of sepia liquid.

'Prune juice,' he said. 'And chickpea and lentil stir-about. I trust it's to your taste.'

I forked the greeny-yellow mush experimentally. 'Oh yes, thank you. I eat most things really.'

The gristle blanched disapprovingly. 'You're fortunate. I have to be very careful. Dairy products, white sugar, gluten, artificial colourings – my system reacts to them with everything from cold sweats to hives.'

'How very difficult for you.'

'Oh yes,' he said, sipping his glass of warm water. 'But then that's the price one pays, in this polluted world, for any degree of sensitivity. I suppose it's something one's born with. Most ordinary people are brutalized by the toxins in our environment. They're so numbed from infancy by the constant barrage of chemical warfare they become anaesthetized. They can't react, so they don't question. I must say, I sometimes envy their ignorance.'

'Really?' I said.

'Oh yes, indeed. If they could see what I see . . . Take this table, for instance –' he gestured at the spotless expanse of white formica between us. 'It looks relatively clean to you, doesn't it? But if you put it under a microscope you'd see it's literally seething with bacteria –'

'Good heavens,' I said, resisting a sudden desire to scratch.

'Just look at the place where your bare arm touches it. Every second your epidermis is shedding tiny particles of dead skin which drift out into the atmosphere as dust mites. Inhale them and they could cause choking, hyperventilation, asthma attacks –'

I withdrew my arm.

'Oh yes. Sometimes I wish I could be desensitized. I truly do.' He closed his eyes, compressed the bridge of his nose again, heaved in breath.

'What is it?' I said, endeavouring to hide my forearms beneath the table. 'Still my scent?'

'No, no.' He paused, sniffing, eyes still closed, like a connoisseur testing the bouquet of a burgundy. 'But there's something . . . Your make-up, perhaps?'

No excess of politeness was going to force me to wash off my make-up. 'It's hypoallergenic,' I lied.

'Hairspray? I'm ultrasensitive to hairspray. My last girlfriend persisted in using it although she knew it brought on my blistery rash. She denied it, of course. But one day, when she was out, I searched her flat, and there, right at the back of her top dressing-table drawer, hidden behind her diary and a packet of Tampax –'

'No. It's not hairspray,' I said.

'Deodorant? I react adversely to all aerosols and even to some roll-ons –'

'No. Not deodorant,' I said cheerfully. 'Just me.'

Andy, 39, 5′11″, floppy hair, swimming Cocker Spaniel eyes. It was nearly closing time in the saloon bar of his Stoke Newington local, and my turn to buy another round.

'. . . I mean, she can't be happy, I mean what can she talk about to someone his age? Acid House parties, or when he's going to get a steady job? The trouble is, when the lawyers get stuck in, it's a roller coaster and you can't get off. Oh Dee, if I promised to drive her to Sainsbury's and put a new plug on the Hoover, if I told her my mother never meant anything by that remark about Weightwatchers . . .?'

90

His eyes, like two pints of Special, were full to brimming. I felt almost tearful myself.

'Well, Andy, you can only ask her. Perhaps it's not too late for Marriage Guidance . . .'

Jed, 47, 5'9", shiny suit, toupée and reptilian eyes. Spare ribs for two at Tony Roma's.

'Of course, love, when I say "unattached" – well, the word's as broad as it's long, isn't it? The wife and me, we've got what you call an open marriage –'

'Mummy, Mummy! Titus pissed on the mat again!'

'Peed, Cassie darling,' said Laura, reaching for a strip of kitchen towel. 'Titus has *peed* on the mat.'

I watched Laura as, wading through a scatter of Lego and building bricks, she seized Titus and, like a machine-tool operator trained to split-second co-ordination, debagged him with her left hand, while her right sponged those areas of his anatomy and the floor which required sponging.

Cassie smiled up at me confidentially. 'Titus,' she said, 'pisses and shits everywhere.'

'Pees, darling. Pees and poohs. The other words are nasty.'

'Titus is nasty,' said Cassie amiably, rising on invisible points, then twirling away to perform her Wicked Fairy dance in the far corner of the kitchen.

'He's just a little resistant to potty training. Perhaps he'll grow up to be a Nobel prize-winner.'

Laura is my oldest friend, we met at university. Together we smoked dope and had nervous breakdowns in the small hours over mugs of Nescafé. Together, in the flowing black rejects of theatrical costumiers, our hair dyed Ravishing Raven, our eyes rimmed with kohl, we prowled the faculty building or lurked in the university library tearoom in search of prey. Later, Laura's 'proper job' did not discourage her from offering me the hospitality of her floor during my starving artist phase. We had our ears pierced, we went to the kind of Eastern European films where the dinner eats the people, we gave parties where everyone wore glitter. We saw each other through an assortment of unreliable men. When Laura married Charlie, I suffered my first real loss, my first intimation that youth might not last for ever. When, at thirty, she gave birth to Dominic, I felt this sense of loss again, more sharply. Three years later Cassandra arrived, and Laura announced she was giving up being a marketing high-flier for full-time motherhood. I, by now dedicated working woman and company director, expressed horror. To pacify me, she would make murmurings about working part-time or starting a local magazine. Then, two years ago, had come the accident of Titus. Now Laura freely opines that work is horrid and offices as unnatural as battery-chicken farms. And I, though I would not confess it, have developed some sympathy with her point of view.

'So tell me, tell me,' I said. 'Nigel Larkin got *married*? I thought he was –'

'Oh, he is,' said Laura, producing fresh shorts for Titus from beneath an anorak and several magazines, and returning to the business of simultaneously grilling fish fingers and knocking up *Poulet Sauté à la Basquaise*. 'She's much older, apparently. They met on an archaeological dig in Tunis and – Titus, naughty! Cassie, stop Titus, will you! And where's Dom? Still playing on Daddy's computer? Titus, darling, no!'

'Titus pissed over Daddy's computer,' said Cassie reflectively. 'We had to get a man in.'

'Cassie, don't let Titus put that in his mouth.'

'Titus pissed in the fish tank. All the fish died. Even the snail.'

'Cassie, shut up! Titus, no!'

I gathered up Titus and extracted the ping-pong ball he was attempting, python-like, to swallow.

He let out a howl.

'Mummy says things just go in Titus one end and out the other. I bet you, Dee. He'll piss over you.'

'Poor Titus.' I stroked his hair. As suddenly as it had started, his howling stopped. He turned upon me a pair of enormous pale blue eyes, ingenuous yet all-knowing, master criminal's eyes. He put his thumb in his mouth, buried his head in my breast and, curling like a cat against me, appeared to fall asleep. Despite Cassie, he had a warm, sweet, flowery smell.

'So you were saying,' I said, 'Nigel Larkin got married. In Tunis. To a woman. But do they . . .?'

'Oh, I shouldn't think so,' said Laura, turning fish fingers with one hand, sprinkling cayenne with the other. 'It's for companionship, I gather. She's a nurse and Nigel, remember, is a chronic hypochondriac, so they've got lots in common – Ah, Dominic, supper's ready. Good grief, you might have warned us it was fancy dress!'

Dominic lolled against the kitchen lintel, his eyes concealed behind over-sized shades, his hair teased into a quiff, his matchstick legs dwindling upwards from flipper-length trainers into voluminous candy-striped trousers hacked off at the knee. He flexed his shoulders, chewed imaginary gum. 'Yo, man!' he said. 'It's cool.'

'Dom! Are those your new pyjama trousers?'

'Bermudas, Mum. They're seriously cool.'

'Hee, hee!' shrieked Cassie. 'Doesn't Dom look stupid?'

'Oh, Dom. You might at least have cut both legs the same length.'

'Mummy, Dee – doesn't he look stupid? Domdom's a dumdum!'

'And if that stuff in your hair's my new bath oil that Daddy brought back from duty free –'

'Domdom's a dumdum! Domdom's a dumdum!'

'It is! Ma Griffe! You'll be reeking for weeks.'

'Actually,' said Dominic with dignity, 'if you weren't so square, Mummy, you'd know Bermudas are what's going down at the moment. Everyone in Covent Garden's wearing them, aren't they, Dee?'

'Domdom's a dumdum! Domdom's a dumdum!'

'Tell Cassie to shut up. She doesn't know anything. She's just a girl.'

'And you're just a boy, so there. A dumdum boy!'

Dominic lunged at Cassie, who leapt sideways. He grabbed her leg and they fell, sprawling.

'Children! Dominic, careful of Daddy's dark glasses. Children! Dom! Let go of Cassie! You'll hurt her.'

'He'll tear my leg off,' said Cassie cheerfully. 'There'll be gallons of blood.'

'Oh well,' said Laura, returning to the stove. 'Supper's ready anyhow. And Daddy'll be home soon.'

I looked down at Titus, oblivious, angelic, contentedly sucking his thumb. I watched Laura as she set plates of fish fingers and peas on the table and hunted for the ketchup. Her hair is sandy now, its natural colour, and gathered up at random away from her face, which, innocent of make-up, is scrubbed a shiny pink. She has gained at least a stone, lives in sweatshirt and jeans, has, to my knowledge, only one evening dress and a mere three or four pairs of heels. Yet I felt a twinge of envy. Laura is no longer obliged to accept questionable invitations on the improbability that her hosts might just also have invited the answer to her life. Laura no longer walks into rooms eyeing every male for potential; she can hold conversations over paper plates of Coronation Chicken without wondering whether the other person is with someone, what he looks like without his clothes, whether he is the kind of man who blows down women's ears. It was a state of mind I could scarcely imagine. I wondered why happily married people ever bothered with parties. I looked down at Titus and sighed.

'How is Charlie?' I said.

'Oh, lovely as ever.' She adjusted gas levels under the saucepans, swept a clutch of cuddly animals from a chair.

94

'Tired, though. Darlings, stop that now! Come and sit up at the table. They work him too hard at this new job. All this protestant work ethic nonsense – in at seven thirty, meetings till all hours. Sometimes, poor darling, he doesn't get home till ten or eleven. Cassie! Dom! I said cease.'

Out in the hall the phone rang. Laura wiped her palms on her jeans. 'Oh dear, I hope that isn't Charlie. He promised to be home at seven, on pain of death.'

Dominic and Cassie had picked themselves up and climbed on to chairs, from which they continued to snipe at each other. Above the uproar occasioned by Dominic trying to force-feed Cassie a fish finger, Laura's voice drifted from the hall.

'You what? Oh hell! . . . But darling, you swore, cross your heart . . . What? . . . Charlie, I can't hear you, it seems to be a bad line, lots of noise and voices your end . . . What? . . . Yes, I'll apologize to Dee . . . Love you, too. Goodbye.'

She returned, shrugging her shoulders. 'That company has more crises than a banana republic. Poor darling, we'll have to keep something warm for him. Dom! Cassie! Sit straight and eat sensibly.'

'Can't,' said Cassie. 'Dom stinks. Pooh! I feel sick.'

'I agree it's a bit like eating in Harrods' perfumerie. Dom, darling, go upstairs and wash that stuff off your hair. Dee, you'd better pass Titus over to me.'

Titus, as if on cue, stirred in my arms and let out a soft, luxuriating sigh. A stench of ammonia and Brussels sprouts rose up powerfully to compete with Ma Griffe.

'Pooh!' said Cassie. 'I told you so! I told you so!'

'Oh Titus, you little monster,' said Laura. She laughed as, handing him over, I lowered an anxious glance into my lap. 'That's marriage for you, Dee. Hooligan children, an absentee husband, and a potential Nobel prize-winner who won't be potty-trained. How wise of you not to touch it with a barge pole.' But the smile she shot

95

me as she moved to the door, cradling Titus, was unpardonably smug.

Almost before I could remember, my mother had operated scorched earth tactics against my father. At first she worked under cover. There was the pretext, for instance, of taste – since she could not hang our walls with Renoirs or Cézannes, we should have to make do with bare distemper. Then there was convenience: 'What's the point of having ornaments, Deedee? They only gather dust and you know how much time I have for cleaning.' Or the ever-present issue of economics: 'We can't afford a new hall runner. We'll just have to put up with lino. Your father won't care, he won't even notice.'

The Evanses up the road were as poor as we were, but they had pictures – old photographs and the little Pears Soap boy blowing bubbles. Mrs Linsey opposite had a green-faced woman and a charging elephant, despite her being a widow and having to take in a lodger. The Evanses' house was brown like gravy; brown-painted doors, looming brown cupboards, saggy brown armchairs, and a dark brown smell, compounded of furniture wax and pipe tobacco and things from the butcher boiled for the cat. The Evanses were old, with grown-up children, and I knew my mother thought the house antiquated: but, to me, it was comforting, like a battered leather book of favourite stories. Mrs Linsey's house was as bright and frilly as she was, with cushions and vases and a great many cacti in pots on the window-sills. Mrs Linsey had fawn carpets you had to take your shoes off to walk on and, in front of the lounge gas fire, a white fluffy rug with a furry black spider squatting in one corner. I tried to scorn the spider as I knew good taste required; but, crossing the road to the spartan utilitarianism of our house, I would feel a guilty longing for it, like someone hankering after a perversion.

My mother was right, of course. My father did not

appear to notice the bare lino in the hall, or any other aspect of our domestic deprivation. My mother, infuriated, translated his passive indifference into an active, threatening force. My father's elbows scuffed walls, his hair made greasy patches on armchairs, his feet wore holes in the toughest carpets, his very presence necessitated a battening-down of hatches. 'That's the third cup gone this week, Dee. Your father says they just come to pieces in his hands.'

It was true that my father was not adept at household tasks, hammering his thumb as often as he hit a nail, and failing to distinguish seedlings from weeds (it usually fell to my mother to unblock drains or minister to the Hoover when it had one of its seizures). But my mother seemed to nurture his clumsiness like a culture, so that the more it was remarked upon the more it grew. We accepted the need for stringent precautions: the china was replaced with school-canteen Pyrex, the wedding-present silver with stainless steel; when the coal scuttle disintegrated, we sat nightly round a hearth adorned by an aluminium garden bucket. But still the scope of my father's clumsiness grew until, like a poltergeist, it took possession of the entire household. My mother's very body became threatened and fragile. 'Ouch!' she would cry, 'that's my arm!' or 'Ow! My leg!' as though my father's touch would chip or crack her. I began to catch her watching me for tell-tale signs – 'After all, Dee, you're your father's daughter.' Even the supernatural was not immune from the general contamination: Father Christmas was too hamfisted for fiddly stockings and darkened bedrooms, dumping a haphazard pillowcase outside the door; the tooth fairies lacked the finesse for nocturnal juggling with molars and sixpences and were obliged to make their exchange beneath an upturned egg cup on the kitchen table.

My father continued uncomplaining, seemingly oblivious of the wasteland around him, accepting his reputation

97

as demolition expert without demur. But when I was nine he made a fatal mistake.

My mother, going on the offensive suddenly, demanded a rise in her housekeeping. My father fell into the ambush. Surely, he suggested, there were ways of shopping more cheaply? Surely, she retorted, if he was so clever he should try it? My father tried it. My mother inspected the contents of his shopping bags and told him, fine, he could cook it. And so began my mother's cooking strike, which lasted nearly four years. For four years we lived on a rotation of rump steak, lamb chops and pork chops, with tinned peaches, pears or mandarin oranges for pudding. (I suppose my madeleine is a tinned mandarin orange slithering in its metallic juice like a day-glo slug.)

Often, as I watched Mr Evans put the finishing touch to one of his balsa-wood aeroplanes, or observed Mrs Linsey's lodger handling a bone china cup without mishap, I would ponder the curse that had devastated our household. The Evanses and Mrs Linsey looked the same, inside their houses or outdoors. We looked normal enough, too, when we set out each morning, I in my school uniform, my father in his grey suit for the office, my mother in her smart, if well-worn, navy blue. Even the house, though a little dilapidated, did not look strikingly different from all the other semis in the street. It was just when you opened the front door that everything changed – like one of those film effects where the hero crosses the threshold and finds himself suddenly in the Arizona desert. People did not visit us, not even the Evanses. 'After all,' said my mother accusingly, 'how could you invite people into a place like this?'

It was around my thirteenth birthday that my mother declared all-out war. She got promoted to assistant buyer, and treated herself to a new overcoat and three new frocks. My father, snoring over the newspaper in his usual armchair, did not notice. My mother took the armchair into the garden and chopped it up.

My mother went to the hairdresser's and had her hair dyed a coppery red. My father said: 'God, what do you look like?' My mother rolled up the dining-room carpet and left it out for the dustmen.

My mother bought more frocks, and French knickers, and a chiffon nightdress trimmed with lace. My father said: 'What d'you want to buy a thing like that for?' My mother announced she could not sleep because of his snoring and relegated him to a camp bed in the living-room, which was made up each night and dismantled each morning.

My mother acquired a passport and a whole set of matching suitcases, including a vanity case. My father said: 'What for? You're not going anywhere.' My mother said mysteriously: 'You just . . . never . . . know.' Then she gave the living-room curtains to the rag-and-bone man.

Paint flaked, wallpaper peeled, the Hoover had a terminal seizure and was not replaced. My mother trained her full fire-power upon my father. She could not stand his jaw cracking as he ate his burnt chops; she could not stand his snoring, which she could still hear through the ceiling; she could not stand his rattling the coal bucket or the noise his shoes made or his cricket club tie or the way he put his tongue out when he was concentrating.

Then, one day, my mother became strangely quiet and withdrawn, as if she had exhausted her ammunition. A few weeks later, without a word, she resumed shopping and cooking. She bought a television set and (after my father and I had been instructed at length about switching it on and off lest we should do our worst to the cathode ray tube) the contours of our desert vanished into shadow as we sat, mesmerized to silence, within its blue glow.

'Chrissie says I should give up searching for Mr Single and make do with Mabel.'

'Ah,' said Gilda, spearing the cherry in her manhattan. 'I hardly dared bring up the subject again. Still no dice?'

'I'm working on it.' I said.

'You know, you're insane to turn down my offer. A casting session would be such fun. We could follow all the rules, just as if it were for microwave pizzas or dandruff shampoo. Of course, we ought to start with a detailed casting brief.'

' "Personable, dynamic, authoritative, aspirational, yet friendly and approachable, someone who will appeal to the C2,D,E housewife as a credible dandruff sufferer"?'

'Well, what did you say in *Bright Lights?*'

'Tall, slim, attractive –'

'Handsome, darling heart! Attractive could mean anything. Even Frankenstein's monster appealed to Frankenstein – at least, to begin with.'

'Tall, slim, handsome, unattached man, 40–45 . . .'

'Yes, go on.'

'London only, send recent photograph.'

'Yes?'

'That's it.'

'A trifle bald, perhaps.'

'Oh no, I'd prefer to avoid baldies. And men with dandruff, come to that.'

'Idiot child!' said Gilda, craning after the barman. 'I mean we need lots more detail. For a proper casting brief.'

'But we're not writing a proper casting brief.'

'We could, dear heart. Just as a game. To pass the time while irresistible forces chain us to these bar stools, compelling us to consume sinister, mind-altering cocktails. Just as a game.'

'All right then. Just as a game.'

'Splendid.'

'Well, where shall we begin?'

'Darling heart, don't ask me. You must know what you want.'

I licked the salt from my margarita glass reflectively. 'I do. Of course I do. But . . .'

'Then let's work from what you don't want, that'll be easier. No bald men with dandruff, for starters. Tell me, how do you feel about dentures?' Producing a pen, she abstracted the paper napkin from beneath our dish of peanuts and began scribbling furiously. 'Tall, slim, handsome man, 40–45, own hair and teeth . . .'

'And I'm not mad about men who don't change their socks.'

'Own hair and teeth. Stylish . . .'

'Or men who talk informatively about pension funds and life assurance –'

'Creative.'

'Or about who scored what for Liverpool in the Cup.'

'Cultured.'

'Or men who tune into the World Service on your left nipple.'

'Sensitive.'

'Or men who refer to "my other half" or "the old woman".'

'That goes without saying.'

We both drained our glasses. I signalled to the waiter while Gilda scribbled.

'What about financial circumstances, darling heart?'

'Mmmm. I'm relatively relaxed there.'

'Come, come, my dear. You don't want to keep him. So tiresome when you take him out to dinner and he insists on seeing the pudding menu. Besides, what if it doesn't work out? There's the palimony to consider.'

'That's mercenary, Gilda.'

'Nevertheless, I'll put down "well-heeled". What kind of car?'

'Oh, I don't think –'

'Well, you've never got round to taking your test, and I feel drained just watching you sprint after taxis.'

'I suppose it would be useful for carting Mabel to the vet.'

'Morgan? Aston Martin? Maserati?'

101

'How about a 1953 racing-green Bentley Continental?'

'Narrows the field a bit, don't you think? Tell Mabel she's got ideas above her station. Mmmm! The manhattans are good here – though, mind you, I only drink them for the cherries. Why don't you catch the eye of the person with the shaker while I look over what we've got so far and give it a little polish.'

By the time fresh drinks had arrived, Gilda was on her second paper napkin, with many crossings-out and parentheses. Abandoning the refinement of cocktail sticks, she delved with her index finger for the cherry, balancing it on the underside of her elegant talon and surveying it for some moments, before suddenly devouring it like a sealion thrown a fish. It seemed to provide the necessary inspiration for, after another bout of writing and several more decisive crossings-out, she gathered up the napkin with a flourish.

'How does this sound, darling heart? "Casting Brief – Mr Superlative Single. Client: Dee Devlin. Casting Director: Gilda Kominska –" '

'Sounds just right, so far,' I said, unaccountably missing the bar top with my elbow.

'Shush, dear. Listen to your kind Auntie Gilda. "Our hero should be a tall, handsome six footer, between 40 and 45, with an attractive smile and a good head of hair (the Harrison Ford or Jeremy Irons type). His wardrobe should be elegant, yet informal (designer casuals rather than stuffy business suits). Though he should exude an aura of status and wealth" – I like that, don't you, "exude an aura"? – "this should be underplayed and never vulgar. Whether at the wheel of his high-powered sports coupé, discoursing upon art and literature, or throwing together a delectable paella in the kitchen of his post-modern apartment, he should at all times appear relaxed, confident, at ease, not only with himself, but with the world. He is the man who knows his way round a wine list, who always commands the best table in a restaurant; his car is never wheel-clamped,

102

he never loses his credit cards or phones to tell you the show you want to see is booked solid until after Christmas. Yet, despite his assurance, he has hidden depths –" '

'Sounds like *The Wanton Waves*.'

'What, dear?'

'Nothing, Gilda.'

' "– He has hidden depths. He should convey that his cool exterior conceals a man of sensuality and passion, an imaginative and proficient lover. He firmly believes that women are equal participants in society and sends everything, even his socks and underpants to the laundry" (I put that bit in for obvious reasons).

' "Given the client's requirements, it goes without saying that those called for casting must be single or divorced (no live-in girl-friends)." ' Taking a gulp of her manhattan, Gilda sat back in triumph. 'What do you think, darling heart?'

'Inspired, Gilda.'

'Isn't it just?'

'Truly inspired. But all the same . . . I don't know . . . somehow, there's something missing . . .'

'When I said specific, dear, I don't think we can be *that* specific. Unless – I seem to remember from my straight days, extremities are a good guide. We could specify nothing under a size ten shoe.'

I laughed. 'Gilda, you're evil.'

'And if you're seriously worried, we could recall the short list for a run-through of the script, a quick rehearsal to see what their form is.'

'Oh, Gilda –'

'But otherwise it seems to me pretty comprehensive.'

'Mmmm,' I said, gazing fixedly at my empty margarita glass. 'Comprehensive's the word. But all the same . . .'

'Well, check it yourself,' she said, thrusting the napkin at me. 'Run your eye over it, while I attract the person with the shaker.'

Somehow my eye obstinately refused to run over it – or

perhaps it was that Gilda's intricate scrawl seemed rather more intricate than usual.

'I don't know,' I said, handing it back to her. 'I think perhaps . . .'

'Of course, you're aware it's not my cup of darjeeling personally. I've simply approached the task with my usual ruthless professionalism –'

'Very noble of you, Gilda.'

'And I'll agree in one or two places it may go over the top – perhaps I should axe "post-modern" and that bit about the wheel-clamps. On the whole, though, it's better to aim high at the start – gives you somewhere to pull back from.'

'Very true, Gilda. But . . .'

'But what?' said Gilda, attempting her sealion trick with the cherry again, and this time failing dismally.

'I still think there's something missing.'

Magnetized, Gilda watched the cherry as, laying a slimy trail, it rolled down her blouse, across her lap and, bouncing from her knee, landed neatly in her discarded left shoe, where it disappeared into the toe. 'What, dear heart? What could possibly be missing?'

I stared lugubriously into the depths of my margarita. 'I'd like him to be . . . nice.'

'Nice? What sort of a word is that?'

'A very important word.' I sighed. 'I'd like him to be nice. And love me.'

'There's no need to get maudlin, duckie. Besides, the video camera can't pick up that kind of thing. You're getting harder to please than Zig Zigeuner.'

'Anyway . . . it's only a game.'

'It doesn't have to be. I've got the brief now, I'm poised ready for you to galvanize me into action.'

'It's just a joke, that's all.'

'I'm not joking, darling heart. While I deplore your recidivist tendencies, I'll always help out a friend in extremis.'

'Sweet of you, Gilda,' I said, failing once more to connect my elbow with the bar counter. 'But let's just leave it, shall we?'

'Why? Why leave it, when it's such an utterly inspirational solution to your problems?'

'Because. That's all. Because.'

'Because what? If it's money that bothers you, I'll donate my time and pay for the studio booking. After all, your birthday's coming up. Jamie-Beth and I have decided to swallow our principles and treat you to this as your present.'

'Generous of you. And Jamie-Beth. But, thank you, I simply couldn't –'

'Couldn't what?'

I drained my glass. 'Gilda, it's a joke. And it's getting a bit stale.'

'Couldn't what, what, *what?*' Pushing her spent manhattan aside, she narrowed her eyes to scrutinize me. She appeared to experience some difficulty in focusing. 'Come on, darling heart,' she said, changing tack. 'You can tell your kind Auntie Gilda.'

I sighed. 'It's a joke in poor taste.'

'Heaven forfend! Where's the person with the shaker, we need another drink. What on earth has taste got to do with it?'

'It's just not on, Gilda. Lining up a bunch of actors on false pretences –'

'If you're concerned about the damage to my professional reputation, I think I might, just might, darling heart, be capable of covering myself.'

'Lining them up, ogling at them with the camera, asking them intrusive personal questions –'

'Men do it all the time.'

'Not in that way.'

'Darling, do you wander round The Casting Couch blindfold? Do you never see those seedy creatures in shiny suits the advertising agencies summon out of the woodwork every time there's a swimwear casting?'

'Well yes, but –'

' "Lovey, there's a strong chance your left ankle may be in shot, so forget the swimsuit, just take everything off, will you – show us there are no scars or deformities." '

'Yes, but –'

'And then the demand for extra tapes of the session. All the girls, even the rejects. So the client can run through it again on his video at home – in his brown mackintosh, while his wife's at her Tupperware evening.'

'I know, but –'

'If they can do it, we can do it. Do you honestly think the seedy brigade, the casting cockroaches, are afflicted with delicate scruples about *taste*?'

'I agree, Gilda. But it wouldn't make us any better.'

'Nonsense. By comparison our intentions are as driven snow. Besides, it would be a positive pleasure to give the male sex a dose of its own paregoric.'

'I'm sorry, Gilda, truly I am. But it just isn't on.'

She stared at me for a moment, her lips pursed. Then she turned irritably to her empty glass. 'Dear me. Saint Deirdre, Blessed Patron and Guardian of the Frail Phallus. Well, we'll see. Now where's the bar person? Or are we suddenly in the Gobi Desert?'

A suspicion drifted hazily into my mind. Slowly its outlines took on a fuzzy but identifiable shape. 'Gilda, what did you do with that brief we wrote?'

'D'you know, it's getting darker in here. And colder. Or is it just me? Perhaps I'm dying of thirst. It's like being the hero in a war movie. At any moment you're going to put a last cigarette between my lips and tell me I'm lucky, I've got a Blighty one –'

'They've turned out nearly all the lights and opened the door. I think they're trying to hint at something. Gilda, what have you done with the brief?'

'Ah yes. I spy chairs on tables. Thank goodness for that. I was seriously worried for a moment. I seem to have lost all sensation in my legs.'

106

'Pins and needles. It's these bar stools. Now, Gilda, please – would you give me the brief?'

'Of course we may have been poisoned by an unseen hand. That would account for the creeping paralysis –'

'Gilda!'

'Something deadly slipped into our drinks.'

'Yes, alcohol, Gilda. Now, please. Where have you put it?'

'Put what?'

'Gilda. Come on!'

She surveyed me for a moment, then, very slowly, she unfastened her bag and drew out the paper napkin. I bent forward to take it, but just as my grasp was about to close upon it she snatched it away.

'Gilda, for heaven's sake!'

'Do be careful, darling heart. So undignified to fall off a bar stool. People cruelly assume you are over-refreshed.'

'Gilda, I want that napkin destroyed. Now.'

A waiter was approaching with a tray of empty glasses. Gilda watched his advance thoughtfully. Then, as he drew level, she screwed the napkin into a ball and tossed it into the tray amongst the debris, gesturing ceremoniously, like a conjuror who has just magicked away a whole top-hat full of his audience's watches and spectacles.

I had racked my brains to think of a suitable venue. Unworthily, I had determined that this time, whatever else, there should be no chance of bumping into someone I knew. A certain insensitivity kept drawing my thoughts towards drag bars, somewhere he/she might feel at home with his/her own kind, but mercifully common sense prevailed. Ms Smith herself had only recently moved from Manchester and lived and worked in Kingston, so the choice was mine. In the end, remembering that a colleague of The Virgin's had proclaimed it the perfect location for tête-à-têtes with headhunters, since 'nobody – but nobody – ever goes there', I had chosen The Shakespeare.

107

The Shakespeare Hotel is a bleak concrete construction, set in the no-man's land behind Oxford Street bounded by Baker Street and the Edgware Road, a desert of function rooms and offices. As I negotiated the automatic doors, tactful spot-lights and an acre of brown carpet told me I was in Hotelville, International-land, The World. Yet, despite its leatherette and brass plate, despite its fielding the requisite number of flunkeys, there is a tackiness about The Shakespeare reminiscent of a railway station buffet, a feeling that your glass will be smeared, that the brass trim will come away in your hand, that unmentionable objects have been swept out of sight beneath the sofas. In The Hamlet Bar (only concessions some etchings of Irving and an ice bucket in the shape of a skull) a haze of pine air freshener failed to blot out lunchtime's beer. On bar stools, two bottle blondes in leather micro-skirts ostentatiously studied their pernods-and-blackcurrant, in stand-off with a party of Arabs, while a third girl jangled her earrings at a solitary businessman. My own blond hair and short skirt seemed to attract unwarranted attention. Nervously, I sought out a pair of elderly tourists in his'n'hers hunting jackets, and settled at the table next to them. I produced my evening paper and endeavoured to avoid everyone's eye but the waiter's.

I wondered why I had come. Curiosity, I supposed. Oh, the letter had been engaging, as had the voice on the end of the phone – Marlene Dietrich with a touch of Lancashire flatness to the vowels. And I sympethized with the need to talk to a woman – it must be difficult, a limbo life, an empty corridor with one door firmly closed behind you and the other refusing to open. Yet, sitting in The Shakespeare, sipping lukewarm Riesling, I felt once again a primitive hostility to someone who, despite the hormones and the painful surgery, must surely only be pretending to be a woman; it was as if, obscurely, my own sexuality were under threat. Why had I let myself in for this embarrassment? True, she (I still found the choice of pronoun difficult) had been chatty, even amusing, over the phone. But nevertheless the husky voice conjured up inescapable images. Peering furtively at the doorway over my newspaper screen, I rehearsed in my mind's eye her spectacular entrance: the sequins, the false eyelashes like centipedes, the architectural hair, the eight-inch patent stilettos, the dated, prancing caricature of all things female. I could almost touch the fox fur stole as she sashayed towards my table and struck the opening pose for her rendition of 'Hey, Big Spender!' I saw the beginnings of shadow beneath the panstick, a tell-tale bristle peeping through the fishnet of her stocking . . .

Of course, there was nothing to stop me leaving now. Six-thirty we had said, and the clock told me I still had three minutes' grace. There was nothing at all to stop me leaving, apart from honour and decency. Gingerly, I lowered the newspaper, looked round for the waiter.

The earring girl and the businessman had vanished and the taller of the blondes appeared to be concluding negotiations with one of the Arabs. Beside me, the tourists had ceased their benign contemplation of the English way of life and were shifting in their chairs uncomfortably.

The waiter stood in the doorway with a tray of dirty glasses, in conversation with one of the flunkeys from the foyer. A joke was exchanged, the two moved apart; the waiter stepped blindly forward and, with Chaplinesque timing, brought his loaded tray into collision with the Arab, who was leaving with the blonde. In the resultant mêlée, the blonde screaming abuse, the Arab gesticulating, the waiter seizing the ice bucket and making apologetic dabs at the Arab's shirt front, I at first scarcely noticed a fourth figure hesitating in the doorway.

Neat floral-print shirtwaister, neat white shoulder bag on a gold chain, sensible white court shoes side-stepping the broken glass; a genteel matron up from the suburbs to choose curtain material at John Lewis. She eased her way carefully past the Arab and the screaming girl, paused, scanned the room tentatively, clutching her bag. Then our eyes met and, with purpose, she moved forward. I strove to conceal my disbelief. A tall woman, slightly stooped with, yes (though I should not have noticed, had she not mentioned it), shoulders a trifle too wide. A broad, cheerful face beneath the discreetly-streaked bubble cut, with pale-rimmed spectacles and slightly protuberant teeth. A light dusting of powder, the merest suspicion of pink frosted lipstick. A homely figure, deliberately inconspicuous – yet more out of place in The Hamlet Bar than any of my fantasies.

Reaching my table she extended a neatly manicured-hand. 'Dee Devlin?' said the gin-and-cigarettes voice so curiously at odds with the rest of her. 'Hullo, Dee love. I'm Ann.'

'So Somerset House won't change your birth certificate?'

'I could flash my boobs and vagina at them, love, they'd still say I was Andrew.'

Agreeing on the need to escape from The Hamlet Bar, we had spurned the international cuisine of The Twelfth Night Restaurant for The As You Like It Eaterie – stripped pine and Coca-Cola mirrors, pizzas and burgers. Amongst the tourists in their non-iron jersey two-pieces, she merged as if camouflaged.

'That seems so unjust,' I said, 'after all you've been through.'

She dabbed her lips delicately with her napkin. 'You expect a certain amount of prejudice when you're a curiosity like me. It's very brave of you, Dee love, to take me on. It's so nice to talk frankly to someone. I haven't dared tell the girls at work, and the women I used to know in Manchester – well, most of them couldn't cross the street fast enough, after I'd had the op.'

110

'Perhaps they thought you were a spy from the enemy camp.'

Behind her thick lenses her eyes blinked gratefully. 'All the more thanks to you for not thinking the same.'

I tried not to look sheepish. 'Oh, I don't – not now I've met you. Only I am curious. I suppose – well, I suppose I can't imagine why anyone would ever want to be a woman.'

'But I didn't have a choice. I've always been female. Even when I was kicking a football round the school playground, even when I signed up for my apprenticeship in the RAF, I always felt I was a woman inside.'

'You mean you always longed for frocks and make-up?'

'Oh, I adore all that now. Goodness, you've had me rattling on about shops like a tape on fast forward. But no, I just knew, when I caught sight of my prick – which I tried not to do whenever possible – that divine bureaucracy had made a stupid administrative mistake. Within, I had a female soul.'

'Good heavens,' I said. 'I'm not sure if I'd recognize the female soul.'

'You know what I mean, love. Not competitive or aggressive. Sensitive, intuitive, yielding – caring. And oh, isn't it lovely to have a really good weep when you want one?'

I smiled wryly. 'Women aren't supposed to cry any more. They're supposed to wear stiff upper lips and smart little business suits, and be just as competitive and ambitious as men – without, of course, compromising their essential femininity.'

'Well, obviously I don't approve of all that. What's the point of women's lib if it just confuses everything? Who wants to be strong the whole time, and watch your back, and know you've got to keep climbing that ladder because you're the breadwinner and anyway, you've got no role in life if you don't? Strikes me, it's a bit of a mug's game, being male.'

111

'It's still a man's world, though, in everything that counts. The middle-class Caucasian male still inherits the universe.'

'And what price his inheritance if all it amounts to is gastric ulcers and a new BMW with a car telephone?'

I backed off, escaping into laughter. 'Oh, I don't know, Annie. I certainly can't begin to imagine what it feels like to be a man.'

She joined my laughter. 'Neither can I, Dee. Never have been able to. Oh, I love their company. But it's always seemed to me they belong to some club I can't ever join.'

'You can say that again.'

CHAPTER

SIX

A sense of dislocation hit me as I walked into The Casting Couch, a feeling that I must still be drunk from the night before. I seemed to be seeing two of everything. Beneath the window two identical fat ladies in identical frilly frocks sat knitting identical sweaters. Over by the shelves of directories and *Spotlights* two identical bikers flexed identical tattoos. Identical cub scouts with red hair and freckles picked their noses; identical clowns were dialling on the reception telephones. On the far wall two identical trouser-suited wives with identical sports-jacketed husbands sat like a row of book ends; I retreated from the eerie gaze of two sets of four identical eyes. Mercifully, there was still only one coffee machine, and one Samantha, fully occupied on the switchboard as usual, being officious to a client. I raised my eyebrows, swivelling my gaze to take in the room. 'Weird!' I mouthed. She shrugged a sour shoulder at the Studio One board. 'Zig Zigeuner,' it read. 'Masuji Stereo Systems.'

A new novel lay open on the desk. *Heart By-Pass*. In a grimly lit corridor two gowned and masked figures clung to each other, their rubber gloves entwined. 'He had promised her intensive care. But would their love

113

end up in Casualty . . .?' Coming abruptly off the phone, Samantha snatched the book away with a sniff.

She, too, looked different this morning, I thought, though perhaps it was the effect of her singularity in a world that was suddenly double. Her jaw seemed heavier, her lashes scantier, and there was a pustule on her upper lip. Altogether, she appeared to have diminished in lustre, as if some important component of her mechanism were missing. Even in delivering her litany about the messages – 'Only a Miles Jangle for Zig Zigeuner' – she seemed bereft of enthusiasm; and her refrain of 'No one loves you this morning' was positively half-hearted.

Closing my office door on the world of stereophonic cub scouts, I lit a cigarette and sipped my coffee. On the third floor they had finished casting the Alex Power feature and were beginning a TV series about plumbers. Nobody loved me this, or any, morning. Gilda was right. Apart from providing me with an insight into the pitfalls of being a transsexual and an encyclopaedic knowledge of the seamier watering holes of London, the advertisement had proved a complete failure. Perhaps I had been wrong to dismiss a casting session out of hand. Perhaps I should advertise again. Or perhaps I should simply accept that, in a binary universe, I was doomed to be a perpetual odd number.

Staring into space, I contemplated a life of celibacy. After a few minutes of this – maybe due to the oppressive heat, or to a mocking association of ideas – I felt my pelvic muscles contract hungrily. I thought of The Virgin. Three weeks, four days, and he had not once phoned me. Not that I wanted him to phone, not that I was prepared, under any circumstances, to speak to him. I had excised him at last, like a painful corn. I stared at my photograph of Mabel, as if to confirm my strength of mind. Mabel's round mustard eyes stared back at me blankly. My pelvic floor continued its involuntary contractions. The telephone rang.

114

'Hullo, Dee,' said The Virgin.

'Ker–sploosh!' I said, choking on my coffee.

'Dee? Dee! Are you OK?'

'I'm fine. Wonderful. Or I was until I picked up the phone.'

'Thing is, Dee, I know you're angry with me. But we've got to talk.'

(Tell him to take a long promenade off a short pier. Or, better still, just hang up.)

'I've been trying to get through to you for three days.'

(He misses me. He's discovered how much he loves me.)

'I knew you were angry when you didn't return my calls.'

(Don't fall for it, Dee. Just this once, don't fall for it.)

'Pull the other one,' I said. 'There haven't been any messages.'

'I've been leaving them every day. I was frantic –'

'Here? At the office?'

'With Whajamacaller.'

(Samantha! I am going to kill Samantha!)

'Thing is – something's happened, something unforeseen (My God! His wife's agreed to a divorce.)

'I had to call you – talk to you about it –'

(A divorce? It's the usual tissue of lies. For heaven's sake, just hang up, you fool!)

'I've been really desperate, Dee. In a terrible state. Ever since – well, ever since three days ago, when I found out . . .'

The line went dead. I shook the receiver, I hammered at the phone, I bounced it up and down. Stone dead. The Virgin had found out three days ago that he could not live without me, had persuaded his wife to divorce him, had been living in hotel rooms, walking the streets, declining into despair with every futile phone call, every unanswered message. And now, now when at last he had got though to me – Samantha had cut him off. I would

115

batter Samantha with The Brides Book, suffocate her with her St Michael silk négligés, force her to swallow her diamond solitaire –

The phone rang. I snatched it up.

'Zig?' said a voice. 'Is Zig there?'

'Please –' I said.

'Tell Zig it's Mel. About the fountains. I need a decision.'

'Please,' I said. 'Go away.'

'Sorry? Is that Julie? Can you get Zig to the phone? Or tell him I've had a look at the ground plan of A Stage and it's no go. Tell him if he wants two life-size Trevi fountains, plus a bandstand, plus a throng of peasant extras, he's going to find his peasant throng shuffling round crabwise like commuters in the rush hour –'

'Please,' I said, 'you have the wrong number. Could you get off the line.'

'You mean I'm not through to The Casting Couch? But I spoke to the switchboard.'

'You want Studio One. This is not Studio One. This is my line and you're interrupting a very important call –'

'Then could you transfer me?'

'I was on an important call, a matter of life and death. If I transfer you, you'll block my line. Please put your phone down and call again.'

'You're kidding? It's taken four goes to get through this time.'

I gritted my teeth. 'Then leave a message.'

A gale of laughter assaulted my ear. 'Now I know you're kidding.'

My patience snapped. 'Are you by any chance Miles Jangle alias Jingo alias Jello?'

'Jago. Mel Jago.'

'Well, whatever you're called, I think you have a nerve to complain about our message service. We could paper our walls with your messages. In fact, you are exceptionally privileged. Our entire corporate message-

116

taking capability appears to be devoted exclusively to you. Anyone else who phones this company finds their messages automatically diverted to The Bermuda Triangle or swallowed up in a deep black hole. But you – you have the incredible fortune to penetrate the super-efficient security of our message-shredding system, to slip messages under the net – you, alone, of everyone else in London, and probably the world. Just tell me, Miles Jingo, what is so special about you?'

'I think it might be faster if you just transferred me to Zig. I do need a decision on those fountains.'

'I do not care about your fountains, Miles. I do not care if you, and Zig Zigeuner, and your entire troupe of shuffling peasants fall into them and drown. I was in the middle of a very important call when your call cut me off, and you are now blocking my line. I have asked you to replace your receiver and try again. Since you are apparently too much of a creep to do so, I shall now take the only course left to me and replace mine!'

In fury, as I tore the phone from my ear, I heard his voice drift back sweetly: 'Great talking to you too, darling. Have a nice day.' Partly to get my breath back, and partly to make sure he had gone, I forced myself to count to ten before dialling The Virgin's office. On nine, the bell went.

'Please, Dee – I know you're angry, but please, listen to me –'

'Darling!' I said.

'Please don't hang up on me again.'

'We were cut off,' I said. 'Oh darling, I wouldn't do that to you, how could you even think it? It's wonderful to hear from you. But tell me, what's happened? Are you all right?'

'Thing is, it's difficult. Where had I got to when you hung up?'

'You were in a terrible state. And three days ago you'd made this incredible discovery . . .'

117

'Ah. Yes. Well –'

'I'm listening, darling.'

'Well – thing is – it's Meaty Doggi-Chunx.'

'Oh?'

'We're making this commercial and I promised the client I'd supervise it personally. Every step of the way.'

'Oh?'

'Well – thing is, we're shooting with Zig Zigeuner.'

'Oh!'

'And he always does his casting at The Casting Couch.'

'We don't cast dogs. We don't have the facilities.'

'Oh, we're getting the dogs from Cute Canines. But we need two housewives, a bishop and a retired colonel. And, thing is –'

'Yes?'

'We're booked into Studio One, right next to your office. So I thought –'

'Yes?'

'Well, I thought, after all that's happened, it might be embarrassing if we bumped into each other. I thought I'd better warn you, so you could be out.'

'I see.'

'It's Monday afternoon, two thirty to six, if you want to put it in your diary.'

'Thank you. Very thoughtful of you.'

'I just didn't want you to have a nasty shock.'

'Well, thank you. I'll make a note of it. How kind of you to call and let me know. Shame you had such trouble getting through. Thank you – and goodbye!'

When I had replaced the receiver, I stared at the phone for a while. I lit a cigarette. I picked up the phone and spoke for some moments to the receptionist on the third floor. Then I stubbed out my cigarette, smoothed my hair, and strode purposefully into the outer office.

'Samantha!'

The double images had altered, shifting or reshaping themselves. The cub scouts still lolled in a corner, kicking their heels, but a pair of pony-tailed nymphettes had replaced the bikers by the bookshelves and, under the window, a duo of spinster ladies now plied their needles, one at either end of a single strip of petit point. It struck me, as I waited for Samantha to come off the phone, how the double image was, after all, an illusion, how in every case one twin was more vivid, indefinably more substantial than the other, as if I were merely observing a trick performed by blotting paper.

Samantha came off the phone. Her eyes appeared lashless now, her nose red and squashed, giving her the look of a disgruntled Pekinese.

'Helen from Studio Three will be down to take care of the switchboard,' I said. 'Please come into my office. And bring the message pad with you.'

Samantha sighed. 'But there aren't any messages.'

'That is precisely the point I should like to discuss.'

She stared up at me sullenly. Then a curious upheaval began in her face, a tremor spreading, swelling into an earthquake, shaking eyes, nose, mouth into a formless scarlet blotch.

'Owow!' she howled. 'Owowowow! Owww!' as from all sides, matching pairs of eyes widened in astonishment.

She put her hands up as if to hold in check her disintegrating features. And now, at last, I observed the conspicuous absence of the diamond solitaire.

'He says he's too young to get married. We've found a nice house only two streets from my mum and dad, nearly saved the deposit. My dad's promised us the carpets as a wedding present, my Uncle Ron says he'll do us the fitted kitchen cost price, my nan'll make the curtains. And now Wayne says he wants to smoke dope and go out to night-clubs and play the field . . . Owowow!'

I had settled Samantha on my sofa, and found the Kleenex and the office vodka from my desk drawer, and had put my arm around her, but it was fully ten minutes before she had been able to utter a coherent word. Now she sat hunched and shivering, glass in one hand, ball of sodden Kleenex in the other, tears still oozing relentlessly from crimson-slitted eyes.

'Do you think I should have saved myself, Dee?'

'You what?' I said.

'Mum says I should have saved myself. I thought it would be all right once we got engaged. But Mum says I should have waited till I had the wedding-ring on my finger.'

'A touch old-fashioned perhaps. And it does rather smack of commerce. Like waiting for the bank to clear the cheque.'

'He's not a teenager any more. He's twenty-three. All our mates are settling down. He's got a good steady job in my dad's removal business, we've got money put aside in the building society, my mum would do anything for us – she even pays for us to go to the Algarve with her and dad every year.'

'Perhaps he feels a bit smothered.'

'Smothered? Wayne? It's me that gets smothered. Six years I've given him, going to football with him on Saturdays, taking cookery evening classes, getting to appreciate Heavy Metal, listening to his mates swapping smutty jokes in the pub. And now, come the crunch – he says he's sick of babysitting in front of the telly, says he's got to go off and find himself!'

'Well . . . maybe . . . I mean, now this has happened . . . maybe you should try it, too.'

She gaped at me. 'Try what?'

'Finding yourself.'

'But I have found myself. I want to get married and have a family. I'm twenty-four years old. Both my best girl-friends are married. Mum and dad were married when they were nineteen.'

'All the same, there can be more to life, you know.

120

Cultivating your own interests . . . developing your career . . .'

'And end up like my Auntie Sandra? Wake up one day and the good men have gone and all I've got is a boring job and a flat smelling of cat's pee and I'm the wrong side of thirty and well past it? Oh –' She crammed the Kleenex into her mouth in consternation. 'Oh, I'm sorry, Dee. I didn't mean – oh, and you've been so nice . . .'

I reached for the vodka bottle to counteract this fresh spate of tremors, on second thoughts pouring myself a stiff one too. 'Being single does have its compensations,' I said brightly, handing her the tissue box while I strove to muster them. 'And, after all, it's important to any relationship to feel secure in your own identity, so you don't get submerged.' I expatiated at some length on the joys of being independent, of learning to know one's self and feel comfortable in one's own company. I dwelt upon the satisfaction of achieving one's potential. I enlarged upon the necessity of rejecting gender stereotypes and understanding the modern, multi-faceted role of woman until Gilda and Jamie-Beth would have been proud of me. I was not sure that Samantha grew convinced, but the rise and fall of my voice, combined with the vodka, seemed to have a sedative effect.

'And anyway,' I said, my enthusiasm faltering, 'once Wayne sees what a fascinating, independent person you've become, maybe he'll have second thoughts. Maybe he'll even get a bit jealous . . .'

This brightened her immediately. She swabbed her nose, began to scrub the mascara from her cheeks.

'Oh Dee, you've been ever so kind. I'm so sorry about saying – you know. I mean, you're not anything like my Auntie Sandra. You're really well-preserved for your age.'

'Thanks,' I said.

'And I'm sorry about the messages. I know I've been awful recently. I've had a lot on my mind, what with arranging about the wedding, and now – this.'

121

Her chin trembled, I feared the earthquake again. 'Don't worry,' I said hastily. 'Just try to be more careful in future.'

'Oh, I do try, really I do. But sometimes the switchboard flashes again before I've written everything down, and then I forget. And sometimes I leave the messages on my desk and they just go missing – I think I must bin them by mistake. Even when I do write things down, I'm in such a state at the moment I can't read my own writing.' She picked up the yellow message pad and flicked through it ruefully. 'This one, for instance. I always have trouble catching his name, so I even asked him to spell it this time. But now – for the life of me – could it be Dago? Or Sago, maybe?'

'Jago,' I said.

'He always gets me confused. He has such a lovely sexy voice.'

'Really?' I said.

'Mmmm. All quiet and husky.'

'When I spoke to him just now he sounded like a pushy, insensitive, patronizing prat.'

She pondered this for a moment, mopping her nose. 'Well, there you are. You just can't tell. You know Wayne can be insensitive sometimes. And pushy.' She drained her glass. She sighed. 'You know, men can be bastards sometimes, can't they, Dee?'

My father believed the world would grind to a halt if he missed the news. Nightly, his single-minded concentration helped Kennedy outwit Kruschev, the police arrest CND marchers and the Tristan da Cuhna islanders flee their volcano. During intervals between bulletins he would strain his eyes combing the morning's *Telegraph* for unread snippets (house fires, inquests, scout jamborees) whose dramatis personae would hang in limbo if they escaped his notice. Often the burden of keeping the earth turning exhausted him. His eyes would close, his mouth would open, his head would loll dangerously from the back-rest of his armchair; whereupon his neck would snap upright, rocking him forward and transforming his nascent snore into a grunt.

This evening the sea-saw of snorts and grunts had been set in motion earlier than usual, leaving a murderer bereft of a verdict and the whole Scottish Premier League awaiting the final whistle. My mother waited too, rustling sweet papers irritably on the sofa: she had recently been promoted to buyer, but her new suit and her hair, now a vibrant chestnut, had been received without comment.

My mother rose abruptly and switched off the television. My father lurched forward with a volley of grunts.

'Have a heart, Kitty. I was watching that.'

'I want to go out,' she said. 'You go drinking every Saturday with your cricketing cronies. All I do is sit here, entombed, listening to you snore.'

'Come off it, Kitty. I wasn't snoring.'

'I want to go to The Rose and Crown for a drink. If you won't come, I'll go by myself.'

My father jerked upright, clutching his newspaper to his chest like a shield. 'Don't be a bloody fool, Kitty.'

'I've been a fool all my life. Only a bloody fool would put up with this.'

'Deirdre,' said my father, 'go up to your room and finish your homework.'

'I'm getting my coat,' said my mother. 'I'm going now.'

'Please,' I said. 'There's a Western on ITV in ten minutes. It's got John Wayne in it. Couldn't we switch the telly on again?'

'Do as you like,' said my mother. 'I'm going to The Rose and Crown.'

'Deirdre, will you go upstairs to your room.'

'But I've finished my homework.'

'You should obey your father.'

123

'Oh, leave the child alone.'

'Please, Mother. Let's watch John Wayne. Please don't have another row.'

'It's none of your business, Deirdre,' said my mother.

'Do as I say,' said my father.

'Deirdre,' said my mother, 'do as your father says.'

I paused on the stairs, listening to the echo of the slammed living-room door. I could go to my room and unearth the lipstick and eyeshadow I had filched from my mother's dressing-table. I could drape myself in the imitation shot silk bedspread and, teetering on my mother's evening sandals which she never had occasion to wear, I could pose before the wardrobe mirror admiring my years-older-than-thirteen image, letting the orange-green material slide down to expose my breasts. But, however hard I concentrated on being a film star with a mink coat and a white telephone, I should still hear voices from down below. On the whole, it was less painful to listen properly. I settled on the top stair.

'A woman,' my father was saying, 'going into a pub on her own –'

'I asked you to come with me. But oh no, you'd rather sit here getting square eyes.'

'Do you think I want to watch you making a fool of yourself again? Throwing yourself at men, imagining they're attracted to you.'

'If you're referring to Roy Bellstead, that's all you know.'

'I do know, as a matter of fact. I know it was just in your mind.'

'So what are you now, Gerald? Besides being judge, jury and prosecuting counsel? Expert psychiatric witness as well?'

'I know. I spoke to him about it.'

A small silence fell.

'You – did – what?' my mother said.

'As your husband, I thought I should take him aside,

124

man to man. He said there was nothing between you, that you'd invented it.'

Another silence. My mother's voice came out of it, softly at first, but rising. 'So that's why he doesn't go to The Rose and Crown any more, that's why . . . You bastard, Gerald! You mean, interfering, self-righteous bastard! I want a divorce.'

A further silence.

'Well, say something!' screamed my mother. 'Don't just sit there with that supercilious smirk on your face.'

A pause. 'I'll come to the pub if you want.'

'I don't want to go to the pub. I want out. O-U-T!'

'Keep your voice down, Kitty. The McCreadys can hear every word through the wall.'

'Damn the McCreadys! I want a divorce.'

'I don't want to discuss it.'

'I've got grounds. Mental cruelty.'

'I don't believe in divorce. It's not what I've been brought up to believe. What on earth would people think?'

There was a harsh, metallic sound – the coal shovel, probably, hitting the wall and rebounding on to the television set – followed by scuffling.

'Here, go easy, Kitty,' said my father breathlessly.

The living-room door burst open and my mother issued out of it with my father catching at her elbow. She shook him off and ran towards the front door.

'Go easy, Kitty. Steady on!'

My mother tore at the Yale lock, breaking her finger-nails. 'Leave me alone. Just leave me *alone!*'

'You haven't got your coat. You can't go to the pub without your coat.'

'I'm not going to the bloody pub! I'm going for a walk. Anywhere to get out of here!'

My mother had managed to prise the door open. My father grabbed her by the shoulders, forcing it shut.

'Whoa there, Kitty. Whoa there!'

125

'I'm not a bloody horse!' screamed my mother, hacking at his shins and wrenching the door open again. They struggled on the threshold. My mother bit my father's hand.

'Do you want your precious McCreadys to hear us fighting on the doorstep? Perhaps they'll call the police. And then, Gerald, what would people think?'

My father let go of my mother. 'Have a heart, Kitty,' he said, as the door slammed behind her. 'Have a heart.'

He hovered purposelessly for a moment. Then, looking up, he saw me at the top of the stairs. 'Deirdre, I told you to stay in your room and finish your homework.'

'Why don't you let her go?'

'A woman can't sit in a pub on her own.'

'I mean a divorce. Why don't you give her a divorce?'

My father looked up at me. The small tight smile my mother described as his supercilious smirk crossed his face.

'I don't care if you get divorced.'

'It's none of your business, Deirdre.'

'You're my mother and father, aren't you?'

The small smile continued to play on my father's lips.

'I want you to get a divorce. It would be better than this.'

'You don't understand, Deedee,' said my father. 'Your mother is a woman over forty. Where would she go? Who'd take care of her? She wouldn't manage on her own.'

I buried my face in my knees. 'Oh Da! I can't stand it. I can't stand any more rows.'

'Dinna fash yourself, Deedee. Dinna fash yourself.'

I looked up. I stared at him. 'Don't say that!' I screamed. 'It's horrid. It doesn't mean anything. Why can't you say things properly? Why can't you use real words?'

'Deirdre, don't speak like that to your father.'

'I'll speak to you how I bloody well like!'

'Show some respect. You should respect your father.'

126

'Why? Why, why, why?'

'Because I say so. Now go to your room!'

'I won't. I bloody well won't!'

My father favoured me with the smile again, his cheek muscles stiff, his upper lip curled. Then he went down the hall to the living-room. Seconds later from behind the closed door came gun-shots and menacing music, and I knew he was sitting there impassively, waiting for the late night news bulletin, making sure he kept world events on their course.

The July sales were in progress. I have always disliked sales, viewing them as an irritating interruption to serious shopping. Firstly, who wants to buy something which is, by definition, already *passé*? Secondly, half the pleasure of shopping is in the impulsive spending of money you do not possess: to hedge this pleasure, and its attendant guilt, with spurious justifications about 'savings' and 'bargains' is to taint the purity of the experience. And thirdly, sales tend to attract amateurs, who are content to mill about, browsing.

The serious shopper will never go into a shop just to look. Oh, she may claim that is what she is doing, she may even have committed herself to a quest (for the ultimate pair of non-see-though white trousers, for instance, or another go-with-everything black polo neck). But, once over the threshold, she is committed to buy if there are things to be bought. She does not thumb through the racks speculating how she might look in fuchsia or whether she should try a second go at culottes. She homes in with laser precision on what she feels is inescapably 'her', items she knows she will hanker after regretfully for weeks if she fails to snap them up. The ultimate white trousers quickly transform themselves into a batik shirt, two pairs of shoes and a cream silk peplum jacket. Decisiveness, efficiency and speed are of the essence, so that she can move on to the next shop. Myself, I never waste time with changing

127

rooms. If that slinky fake leopard skin skirt won't zip up over jeans and a baggy sweater, it probably won't zip up anyway. My idea of heaven is a near-empty shop with this season's stock fresh on the rails – a clear run through, a thrust of the credit card, then out into the street again clutching my trophies.

I wasn't, in truth, quite sure about the batik shirt, its combination of green, ginger and aubergine being something of a departure for me. But two shops along I found a khaki Bermuda shorts suit with which it looked staggering. A pair of cowboy boots and a hat pin later, I consulted my watch. Two fifteen. Though I should have to suffer the indignity of sandwiches at my desk, I was determined to be back at D'Arblay Street in a quarter of an hour. Monday, 2.30–6 p.m., Meaty Doggi-Chunx casting. No man was going to dictate to me when I should, or should not, be in my own office.

'I knew it was a sign', said The Virgin. 'I knew if you were in your office it meant you'd forgiven me. But I didn't expect to find you standing there half naked.'

'Two points,' I said, summoning as much dignity as a person can who is trying to fasten her fly while simultaneously tucking in a sketchily-buttoned batik shirt. 'First, I am in my office because I happen to work here. Second, when your casting session finished, over an hour ago, and I concluded the building was empty, I was scarcely to know you were still skulking around like a bit part from a bad spy movie.'

'I went for a quick drink with Zig's producer. And when I came back, there you were waiting for me – in nothing but your bra and cowboy boots.'

'Third, I am changing my clothes because I am going out to dinner. Now.'

We surveyed each other across a sea of carrier bags, tissue paper and scattered clothing. Determinedly, I seized my make-up pouch and turned to the mirror.

128

'Thing is, Dee – I've missed you so much.'

I heard the crackle of footsteps on tissue paper.

'I wanted to say I'm really sorry.'

I lifted my mascara brush to my lashes and found, with irritation, that my hand was shaking.

'I – I've brought you a present, Dee.'

I turned. He was standing five paces from me, holding out a Foyles paper bag.

'A present. To say I'm sorry.'

I put down my mascara brush and took the paper bag, carefully avoiding touching his fingers. I laid it upon my desk. 'Thank you.'

'Aren't you going to open it? It's a book.'

'D'you know, from the shape, size and wrapping I'd never have guessed. A book. You always buy me books when you're feeling guilty.'

His squirrel nose twitched agitatedly. 'Please, Dee –'

I took up the paper bag again and extracted its contents. '*Nuclear Winter: A Marxist Analysis of Political Economy and the Class Struggle in the Aftermath of the Third World War.*'

'You haven't got it already?'

'Not that one. Thank you.'

'I thought it would interest you, Dee.'

'Oh, it does. No, don't spoil it for me by telling me the plot. I want to be kept guessing till the very last page.'

His eyes glittered, I thought for a second his chin quivered. 'Don't hurt me, Dee. I love you so much. I don't deserve to be hurt.'

'You hurt me,' I said.

There was an ink smudge beneath his left ear, I noticed, and two of his shirt buttons were missing.

'You're the only one who understands me, Dee. The only one who listens to me. I was talking to Rosemary about the ozone layer last night, really trying to outline the major issues, and all she could say, after an hour, was, "I think The Dog needs a walk".'

'How is The Dog?'

129

'The new vet's diagnosed a hormone imbalance. I think of you all the time, Dee, in board meetings, in Meaty Doggi-Chunx presentations –'

He had advanced a few more paces, so that by now I was backed up against the mantelpiece.

'I think of you when I'm lying awake listening to Rosemary grinding her teeth. I have to creep to the bathroom to put myself out of my misery. We went for a curry – one look at the menu, and I was in agony –'

'I'm going out to dinner. I've got to get ready.'

'I can't stand you looking so sexy in those cowboy boots.'

'I'm having dinner with Ambrose and Sergei. I mustn't be late.'

'I think of you in bed with other men. It drives me wild.'

'Sergei's making Tapas. He's been cooking since Saturday –'

'Oh, Jeez, why do you do this to me? Why are you going out to dinner without your knickers? A blind man could tell you're naked under those shorts.'

'VPL. Please, I must finish my make-up.'

'Vacant Pussy to Let? Very Provocative Labia?'

'Visible Panty Line. Now – go away!'

Grabbing me round the waist, he pressed his mouth on mine.

'No,' I gurgled.

'Yes. Oh shit. Oh yes.'

'No,' I grunted feebly, realizing my hand, from force of habit, had already strayed to his fly.

'Yes,' he said, tugging at the buttons of my waistband.

'No. You'll make me late for dinner.'

'Yes,' he said, pulling my shorts down to my thighs.

'And anyway, what about Rosemary?'

'It's her Assertiveness Training evening,' he said, falling to his knees and sliding his tongue stealthily towards my

clitoris. 'Oh shit, Dee, you're so naked. And – mmmm
– so wet.'

I wound my fingers into the chewed strands at the nape
of his neck. I crushed his face into my pubic hair. I arched
my back.

'Oh God!' I moaned.

'Mmmm.'

'I've just remembered –'

'Mmmm. Mmmm.'

'I'd better lock the front door!'

Pulling on my shorts, pretending to search in my briefcase for the keys, I surreptitiously pocketed my Dutch cap.
'I won't be a minute,' I said.

'Hurry,' he said, struggling out of his Levis.

'Oh, I shall. I will.'

I rushed downstairs, locked the front door, then tore into
the lavatory. There, as well as inserting my diaphragm,
I stripped off my bra, cramming it out of sight behind
the cistern. In the dash upstairs, the abrasion of my nipples
bouncing against the stiff cotton of my shirt made my
stomach tighten.

'Leave your boots on,' said The Virgin, as I burst
through my office door.

'Ohmigod!' I said, tearing off my shorts. 'You're going
to make me so late for dinner.'

'What did you say Sergei was cooking?'

'Tapas,' I gasped, as we toppled together on to the
sofa.

'Tortillas,' said The Virgin, squeezing my breasts
through the batik.

'Chorizos,' I said, feeling his erection stabbing at
my belly.

'Gambas al Ajillo,' said The Virgin, working his finger-
tips between my legs.

'Patatas Bravas.'

'Calamares.'

'Pimientos Fritos.'

131

'Meat balls,' he groaned, plunging into me. 'Albondigas.'

'Albondigas. Oh, Albondigas!'

'Huevos.'

'Huevos con Morcilla.'

'Oh shit, Blood Sausage. Put yourself on top of me so I can see your boots. Morcilla! Morcela – !'

We tried to roll over, made a false start, collided with the back of the sofa, rolled over again the other way, felt too late the seat cushions sliding, found ourselves slithering with them, rolling all knees and elbows and cowboy boots to the floor, crash-landing into a heap of carrier bags. At the precise moment we hit the ground I was aware of the door being flung open. There was a gasp. Then an ear-splitting scream.

'Oh my God!' said The Virgin, declining from blood sausage to chipolata.

'Oh my God!' I said, struggling up from underneath him. 'Samantha!'

She was nearly at the corner of D'Arblay Street and Poland Street when I caught up with her.

'Oh Dee, I'm sorry,' she sobbed. 'I'm so sorry.'

'Nonsense. It's me who should apologize. But I thought you'd gone home hours ago. Why ever did you come back?'

'It was the messages.'

'Messages?'

For a moment she was too convulsed for speech. Passers-by slowed to stare at us curiously, at her, crimson-faced and howling, and at me, lipstick-smeared, wild-haired, one shoulder exposed by my flapping batik shirt.

She wiped her nose with the back of her hand. 'I promised I'd try, Dee. And I have, ever so hard. But then, when I was on my way home on the tube, I went to my bag for some mints . . .'

Unzipping her handbag, she began to pull out an

assortment of objects – hairbrush, travel card, nail varnish, curling tongs. Hopping on one leg, she juggled them with her left hand while her right continued to rummage.

'Please, Samantha,' I said, 'there's really no need . . .'

'Here we are.' Triumphantly, she produced from the depths a dog-eared paperback. 'I can't think how they got in here. I haven't been reading it recently – I sort of went off it when Wayne – well, you know . . .'

She flicked through *Heart By-Pass* until, from somewhere amongst the concluding chapters, she extracted a sheaf of sticky yellow message slips.

'I thought, Dee'll never forgive me, she's been so nice and they might be urgent. So I got off the tube and took the opposite line straight back to work. Well, when I found the door was locked, I thought, no point in all that effort wasted, I'll let myself in with my key and go up and leave them on her desk so she'll have them first thing in the morning. And then, when I got to your door and I heard noises – I thought – I thought it was burglars and I was ever so frightened . . .'

She began to howl again. I put my arm around her heaving shoulders. 'You were very brave. And very conscientious. And I'm sorry my friend and I scared you.'

She sniffed and, pausing mid-sob to glance at me, suddenly let out a hiccupping giggle. 'I suppose it's quite funny really. You did both look ever so funny, you in those boots and your friend with his bum in the air and a sofa cushion on his head. I suppose the two of you was just hunting for his contact lens?'

I straightened my shirt. 'Perhaps, Samantha, you'd better give me the messages, since you've come all this way with them.'

I flicked through the yellow sheaf. All the messages dated back to the previous week. And every one was from The Virgin.

★ ★ ★

133

The Virgin was fully dressed when I returned, and clutching the telephone receiver. 'Jeez,' he muttered. 'Jeez, what a disaster.'

'Yes,' I said, beginning to gather up clothes and carrier bags. 'I'm going to be hours late for dinner.'

'Thing is – I've tried to call Rosemary twice and she's not in.'

'You said it was her Assertiveness Training evening.'

'Yes. But I thought I'd better call her – just in case.'

I paused in the act of straightening the sofa cushions. 'Oh, for heaven's sake,' I said.

'You talked to Whajamacaller?'

'She was very upset, poor love, But she's fine now.'

'But you set her straight – told her you'd fire her if she said anything.'

I had been groping under the desk to retrieve my hairbrush. I reared up sharply, bumping my head. 'I most certainly did not. Poor Samantha. She was only trying to be helpful. It's scarcely her fault if she walks innocently into my office and finds us auditioning for a porno movie. What do you think she'll do? Rush off and sell her story to the *News of the World*? "Knickers off in Casting Couch Canoodle. Company Director and Convent Girl Surprised in Steamy Sofa Sex Session"?'

'Half of Soho comes through this studio every day. She'll tell Zig. She'll tell Zig's producer. It'll get back to the agency. Someone's bound to tell Rosemary.'

I sighed. 'Samantha's in a delicate emotional state just now. She's got more on her mind than a three-second glimpse of your naked buttocks. I doubt if she'll gossip. But even if she does, it's quite unlikely to go any further than her mum, her dad, her Uncle Ron and her Auntie Sandra.'

'But how can I chance it? What about Rosemary?'

I bent to my desk drawer for the office vodka. 'More to the point,' I said, pouring two generous measures, 'what about us? That was going to be entirely wonderful until

134

Samantha's spectacular entrance. Now I'm like an Alka Seltzer in a glass of water that somebody knocked over – plink, plink, but where's the fizz?'

His hand, as he took the vodka, was shaking. 'Thing is, you don't understand, Dee. My wife is a –'

'A very jealous woman. I know, you told me. She'll do you over with the upholstery mallet, extract your toe-nails with the can opener, put the poor old Morcilla through the mixer blender.'

'It's not funny, Dee. She's bound to be suspicious.'

I surveyed him over the rim of my tumbler. His nose twitched, his eyes darted, the spikes of his hair prickled like exclamation marks. 'She will be if you don't calm down. You look as if you'd been stopped for speeding with a body in your boot.'

'Dee, I've done a rather stupid thing.'

'Oh?'

'I went to the gents – you know, to have a wash – and well, the basin was rather small to do the job properly. But there was this big can of air freshener. So on the spur of the moment I gave myself a good spray inside my Levis. I just didn't think.'

'So?'

'Thing is – now how do I explain to Rosemary why my boxer shorts stink of Spring Freesias?'

He gazed forlornly at his crotch. I took in his chewed hair and ink-smudged face – he had, I noticed, shed a third shirt button. Then I burst out laughing. 'Oh my love, you are a klutz!'

I went over to him, taking him in my arms and burying my face in his neck. He froze. I drew away.

'What's the matter?' I said softly.

He avoided my eyes. 'I can't – I mustn't –'

'What?'

'Thing is – I'm going to have to keep a low profile for a bit. You know, avoid arousing Rosemary's suspicions.'

135

I removed my hands from his shoulders, stepped back abruptly.

'Don't look like that, Dee. I've got to think seriously about my marriage. I can't hurt Rosemary.'

I picked up *Nuclear Winter: A Marxist Analysis* and hurled it at him with all the force I possessed.

CHAPTER

SEVEN

DEAR ANGELA ADVISES: What is wrong with me? I try to give men love and friendship, but they just treat me like an unpaid hooker. When, oh when, will a man return my love?

PS Don't tell me to save myself as, while I know men are only after *one thing*, I like it too.

ANGELA ADVISES: Pull yourself together, lovey. Self-pity never got those wedding bells ringing. Cultivate hobbies to make yourself a more interesting person – Cake Decoration or Multi-Cultural Doll Making always stimulate conversation. Or try books to improve your mind (they do say J. R. Glob's *Nuclear Winter: A Marxist Analysis* is a very good read).

Remember there is someone for everyone in this world and it is just a question of waiting patiently until you and he find each other. Mind you, knowing your luck, he could be waiting patiently in Patagonia. And if you haven't bumped into him at your age . . . On second thoughts, lovey, I wouldn't bother with this save-yourself business. Frankly, in your case it's a bit like saving yesterday's loaf.

'So talented!' said Mrs Hernandez, manoeuvring her

coffee to escape the sweep of Mabel's tail. 'That is what I tell my friend Irma. My friend Dee have talent and a nice job as company director and a glamorous life.'

'Thank you, Rita,' I said, 'but you are exaggerating somewhat.'

'Not a bit. And – I tell Irma – Dee have good sense, too. She get all this by her own work – she don't lumber herself with no man.'

Although I had risen early with the intention of spending a hard day at my easel, I was grateful for Mrs Hernandez's interruption. Rita Hernandez cleans my flat and generally prevents my life from disintegrating, coping, while I am out, with the washing-machine repair man and Harry the Greatest Plumber in the World and Tom, who cleans the windows, first Friday of every month. It is part of the ritual that, if I am in on one of her mornings, Mrs Hernandez and I drink coffee and exchange cigarettes, while she up-dates me on the fortunes of her numerous friends and relatives, an intricate and action-packed account, delivered without background explanation or connecting links, at a speed which used to leave me dumbfounded, although after seven years I have now almost broken the code.

We had arrived at an uncharacteristic pause, while Mabel, whose limited brain nevertheless retains the fact that Mrs Hernandez often harbours cat treats in her bag, resettled herself so that her mustard eyes gazed up into Mrs Hernandez's black, heavily-shadowed ones imploringly. I had been working on the painting of the trio on the bench, abandoning the waif-like girl and instead elaborating her counterpart, the woman in the hat. Under my brush she seemed to have grown larger, with barrel thighs and bolster breasts, and in her expansion to have assumed a darker, more sinister identity, like a female spider lying in wait. Mrs Hernandez surveyed her thoughtfully.

'She like me,' she said, drawing on her cigarette. 'She need Weightwatchers. Maybe she eat the other

138

girl. She look like poor little Mabel, very, very hungry.'

'Mabel is a con artist,' I said. 'But – your friend Irma – I didn't quite catch – does she have a problem with her husband?'

'Oh, don't get me wrong. Irma's Reginald is a good man, a very extinguished man. But Irma like to boogie. Reginald, he don't like to boogie. He like to play golf.'

'Boogying isn't all it's cracked up to be,' I said. 'She's got someone to look after her, to share the important things, someone who'll always put her first. She wouldn't like my life.'

'All the same, is nice to boogie sometimes.'

'But you're lucky, Rita. You've got Xavier, who adores you. He's always taking you out for meals and buying you presents.' Indeed, Mrs Hernandez's whole glossy person, from her plump breasts and her gold rings to her immaculately-lacquered film-star mane, seems a testament to Mr Hernandez's adoration.

'Oh yes, Xavier is a fine man, an angel – although he ain't no millionaire, that's for sure. We got a nice place, four fine sons, we don't spend a night separate in thirty years. He tell me he still in love with me like he was on our wedding-day. He swear if I die first, he just turn his face to the wall.'

'Sounds like we should clone him,' I said. 'Or declare him a protected species.'

Mrs Hernandez surveyed her rings. She sighed. 'Ah yes. An angel I marry.'

'Anyway,' I said, 'I've decided to give up men altogether. Men, boogying, the lot. I'm going to work really hard from now on and get my exhibition together.'

She raised her eyebrows. 'The one with no shirt buttons – you give him the heave?'

'All over. Finito. Very definitely kaput. It's hard work from now on, Rita, and no distractions.'

She proffered a sympathetic cigarette. 'Never mind.

139

You wait. You know what they say – there's plenty more men in the ocean.'

I don't know why I thought The Virgin would phone me, since I had been explicit, not to say vehement, in outlining the means by which he might effect self-extinction. I don't know why I thought sitting in my studio with a bottle of Rioja and staring at the telephone would bring on his call, as a witch doctor might conjure rain. I had deliberately kept myself from knowing his home number and I was fairly certain, in any case, that he had said he was ex-directory: I don't know why I imagined phoning several wrong numbers with similar initials would be either productive or encouraging. As the Rioja diminished I was less and less certain what I wanted to say to him anyway, except to tell him what a bastard he was. Pouring the last glass, I contemplated phoning his office. True, it was eleven-thirty. But perhaps there was just a chance he was working late.

I stared at the telephone. Its ten baleful eyes stared back at me, shifting their focus, then multiplying alarmingly like the eyes of a horror-movie Thing.

The Thing, shiny, black and protean, began to emit a high-pitched screech. I stared at it in appalled fascination. Then all at once it dwindled, solidified, transformed itself back into an innocent domestic object. I lunged at it, slopping wine on the carpet. 'Yes,' I breathed.

'Deedee sweetie-pie,' said a familiar voice.

'Oh – hullo, Mother.'

'Well, try not to appear so enthusiastic.'

I settled back in my chair, wiping my dripping glass on the leg of my jeans. 'Mother, you've taken your teeth out again.'

'And so, by the sound of it, dear, have you.'

Dignity required me to ignore this. 'Mother, it's very late for you to phone. Aren't you usually in bed by now?'

'Yes, dear. But I can't sleep.'

140

'Oh, I'm sorry. Is it your fibrositis again?'

'No, it's – I, er – Deedee, I'm in love.'

I slopped more wine.

'Deedee? Hullo, are you still there?'

'Yes, Mother. Well – that's marvellous, fantastic! Where did you meet him? Who is he?'

'His name's Bill and he's retired from the Gas Board. Mrs Thing – you know, in the house with the blue door opposite the garage – the one whose daughter had that nasty experience on a package holiday in Greece – well, she invited me round for a bridge evening.'

'But Mother, you hate bridge.'

'I went for the company and he was my partner. When I bid three clubs I thought he was kicking me under the table like they usually do. Then I realized he was playing footsie.'

'Great. And is he tall, dark and handsome?'

'Well, not handsome exactly. Sort of, you know –'

'Extinguished-looking, as Mrs Hernandez would say?'

'Deedee, are you still there? We seem to have a lot of distortion on this line. You know old Thing in that TV series – the one who was going to marry the sister, only the brother was diagnosed as having a fatal hereditary illness, and his second wife's cousin, who everybody thought had been murdered in Australia, turned up for Sunday lunch – you know, Thing with the grey hair, slightly balding – well, Bill looks a lot like him.'

'And is it serious, Mother? Do you – are you –?'

'You mean, are we having an affair? Well, yes we are. That is – sort of – almost . . .'

'How do you mean – almost?'

There was a pause. 'Oh Deedee, I'm so lonely. Bill's in hospital.'

'Oh Ma, I'm sorry. Oh . . . don't cry. Poor you. Poor Bill. Is he very bad?'

'You see, he came round yesterday while his wife was doing her Meals on Wheels –'

141

'His wife?'

'Well, we were just about to – you know – when his disc went.'

'You didn't mention he was married, Mother.'

'It was very embarrassing. We had to say he was trying to mend that wonky light above my bed. We had to get the doctor. And an ambulance. And now he's in hospital, lying on a plank, and when I spoke to him on the phone he said I'd better not visit because it would look suspicious –'

'Mother, are you having an affair with a married man?'

'He says they don't get on. She nags him all the time. He says there hasn't really been anything between them for years.'

'Mother, you've got to be very careful. Otherwise you'll only end up hurt.'

'But I love him, Deedee. And he says he loves me. Do you think when his disc's better he'll leave her? From things he's said, I know he –'

'Mother, please listen to me. Married men never leave their wives. Oh, they say they will. But when it comes to it, there's always the mortgage, or what their children think, or their discs or their wives' discs or the fact that their car won't start or the dog's got mange or your Yorkshire puddings aren't as crisp as hers. Married men are always promising to leave. But they never do.'

'Alex did. Alex got a divorce.'

I bit my lip. 'Only,' I said, 'when it was too late.'

'Anyway, dear, Alex was too old for you. I always said he was a very nice man, but eleven years is too big a gap –'

'Mother, you must listen to me. Married men are bad news. However charming they are, however much they say they love you, they're only after what they can get. You've got to be strong about this.'

'Are you saying, give Bill up?'

'You don't want to spend your life miserable and lonely, sitting by the telephone.'

142

'But I was miserable and lonely and sitting by the telephone anyway.'

'Ma, you know you can always call me, whenever you want. But please be careful. Look around your upholstery class, keep going to bridge evenings, find yourself someone single –'

'Deirdre, I'm older than you are.'

'Yes, Mother, I know.'

'I'm sixty-nine. Most men of my age are married. Or dead.'

'Yes, Mother, but –'

'What I'm trying to explain to you, dear, is that I'm not exactly spoilt for choice.'

I sighed. When she had eventually rung off, I drained my wine glass and dialled The Virgin's office number. The Scots night-security man answered. I hung up.

The orchestra had broken into 'Congratulations and Celebrations', setting up a flutter at one of the tables bordering the Waldorf's marble dance floor. 'A request for Frieda and Colin on their Golden Wedding Anniversary,' boomed the vocalist into his microphone, while she, plump and blue-rinsed, covered her face, giggling, and he, beetroot to his crown, adjusted the knot of his tie. The band struck up the opening bars of 'True Love' and chair legs squeaked as elderly couples rose stiffly for the waltz. From the balcony, while the waiter arranged our table with sandwiches and a pot of Earl Grey for two, we followed the swish of chiffon and rayon jersey, the artful configurations of silver shoes long practised at evading treacherous black brogues.

'This is nice,' said Ann Smith, reaching for the teapot. 'I can't say I really cared for The Shakespeare.'

I watched her movements as she poured the tea, filtering it carefully through the silver strainer, judging just the right amount for each cup. Here, indeed, she was in her element, neat in her pearls and her pink linen two-piece and her feathery cap of streaked hair; somebody's mother up from Worthing or Guildford, enjoying the tea dance between shopping and the theatre. Only the voice, despite its careful modulations, was out of kilter.

'Do you know, I was walking past a building site yesterday and one of the workmen gave me a wolf whistle.'

I laughed. 'I hope you walked on, eyes front, with a disdainful air.'

'I did not. I turned round and gave him a great beaming smile. He nearly fell off his scaffolding. I've not had time to get blasé about these things, love. Grateful for what I can get, that's me.'

'You'll learn,' I said.

She extended delicate fingers for a cucumber sandwich. 'Will I, though? I'm not sure if I want to. I do so love it all. I adore taxi drivers calling me "ducks" and offering to carry my suitcase. I love men holding doors open for me and helping me off with my coat and assuming I can't change a tyre or put on a plug.'

'You don't find their attitude just the teeniest bit patronizing?'

'I like being made to feel fragile and helpless. And you can overrate wiring a three-pin plug as a means to personal fulfilment.'

I paused, itching to respond, yet not wanting to offend her. 'True Love' had metamorphosed with a dramatic swirl of chords into 'Surrey With The Fringe On Top', chacha tempo. Below us a splendidly preserved strawberry blonde clicked smartly into the rhythm, while her grey-suited husband, hampered by a rigidity of back and knee, extended her upon his arm so she could twirl at will. A curious couple who had soldiered through the waltz by taking long gliding walks with the man travelling backwards hiccuped to a halt, recovered gallantly, and resumed their mysterious trance-like glide, each focusing steadfastly on the other's feet.

'It's still a man's world,' I said. 'You're a qualified engineer, but now you work as a book-keeper.'

144

'It suits me. It's a nice clean office and I've my own tidy little desk with potted plants and a space to pin photographs. Not too much stress or responsibility, the other girls dropping by for a cup of coffee and a gossip. And proper gossip, too, about whose daughter's just had a baby, and what's the best remedy for cystitis. None of this guarded stuff about camshafts and soccer scores that men go in for like warring powers seeking neutral ground for negotiation. No struggles to remember the punchline of the latest joke.'

'But' – I fought with my irritation – 'you make it all sound so trivial.'

'Are babies and illnesses trivial?'

'No, Annie, of course not. But women want more now. We want the real world, real power. God, it makes my blood boil when some pimply youth calls me "love". He's assuming he's superior, he's in control, just because he's a man –'

The waiter arrived with muffins and scones, and I bit my lip, liking her, not wanting to be angry. For some moments we were preoccupied, spreading preserves and clotted cream. Below, the dancers were rumba-ing to 'They've Got An Awful Lot Of Coffee In Brazil'. The strawberry blonde skipped and swayed proficiently from the tips of her partner's extended fingers like a Morris dancer circling a maypole. The gliders continued their steady bumper-car progress, daring an occasional hop in concession to the rhythm. They were altogether an incongruous couple, he very small and hunched in his blazer, she towering in a dress flounced and frilled like Tyrolean peasant costume : Beauty and the Beast. The Beast had a head too large for his body, with a brillo-pad mane and a face grey and knobbly as a venerable potato. Beauty wore her auburn tresses waving down her back à la Rita Hayworth, caught up at the nape of her neck by a pearl and *diamanté* bow, and dressed on top in an elaborately curled pompadour that must have necessitated a hedgehog of

145

pins. Her lips were cupid carmine, her eyelids baby blue;
yet, despite her girlishness, she, like her partner, would
not see seventy again. We watched them as they glided
past, isolated from each other by their downcast eyes, yet
bound together nevertheless by age, by ugliness, by that
fixed, trance-like concentration on their footwork.

'Do you think he gets disorientated?' I said. 'Walking
backwards all the time?'

Annie giggled, licking cream from her fingers. 'Oh,
goodness no. It's obviously a technique they've evolved
together over the years. Suits any pace, any rhythm. And
have you noticed, although they always seem about to hit
something – a chair or another couple – they never do? Just
as you think there's bound to be a collision he puts some
sixth sense to work and they do a complete about-turn.'

'All the same, she does look like a very large nursemaid
pushing a very small pram.'

'They haven't sat out a dance, though, not for the last
half-hour. They're enjoying themselves, love. And that's
the main thing, isn't it?'

I felt the need to make reparation. 'And you're enjoying
yourself. Being female. That's the main thing, too.'

'You know I am, love. Despite the difficulties. You
know I adore being Ann.'

'I was wondering,' I said, larding my scone with
cream, 'why Ann? If I had to change my name, I think
I'd go for something really glamorous. You could have
been Annabelle and kept the same initials. Or Amanda or
Araminta. Or even Amaryllis.'

She laughed. 'I like Ann. It's nice and plain and normal.
Like I want to be. An ordinary, normal woman.'

I felt myself rising again, attempted to smother my
question in a mouthful of cream, failed. 'Is there such a
thing? What is an ordinary, normal woman?'

'Well' – she eyed me circumspectly – 'I couldn't wear
my hair as short as yours, for instance. And I couldn't
get away with your style of dressing. Oh, don't mistake

me, love – you always look very striking. But I couldn't carry off those trousers. I do like the feel, the femininity of a skirt.'

'I have a friend who claims that history forced women into skirts merely to give men easy access.'

'She sounds a touch cynical, your friend.'

'A healthy dose of cynicism comes with the female survival-kit these days. Stuff words like fragile and intuitive and helpless. They're just a put-down, a man's view of women –' I wriggled, knowing I had gone too far. I assayed a laugh. 'Who wants to be fragile, anyway – just so some macho male can come and stamp all over you?'

She eyed me from behind her spectacles, not offended so much as puzzled and concerned. 'Dee love, you make the whole thing sound like war.'

I thought for a moment of telling her about The Virgin, knowing she would listen sympathetically. But guilt for my hostility, my unkindness, barred me from trespassing on her good nature – and, besides, she had problems enough of her own.

'Well, isn't it?' I said.

'Is that war down there?'

I followed her gaze towards the dancers, the strawberry blonde pirouetting around her human maypole, the gliders pursuing their mysterious course.

'Don't you think it's grand, all those devoted husbands and wives, together for years, yet still wanting to dress up and go out dancing? Don't you think it's touching the way they've worked out their little routines? The old gentleman who's determined his arthritis won't stop his wife showing off her gold-medallist skills. And even the strange couple – well, it's perfect teamwork of a kind, isn't it? And how chivalrous of him to be the one always with his back to the engine.'

I laughed.

'Oh, I know you think I'm old-fashioned, Dee. But I

147

like the traditional ideas. I like chivalry, I like the thought of men cherishing and protecting women.'

'If women need protection, it's probably against men in the first place.'

'There you go again, love. I know I'm a novice, but surely it's give and take? Men like to think us women need looking after. Oh, I don't mean we actually have to be fragile and yielding. But if men think we are, it gives them a chance to show the gentler side of their natures. If we're as tough as they are, they have to cover up their feelings like they do with other men.'

The waiter arrived with a tray of pastries and after the traditional protests about the effect upon our figures, we each selected two of the stickiest. Below us, the dancers tangoed to Hernando's 'Hideaway'. Wistfully, Annie licked chocolate from her lips.

'Well, I think it's grand. The comfort, the companion-ship. I'd like that myself, wouldn't you?'

I stared at the gliders, blindly negotiating their fellow dancers. I thought of The Virgin. I sighed. 'You're being romantic, Annie. They probably drive home to Weybridge or Sunningdale and have appalling rows about which end to squeeze the toothpaste.'

She turned to gaze at me over the rims of her glasses. Her eyes were kindly but troubled, as if it were I, not she, who had problems of adjustment. 'Dee, love, don't you like being a woman?'

There was a film on TV, Fred Astaire and Ginger Rogers, but neither of us was watching. I was pretending to knit, but my ear was trained for the sound of my mother's door key. My father, as usual, was peering at the *Telegraph,* ensuring by his perusal of the obituary column that the soon-to-be-buried could safely be consid-ered dead.

'Oh, I'd love to climb a mountain,' sang the TV screen. I shivered. The fire was almost out, but my father,

Master of the Bucket and Coal Shovel, appeared not to
have noticed.

Oh, I'd love to go out fishing
In a river or a creek,
But it wouldn't thrill me half as much
As dancing cheek to cheek . . .

I stood up and walked over to the light switch. 'What
d'you want to do that for?' said my father, blinking.

'Don't you think you should go out and look for her?'

'Have a heart, Deedee. I've tried once. There's no sign.'

'But it's freezing. And it's getting really late.'

'So it is. Long past your bedtime. Go to bed, there's a
good girl.'

Bending to the television, I turned down the sound.
'Please,' I said, 'I'll go and look this time.'

'You will not,' said my father. 'Now do as you're told
and go to bed, young lady.'

I sat down opposite him. He raised his newspaper,
rustling the pages.

'Why did you let her go? Why didn't you try to
stop her?'

He lowered the newspaper again. 'You know there's
no stopping your mother when she decides to take one of
those walks of hers. Now go to bed, Deirdre.'

I made no move to obey him. We surveyed each other
silently. His lips curled into the smirk, he turned back to
the obituaries with a dismissive little laugh.

'You don't care, do you? You drove her out, but you
don't care. You don't care about anything but that mouldy
old paper.'

The smirk tightened, as if he were trying to swallow his
lips. 'You're just like your mother, Deirdre. You have no
compassion.'

At that moment, the door bell shrieked. We froze. My
father, closest to the doorway, got up and went quickly
into the hall.

The voice on the doorstep, a man's, was quiet and, since my father had opened the door no more than a third, blocking the gap with his body, I could not see its owner. Only when I had hoisted myself on to the fourth stair did I glimpse the shiny crown of a policeman's cap. He was asking if my father was Gerald Devlin, and other things afterwards I could not quite hear. My father said: 'Yes', 'Yes', 'Yes', and then 'Oh God!' Then he said: 'I'll come with you now, just give me a minute,' and shut the door.

'Da, what's happened?' I whispered.

His face, pale at the best of times, was the colour of curdled milk. 'There's been a bit of an accident, Deedee. A little bit of an accident.'

'What sort of an accident?'

'A car. Hit and run.'

'Is Ma bad?'

'They . . . they didn't say.'

'They must have said something.'

We stood for an instant or two, staring at each other. The naked bulb blazed cruelly upon the bare walls and torn lino, the emptiness of the hallway.

As my father came towards the stairs, I put out my arms. 'Oh Da!' My hands touched his sleeves, the gritty, tobacco-smelling material of his jacket.

'Dinna –' he said, then stopped. He turned his face away, pushed past me up the stairs. 'Don't worry, Deirdre. I've just got to go with them to the hospital.'

I followed him, fetching my coat as he fumbled for his keys on my mother's dressing-table.

'It'll be all right, Da.'

He reappeared on the landing as I was pulling on my overcoat. He stood for a moment, looking at me as if there were something he did not understand.

'It'll be all right,' I said. 'We'll go to the hospital and it'll be all right.'

'No, Deirdre. You stay here. Go to bed.'

'I'm coming with you. It'll be better, the two of us.'

'Do as I say, Deirdre. The hospital's no place for a child.'

'But I'm fifteen.'

He took hold of my elbow, pushing me towards my bedroom door. 'I don't want any of your nonsense. Do as your father says.'

I struggled, panicking. 'But she's my mother. And I don't know what's happened. Please let me come with you. Please!'

'Deirdre! Just for once – obey your father!'

'Oh please, Da. Don't leave me here. I don't know how bad she is. Why won't you tell me anything? Please don't leave me here – !'

He shoved me backwards so that I hit the end of my bed and fell. The door slammed shut, I heard the key turn. I picked myself up and hurled myself at the door handle.

'Please, she's my mother. Don't leave me here. Don't leave me alone.'

The front door slammed. I rushed to the window, tearing aside the curtains and the grimy net. I hammered on the glass. Below, in the street, without looking up, my father climbed into the back of the police Wolseley. The engine revved, the car drove away.

At The Casting Couch, Bert Goldoni was casting babies. In yellow and pink and blue babygros, they seethed upon the reception carpet like maggots. I picked my way to Samantha's desk, shouting to make myself heard. Samantha glowered behind a death mask of make-up. There was a new book open on the desk – not a novel, I noticed, but *Women Who Love Too Much: When you keep wishing and hoping he'll change* . . .

I was amazed that I had ever complained about not receiving messages. My bank manager had phoned, and my dentist inviting me for a check-up. My accountant had called, no doubt with gloomy prognostications about

151

the Revenue's latest demand. Samantha had even (twice) noted down the details of a caller who sounded suspiciously like a life-insurance salesman. Collecting a coffee, I took the yellow slips into my office, where I filed them in the bin.

It was another cloudless day, a day of shorts and panama hats when drinkers would congregate, stripped to the waist, outside the Dog and Duck and secretaries would bare their lunchtime midriffs in Soho Square, a day when half the world seemed on holiday and everyone appeared derisively happy. On the tube, a rash of posters had proclaimed the latest Alex Power blockbuster, *Secret Wounds*. Nursing a slight hangover, I contemplated my diary: empty for lunch, empty, too, in the evening. To make matters worse, I had discovered while dental flossing my teeth, while slicing between molar and incisor, that I did not love The Virgin, had indeed never loved him. The vacuum this discovery created produced no relief, but a pain more intense than any I had previously suffered. I sat for a while with my head in my hands, wishing The Virgin would call so that I could inform him of my revelation. The clock ticked. My phone remained resolutely silent.

I tried calling various friends to see if they were free for lunch. None of them was. I contemplated an orgy of shopping, but somehow lacked the heart for it. The advertisement had failed, I had turned down Gilda's nostrum out of hand, August was a barren month for party invitations: my horizons were blank. A holiday, perhaps? I was too old for 18–30 packages. A cruise on the Danube, a trip up the Nile to inspect the Pyramids, a journey to Istanbul on the Orient Express? I could spend my empty lunch hour hunting for travel brochures. I sighed and, finding two dusty aspirins in my desk, washed them down with cold coffee.

I considered my defiant pronouncement to Mrs Hernandez that I was giving up men. I turned over in my mind a life of solitude and virtue, worthy hours spent

152

slaving over my easel. I surveyed the photograph of Mabel. Her mustard eyes gazed back at me, uncritical, doting. Perhaps Chrissie was right. Perhaps Mabel and I should go it alone against the world.

I was aware suddenly of the piles of paper on my desk, neglected invoices, a document on the rent review, specifications from estate agents of additional premises for Ambrose and me to vet. Perhaps I should begin my new life at once, by catching up on some work.

By lunchtime I was huddled over my calculator, oblivious of the silent phone. I signed cheques, dashed off letters of query for typing, wrote a report for Ambrose on some studio space in Wardour Street. My face wore an expression as grim and purposeful as Samantha's. On periodic trips to the coffee machine I observed that the babies had gone and that Zig Zigeuner was now casting for Chirpy Chicken Canned Fried Eggs. The harassed Zoë, Rodney Peacock's assistant, was pulling actors of various shapes and sizes in and out of two giant yellow Chirpy Chicken costumes. Closing my door resolutely upon the flaps and squawks, I worked on, phoning agencies to find a new camera operator for the third floor, sorting out the mysterious hiatus in our supply of lavatory paper, arranging for the design of a new mail shot to send to production companies who might be ignorant of our services. At five-thirty, Samantha appeared to say that the chickens had strutted their last and could she please leave for a doctor's appointment? Surrounded by paper cups, my hair on end, my make-up gone, I nodded absently, deep in the intricacies of the rent review. By six-fifteen I felt I had evolved an impregnable negotiating position. I stubbed out my cigarette in the brimming ashtray and sat back with a yawn. Though assailed by the pangs of hunger and exhaustion, I was aware of a satisfaction, a new respect for the dignity of labour. Well, I should not stop there. I should go straight home, feed Mabel, hunt in the fridge for something for myself, then write to the bank manager, pay my credit-card bills, do the ironing, dead–head the balcony geraniums, tidy my under-wear drawer, wax my moustache . . . No point in applying fresh make-up and spraying myself with my new bottle of Chloe, no time for such frivolities in this life of virtue. I ran my hands through my hair, tidied my desk, then phoned the second floor, where they were working late, to ask Andrea to lock up. I had just peered into reception to check that the coffee machine had been switched off and was gathering up my handbag and briefcase, when I was all at once aware of someone behind me.

'Excuse me, is Zig still around?'

A tall man carrying a large black portfolio stood in my office doorway – clearly a late-comer whose agent had not apprised him of Zig Zigeuner's working methods.

'I'm afraid your career as a Chirpy Chicken has finished before it began. Zig left nearly an hour ago.'

'Oh shit!' said the man.

He was moderately good-looking, I noticed, and attired with some style in a black unstructured linen suit and a collarless raw silk shirt unbuttoned at the neck. Classic Rodney Peacock casting. Why were gay men always so much better dressed?

'You could get your agent to phone Rodney,' I said. 'You never know, they may go again.'

'My cab was stuck in traffic coming back from Pinewood. I might have guessed Zig wouldn't hang on. He didn't leave a message, I suppose?'

A message? A chord resounded somewhere. Yes, on closer inspection there was something familiar about his tangle of brownish hair and mobile face. A man in his early thirties with long legs and narrow hips. Something about his voice was vaguely familiar too.

'Have we met before?'

'You're Dee, aren't you? Ambrose Glass introduced us. In Groucho's, I think it was.'

154

Yes, of course. Ambrose. Definitely gay.

'I do apologize,' I said. 'I knew we'd bumped into each other somewhere –'

'And we've spoken on the phone.'

I stared at him. I flushed. 'You mean you're – ?'

'Jago-alias Jello-alias Jingo-alias Jangle.'

'Ohmigod!'

'But I answer to Mel.'

I put my hand to my face. 'Oh good heavens. I'm dreadfully sorry. I was unspeakably rude. I think I was having a small nervous breakdown at the time.'

He smiled, not unpleasantly. 'It happens to us all. As a matter of fact, I'm about to have one right now. Do you mind if I use your phone?'

'Please, help yourself. Have a seat. Make as many calls as you like.' I felt my cheeks glowing like bars on an electric fire. 'Oh, I really am terribly sorry. And I mistook you for a Chirpy Chicken, too. Oh God, how embarrassing. It must have been your portfolio. You really don't look like credible chicken casting. Those fluffy yellow feathers wouldn't suit you at all.'

He glanced up from stabbing at my telephone dial and laughed. 'If I don't catch Zig, I may just lay a tinned fried egg. I was meeting him to get his OK on some set designs. It's a week's build and they need to start next Thursday.'

'The fountains?' I enquired.

'The fountains were axed. No, this is the Chirpy Chicken Barnyard. "Make it stylized", he says. "Think technology, think futuristic, think – *cans*. I've got it, Mel! Give it the feel of Fritz Lang's *Metropolis*. That'll be ace'."

'Really?' I said.

'Really. So anyway, mine not to reason why. But just in case – just in case, mind – the Chirpy Chicken Corporation has a teeny problem, I'd like to know in good time. Otherwise I'm burning the midnight vodka with a bunch of expensive set builders sitting around at Shepperton playing paper darts with the *Sun*.'

He hung up on the number he had dialled and, consulting his address book, began to punch out another.

'Is there anything I can do to help?' I said. 'To make up for having been such a prat?' I remembered suddenly that Gilda had deposited a bottle of Pouilly Fumé in the fridge. 'I know – would you like a glass of wine?'

He looked up, smiling again. (He had, I observed, an agreeable smile.) 'That would be very civilized. As Zig would say, ace.'

I opened the bottle while he made two or three more unproductive calls. Eventually he replaced the receiver with a shrug.

'No luck?'

'He could be anywhere. I should know better by now. The Chirpy Chicken Corporation's his look-out, after all.'

'He does seem a trifle erratic.'

'Oh, Zig's OK. He's been like this since art school. Makes too much adrenalin, gets ahead of himself. By this time of the evening he's usually somewhere in the middle of next week.' He took a large, grateful gulp of the wine, settled back in my desk chair. Then his glance drifted to my briefcase and handbag on the carpet by the door. 'Sorry, Dee. Am I making you late for something?'

I thought of my ironing and my underwear drawer, and of Mabel, curled up in the airing cupboard, little knowing she had been awarded an early dinner.

'Nothing that won't keep for half an hour,' I said.

We began to talk politely about Ambrose and Sergei. It transpired that Mel had been at art school with Sergei too. He had even been invited to the Tapas evening, but a trip to Denmark had obliged him to decline – a friend in Copenhagen ran an experimental theatre group for which he occasionally designed productions. We talked about experimental theatre. I poured us more wine. As the Pouilly Fumé began its stealthy work, pulling focus on the austerity of my day, I found that, despite my

156

first impressions, I was automatically running his details through my Partner Potential programme. The computer can usually diagnose in minutes whether a man is hetero-sexual (an invaluable piece of software which saves weeks, even years of frustration) – it just flashes up a simple code and, if the answer is unsatisfactory, instantly deletes the file. Surprisingly, it was not only refusing to delete Mel Jago, but was also suggesting revisions to my initial entry in the section 'looks'.

He had a triangular face – high cheekbones, narrow jaw and a long straight nose that gave him in profile a stream-lined, feral appearance, like an exceptionally fine specimen of wolf. He had grey eyes, set wide apart, and a disconcerting habit of training them very directly upon me as he spoke. Altogether, there was nothing particularly effete about him – rather the reverse. Did a concern for his wardrobe automatically render a man dubious? Wasn't his turn of phrase more barrow boy than drag queen? And as for the suspect gentleness of his voice ('all quiet and husky' hadn't Samantha called it?), wasn't that merely the wash of elocution upon an undertow of London gravel?

But if he was straight – well, then came the inevitable question: was he single? Here the state-of-the-art software is a long way from perfection. He wore no wedding-ring, I could observe no outward signs of Friday-night supermarketing or car washing on Sundays. But then so many married men come with a complete set of mislead-ing signals as standard. He told me that Ambrose had mentioned my painting. He said that he was a sculptor, of a sort. I poured more wine and we talked about art and exhibitions, the Russian Constructivists and Warhol, and Gilbert and George. He was no effort to talk to, indeed seemed eager to promote conversation.

It struck me with horror that here I was, sitting talking to a potential Single Man with my hair standing on end and my face devoid of make-up. It also dawned on me that, owing to a change of mind about which top

157

to wear that morning, I had left home in a flesh-coloured bra that did not match my knickers. Well, the make-up, at least, I could rectify. I should anchor him to my office with a further glass of wine, then excuse myself and rush to the Ladies.

I proffered the wine bottle. He held out his glass. Then all at once he frowned as if recollecting himself. He covered the rim with his palm, shook his head firmly. 'Better not, thanks.'

Damn the make-up, why hadn't I remembered it earlier? I glanced at my watch. It was ten past eight. More likely his wife had a quiche in the oven, or he'd promised to rush home for an evening of Trivial Pursuit with the neighbours. Oh well, so much for the computer! My geraniums beckoned, and the letter to the bank manager. 'You're right,' I said brightly. 'I forgot to eat lunch today. Another glass and I shall be reeling.'

He rose, reaching for his portfolio. 'I missed lunch too.'

I busied myself screwing the cork into the neck of the bottle. Suddenly my new life filled me with gloom. I wondered whether Gilda was working late, whether Ambrose might still be in Groucho's.

'I was supposed to have dinner with Zig,' he said. 'But of course we never arranged where.'

I paused in the act of stowing the wine in the fridge.

'I take it you're rushing off somewhere glamorous?'

'Well . . .' I said, gathering up my bags, trying to look like a person whose diary would defeat Superwoman. 'Actually, I was going home to the ironing.'

'Shame. If you hadn't got such thrills lined up I was about to suggest dinner.'

As we sat in Orso, discovering acquaintances in common, artists, books, films we held in mutual esteem, the computer kept running further checks on Mel Jago. Hair–yes: beer gut–no: teeth–fine: height–6'2"?: body–yes: without

158

clothes–oh yes: ear-blowing–unlikely. But as to his marital status its screen remained resolutely blank.

True, there occurred in his conversation none of those giveaway references to 'we', 'us' and 'the children'. But perhaps he merely possessed the editorial skills of the dedicatedly promiscuous. Didn't common sense dictate that he was bound to have a wife, or at least a live-in girl-friend? A good-looking man like Mel Jago would be unlikely to exist in monkish solitude – unless there were something wrong with him. And in any case he was younger than me, by a good seven or eight years, so far as mental arithmetic could deduce.

All the same, as the level sank in our bottle of Amarone I thought I could read the portents of imminent sexual encounter: the smiling, the feverish chatter, the wine-glass-threatening moments occasioned by trembling hands. At any minute he would order espressos and Grappa, and the awkward silences would set in. Perhaps, once he was installed in my kitchen for that last cup of coffee, I could sneak off and colour-co-ordinate my under-wear while the kettle was boiling.

Our eyes lighted simultaneously upon the empty Amarone bottle, hovered, met. He grinned. He raised his eyebrows, his lips – I will swear to it – were forming the word 'coffee?'. But then his expression changed, he seemed to pull himself up, just as he had in my office.

'Mind if I get the bill, Dee? I've suddenly remembered – I need to be home fairly smartish.'

A surreptitious glance at my watch assured me it was no later than twenty to eleven. I could not restrain myself. 'I suppose,' I said casually, 'your wife will be wondering where you've got to?'

Was it my imagination, or did he look at me sideways for an instant? 'Hardly,' he said. 'No, it's been a terrific evening, but I – I have to get home. Sort of a crisis.'

No wife? Then what? Was it something I'd said, had he noticed my moustache needed waxing? And what sort

159

of crisis? Men are notorious for their equivocations. No wife, but undoubtedly a jealous lover. Oh well . . . I considered my estimate of his looks, once again revising it downwards. Nevertheless, I felt melancholy descend. I contemplated an early night with a detective story, my bank manager unmollified, my ironing still threatening a takeover in the kitchen. He, too, lapsed into edgy silence as if, having decided to go, he now could not wait. Oh, he offered me a lift in his mini-cab (since Battersea was on the way to Streatham), but the offer was so casual as to seem grudging, and when the car arrived he positively rushed me from the restaurant.

We sat in the back of the mini-cab, his portfolio wedged like a sword between us. I wondered again how I had offended, that conversation, which had been so effortless, was now like squeezing an empty paint tube. I was almost grateful for the reggae blasting into the back of our necks and the admixture of air freshener and sweat which rendered breathing an activity that required concentration. Halfway along the Embankment, as if he felt he should recover himself, he mentioned (or rather screamed above the music) that he had been born in Battersea, but the shouted exchange this generated soon died in strangled monosyllables.

I sneaked a glimpse at his profile beyond the barrier of the portfolio. His mouth was set, his jaw strained, his eyes fixed steadfastly ahead of him. I felt him shift upon the tiger-skin flocking, almost as if my proximity gave him pain. Perhaps he was one of those men who suffered intractable problems with women, perhaps he preferred shoes, or uniforms, or rubber handcuffs in the vacuum cleaner cupboard. Or perhaps the computer had caught a virus, and he was gay after all, with a penchant for waiters or tattooed Irish navvies, perhaps –

As the cab reached the lights at Royal Hospital Road he lurched suddenly towards me, wild-eyed and perspiring, so that I feared a confession to one or all of the above.

160

'Dee –' he began, his words evaporating into the reggae.
'What?' I screamed.
'Forget it. I –' With decision, he brought his hand down on the cab driver's shoulder. 'Stop the car, please. *Stop the car!*'

'No stopping here, man.'

'STOP THE CAR!' As we screeched to a halt in a shudder of furry mascots, Mel's door was already open. We watched, the cabbie and I, as, deftly negotiating an oncoming jugernaut, Mel charged across the road, leapt the small scrub of grass and flower beds bordering the curb, and hurled himself into the bushes that screened the august residences of Cheyne Walk from traffic.

We continued to peer into the shadows until they had completely absorbed the running figure. With a world-weary sigh, the cabbie released his handbrake.

'Wait!' I bawled.

'No waiting here.'

'But – but he'll be back in a minute.'

A second jolt of the brake flung me against the front passenger seat. The cabbie turned to display a sardonic set of teeth. 'Face it, lady. He the one that got away.'

'Nonsense,' I yelled, piqued by the probable accuracy of the comment. 'He's just gone to stretch his legs. Look, he's left his portfolio.'

'Well, I can't wait here. Now I got the pigs up my ass.'

I struggled for an instant with the etiquette of the situation. Surely politesse required, however eccentric one's escort, that one did not leave him inexplicably stranded in the undergrowth near Albert Bridge? But then maybe the cabbie was right and I should gracefully accept his departure as being by way of a hint. Generosity prevailed. Seizing the portfolio, I thrust a note in the direction of the satirical teeth.

'He often does this. It – it's the pull of psychic forces. You know, ley lines and that sort of thing.'

And I was standing on the pavement, clutching the

161

portfolio and pondering the next page in the etiquette book, when all at once a figure stumbled out of the bushes, waving its arms, calling to me across the expanse of roadway, yelling something that sounded like 'Help!'.

CHAPTER

EIGHT

'I'm mortified, Dee. There was I, trying to come on like Mr Cool, hoping to impress you with my scintillating charm –'

I endeavoured unsuccessfully to smother my laughter.

'I reckoned I could hold out until I got back to Streatham. But then – Jesus! What must you have thought?'

'I thought you had a severe personal problem.'

'Stop giggling, woman. This *is* a severe personal problem. I haven't felt so bad since Miss Friedlander made us sit at our desks until somebody owned up to nicking the stuffed armadillo from the nature study room. I think I'm about to have a hernia. And – oh, *please* Dee, don't make me laugh!'

I controlled myself with difficulty. 'Anybody can break a zip,' I said. 'But most people don't sew themselves back together with whaling tackle.'

'It's extra-strong button cotton. I borrowed it from the wardrobe mistress at Pinewood. I didn't want it to come undone.'

'And, thanks to your scout badge in oversewing, it won't, will it? If only I could get some purchase on it.

Ouch, there goes another fingernail! Are you positive you can't just pull these trousers down from the waist?'

'Not unless I fancy singing soprano. Surely that gigantic handbag contains at least one pair of scissors – and some safety pins would turn out pretty useful, come to think.'

'Alas, no. A horoscope book, a two-day-old chocolate croissant, a comprehensive collection of antique bus tickets. But no scissors. No safety pins either. We'll just have to improvise, I'm afraid.'

'Like how?'

'Don't wriggle. I'm trying to think.'

'I'm not wriggling. I'm writhing in a torment of embarrassment and acute physical pain.'

'Well, don't then. I can't concentrate with you writhing.'

'Dee, you don't seem to grasp the urgency of the situation. We're talking desperate measures here.'

'Well . . . I could try setting fire to the thread with my lighter.'

'Not quite that desperate.'

'Or there's a pocket corkscrew in my briefcase.'

'Not that desperate either.'

'Or I could use my teeth.'

'Je-sus! How could you make such a suggestion to a man in my condition?'

I pondered for a moment. 'You know, you should have gone for broke and used superglue. Then we could have sat in Casualty along with the jokers with the telephones and lavatory seats stuck to sections of their anatomy.'

'Dee, could you be said to be taking this seriously?'

'Oh, I'm very serious, Mel.'

'Then do something. Please. Anything.'

'OK. Brace yourself, I'm going in with the corkscrew.'

'Good God, not the corkscrew!'

'Stiff upper lip.'

'Stiff what?'

164

'Only I can't see properly, it's too dark. We'll have to stand under that lamppost.'

'In full view of plutocrat Chelsea?'

'There's no one to see.'

'Yes there is. There's a geriatric dowager just turning out of Flood Street to pooper-scoop her peke.'

'There's no one. Stand still!'

'Her Ladyship's stopped, she's staring at us. Dee, don't get down on your knees like that. Jesus, don't put your face so close! Oh Dee, get up, there's a cop car turning out of Royal Hospital Road. Christ, her Ladyship's flagging it down, she's pointing – Get up, Dee, get up! She's –'

'Got it!' I cried, feeling a snap, followed by a triumphant rending.

'Dee, what's the current sentence for public indecency?'

I scrambled to my feet. 'The bushes!' I gurgled. 'You take the philadelphus, I'll take the laurel.'

I was forking food into Mabel's dish when he emerged from my bathroom. Replacing the needle and cotton on my kitchen table, he slumped exhausted into the rocking-chair. 'You've got to admit I know how to show a lady a romantic evening.'

'Thank heavens those policemen seemed to be rushing home to catch the snooker.'

'And at least there were no witnesses as I crept along Albert Bridge Road like Quasimodo, with my jacket pulled down to my knees.'

'Sorry about the safety pins.'

'Good job I wore clean boxer shorts, like my old Mum always told me.'

We both laughed, polite, nervous laughter suddenly, as if we had shed our camaraderie in my hallway, as if, safely returned from the trenches, we had been metamorphosed back into awkward strangers by civilian life.

Once again I was aware of being fixed by that disconcertingly focused look of his and, avoiding his gaze, found instead that my eyes had travelled unconsciously to his carefully-restitched fly. I glanced away hastily, busying myself with the coffee.

Mabel came over to inspect him, pausing only a few seconds before leaping into his lap like the trollop she is, and endeavouring to bestow his chin with fishy kisses. As we earnestly inventoried Mabel's virtues I felt the air clot with embarrassment. I remembered that the computer had never produced an accurate print-out on his availability, or even, for that matter, his intentions.

'Coffee?' I said, juggling with the *cafetière*. 'And then I'd better phone you a cab.'

'Oh, right. A cab. Of course.'

'I expect they'll be wondering at home where you've got to.'

Once again I fancied he gave me a sideways look. 'Well, yes,' he said. 'Boris will be waiting up.'

The computer threatened error in all drives. 'Boris?'

'He's black and built like a brick shit-house. And yes, he does cut up rough when I stagger home at two in the morning.'

'Oh,' I said.

'Mind you, we've been together nearly two years now, so we're used to each other's little ways. But he can act mean and moody when it suits him. He's a killer when he's hungry, is Boris.'

Bereft of words, I concentrated for a moment on pouring coffee. 'Right,' I said. 'I'll go and ring for that cab.'

He began to laugh. Gathering up Mabel, he lowered her carefully to the floor. Then he stood up himself and, coming over to me, gently removed the *cafetière* from my hands. 'Boris, you crazy person, is a tom cat. And before you call the cab company, I was wondering . . . you don't still happen to have that corkscrew handy?'

★ ★ ★

166

We lay, naked and still connected, on top of my duvet, grinning at each other with ridiculous satisfaction.

'I can't think of a nicer person,' he said, 'to risk getting arrested with.'

'You know, as seduction techniques go, yours is pretty weird.'

'Works, though, doesn't it. I must try it again some time.'

'You're insufferable.'

He pulled me closer so that I shouldn't lose him. 'Anyway, I'm not sure who seduced who, Ms Devlin. You were busy giving me the third degree. Did I have a wife? Did I have someone waiting up for me?'

'I was simply making polite conversation.'

He laughed, pressing his forehead against mine. 'I don't have a wife, Dee. Not even an ex.'

His directness embarrassed me. 'I couldn't care less,' I said lightly. 'In fact, I wasn't even sure you were interested in women.'

'Oh really? I thought I'd convinced you Boris and me were just good friends.'

'I told you, I'd decided you had psychological problems. And anyway –' I wormed my fingers into his artistically-tangled hair – 'you looked far too Men-in-Vogue to be straight-up heterosexual.'

He grinned. 'That's because I'm not a gentleman. I told you, I'm a Battersea boy. I'm your chance at a bit of rough, lady.'

'What makes you think I'm a lady?'

'Not a lot, as it happens.' He slid his tongue over mine and we were silent for some moments. 'Well, am I?'

'Are you what?'

'Interested in women?'

My tongue flickered, snake-like, between his lips. 'On the evidence so far – just a bit.'

'And that was only the rehearsal.'

He shifted his pelvis and I felt him grow hard again.

167

My muscles contracted, my eyes closed. He rolled me over so that I was beneath him.

'Now we're going to take it once more from the top.'

I wriggled and sighed.

'But this time without the overacting.'

I opened my eyes. 'I wasn't acting.'

'You were out-projecting Sarah Bernhardt.'

'Mel Jago! You really are an insufferable creep!' I jerked my hips sideways, dislodging him, trying to work my body free; but his hands went to my shoulders, holding me down, forcing me to look up and meet his unnervingly direct eye.

'Shush, Dee. All I mean is, relax. You don't have to impress me. I'm impressed enough already.'

We remained very still, as if endeavouring to outstare each other. Then he smiled and I found myself smiling back.

'Creep,' I said.

'Mmmm,' he said, keeping his eyes on mine, putting himself inside me again, sliding slowly deeper until we were pressed together, bone to bone. 'Now just relax.'

'Christ!' I said. 'Oh, Christ!'

'Mmmm,' he said. 'All of that.'

Disentangling ourselves, we rolled over till we lay on our sides with our arms around each other's necks.

'All of that. With knobs on,' he said.

We lay gazing drowsily at each other for a while. Then he tightened his arms about my shoulders, drawing me to him until my body fitted the angles of his.

'Dee, beautiful Dee. Horrible on the telephone. But beautiful everywhere else.'

'You have the occasional moment when you're not so bad yourself.'

He stroked my neck. 'What kind of a name is Dee, anyway? Is it short for something?'

I groaned. 'Deirdre.'

'Deirdre. Deirdre.' He intoned it in stage Irish. 'Deirdre of the Sorrows.'

'It's a revolting name.'

'Think yourself lucky, my love. You should try mine for size.'

'Why? What's Mel short for? Melrose, Melville . . .'

'Melvin.'

I let out a hoot of laughter. '*Melvin?*'

'There you are,' he said reproachfully. 'And you think you're lumbered. Many's the time I've cursed my aged mother, God bless her tartan granny basket.'

I levered myself up on one elbow. 'Poor Mel,' I said, kissing his eyelids. 'You don't look a bit like a Melvin. Haven't you got a second name? Didn't you ever think of using that?'

'Yes. And no.'

'You mean you haven't got one?'

'I mean I've never thought of using it.'

I lay on top of him with my face close to his and my chin propped on my arms. 'Why ever not?'

'If I reveal a dark and terrible secret, will you promise never to tell?'

'Cross my heart.'

'Scouts honour?'

'May I have my credit cards chopped up in front of me. May I be visited by a plague of double-glazing salesmen.'

'Very well. When my aged relative was carrying me she went to a matinée of *Singin' In The Rain* at the Ruby, Clapham Junction. She loved the dancing, she swooned over "Broadway Melody". . .'

'So?'

'So my second name is Gene.'

'Melvin Gene! Melvin *Gene!*'

'Stop giggling, you terrible woman! Have you no finer feelings? And stop bouncing up and down on my ribs.'

I began tickling him. He seized my arms and we rolled

169

over and over, kicking and screaming and laughing, until
he had me pinned with my hands above my head. He
bent and kissed my mouth. 'Beware,' he said breathlessly.
'You'll get me over-excited again.'

'Again?'

He rolled over once more so that I was on top of him. I
inspected his erection, running my tongue up its length and
licking away the pearl of moisture at the tip.

'Again,' he said.

Roused by the sounds of Mabel outside the door yowling and
tearing carpet, I realized we had drifted asleep. I moved and
he too stirred, sighing and nuzzling my breast. I struggled into a sitting position. We must get up. I must phone him a cab.

'Jesus, what time is it?' He propped himself on one
elbow to survey my bedside table. 'In this amazing array
of alarm clocks, does anything work?'

I stared at him, puzzled.

'Well, I need to be home around seven. Otherwise
Starving of Streatham will be phoning the RSPCA.'

'You mean . . .?' It took a second or two for the
realization to filter through. 'You mean you're going to
– stay the night?'

'Since it's now a quarter to four that seems the logical
thing. Unless you're the one with the jealous lover, about
to arrive with his bags from Heathrow and threaten to do
me over with his duty-free Swiss Army knife. Or maybe
it's the milkman – his morning for leaving a little extra.
Well, don't mind me, my love. I'm not bothered if you
throw me out half-naked into the darkness . . .'

Laughing, I buried my face in his hair. 'Stop it! I
want you to stay. It's just that I didn't think – I'm not
used to . . .'

I wound the alarms and let Mabel in, and we crawled
beneath the duvet. Though he had settled on my side of
the bed, I felt I would forgive him. He put his arm
around me and I nestled into the warmth of his body. Just

170

as I was drifting off a question occurred to me, although I fell asleep before I could catch his reply.

'Mel, I've been meaning to ask – what star sign are you?'

At The Casting Couch Bert Goldoni was casting Fifties-look boys strumming guitars. But, though the mingled sounds of strumming and scales wafted down to me even as I climbed the stairs, my head felt clear, I thrust open the door with a beaming smile. In Studio One an auditionee was already at work for Bert's delectation, mangling the old Johnny Tillotson number, 'Poetry in Motion'; I caught up the tune, found myself whistling it as I collected my cup of stewed coffee.

Samantha was deep in a tome entitled *What Women Want*. She lowered the book, converting a cursory glance into a prolonged stare. 'Blimey, Dee,' she said. 'It certainly has worked wonders for you, that early night.'

I retired, still whistling, to my office. My desk was tidy, my letters, typed by Andrea during her stint of overtime, were waiting for my signature in a neat pile. I flung my briefcase on to the sofa, kicked off my shoes, settled back in my chair for a cigarette. I smiled to myself, sniffed my bare forearm, fancying I could still smell faint traces of him upon my skin. Then my eye took in the telephone and my euphoria vanished.

DEAR ANGELA ADVISES: Last night I met an attractive unattached man who seemed to like me as much as I liked him. But, though he promised to call me, he didn't say when. Does 'Speak to you soon' mean I'll speak to him soon, or is it only a verbal reflex, like 'Have a nice day'? Was he put off when he saw me without make-up? Could he have noticed my bra didn't match my knickers? Does he still think I act in bed? I can't call him as I don't know his number, either at home or at work. All I know is he lives in Streatham with a tom cat called Boris. Have I been conned into yet another one-night stand? Why, oh why do I always end up hostage to the telephone?

PS If I hadn't remembered to give him his portfolio he'd have been forced to ring me. Why don't I think of these things till too late?

ANGELA ADVISES: Oh dear, oh dear, lovey, when will we ever learn? I can't promise you this man will phone. I can't promise you anything since you know so little about him. You can't even be sure he isn't married. Remember, men *tell lies* to get what they want.

Avoid heartache by throwing yourself into your work. Take an Open University degree. Get the telephone disconnected. Anyway, I thought you said you were giving up men? Send for my pamphlet on the joys of masturbation, 'At Last, Sex with Someone You Can Trust'.

Alternatively, you could phone your partner Ambrose. He's bound to have all the dirt on this Jago person and he might just be free for lunch.

My hand was on the point of lifting the receiver when the instrument squeaked and began to ring.

'Hullo,' said the voice Samantha had described as sexy.

I acquired a momentary paralysis of the throat.

'Remember me?' said the voice.

'Vaguely,' I said. 'Every time I sit or cross my legs or walk upstairs.'

'Don't do this to me, Dirty Deirdre. How am I going to keep my mind on Fritz Lang barnyards?'

I groped for a cigarette. 'Where are you?' I said.

'In Mortimer Street at Maestro Movies having a meeting with Zig. But he got called to the phone – some life or death crisis about a dog food commercial. So I sneaked away to ring you.'

I was seized suddenly by a compulsion to chatter, like a St Vitus twitch. I babbled on, asking him about Boris

172

and Zig, and whether his trousers had held up during the cab ride to Streatham, tumbling over words, blundering through pauses, cutting short his replies.

'Look,' he said, laughing, when I was finally forced to draw breath. 'I can't talk for long. Not while I've got Zig chained to a chair. I really called to find out what you were doing this evening.'

'This evening?' Taken by surprise, I stared at my diary. 'Well, I – er –'

(Don't look too available. This evening? What a nerve!)

'Sorry, Mel, I'm afraid I'm busy.'

'Tomorrow then? Shit, I can't do tomorrow. Friday?'

'Friday, no-o. Some time next week?' I flicked blank pages for authenticity. 'Oh God, next week looks like the Third World War. How about Tuesday? No, Tuesday's out. Thursday – how would Thursday suit?'

(Don't look available? But I am available. Oh God, Thursday. Eight whole days.)

'Well, perhaps on second thoughts Tuesday's possible. I think I could cancel the Tuesday people. Is Tuesday OK?'

There was a brief silence. 'Maybe we could compromise,' he said. 'How about Saturday?'

'Saturday?'

'Yes.'

'But that's the weekend.'

'I see. You weekend on your country estate, do you?'

'No, but I – weekends aren't usually – Yes, Mel. Saturday would be fine.'

(Saturday. Still four long days. Why couldn't I have said I was free this evening?)

'Right,' he said, sounding drier than usual. 'And now we've finished with that one, how about lunch? I'll see you upstairs at the Braganza in an hour.'

Streatham proved to be a converted chapel, and Mel's 'sort of' sculpture chairs. A fibre-glass chair, part hand,

173

part twig, sinister evocation of an Arthur Rackham forest. A throne that looked as if it were made from shards of ice and turned out to be composed of every imaginable kind of knife, welded together and chromium plated. He showed me the sketches of a set of four dining chairs he was making for a friend; wrought-iron serpents undulated and coiled, vanishing into the sinuous curve of a back, re-emerging in a stretcher or the curl of an arm-rest, so that static lines flowed with clandestine movement.

After Sunday lunch, we lay naked on the three-sided mezzanine Mel had constructed as his living area beneath the perpendicular windows. Below us in the studio, amongst the tools and the welding equipment and the beachcomber gleanings of skips, lay Boris, replete with left-over roast beef, a white-spatted, dinner-jacketed, bottle-brush-whiskered cat, whose massive jowls and imposing shoulders looked as if they were hewn out of stone.

Mel lay on his stomach with his head turned aside and his eyes closed. I propped myself up to gaze at him sentimentally. A beautiful body, pale skinned, devoid of spare flesh, with buttocks like green apples. A body whose tastes and smells I knew, whose quirks I had explored, whose semen still trickled between my thighs. Why then could I not understand its owner? He was, I reflected, a mass of contradictions, alarmingly frank one moment, impenetrable the next. Despite the clothes, he was not self-conscious, nor even particularly vain. He sewed, he cooked, but at the same time was resolutely undomesticated, giving the impression that, whether it was an oven or a welding torch, the practicalities barely differed. Even his gentle voice sorted oddly with the spiky gothic of his chairs. He was like Boris, I decided, a street cat, demonstrative when he wanted to be, yet impregnably self-possessed.

Softly I ran my fingers the length of his spine. I kissed

the cleft of his buttocks, fingered the arrow of dark hair and the knot of muscle beneath. I thought of other beds, other skin, another spine hard with muscle. Mel sighed, turned over, pulled my mouth down to his.

We lay for a while listening to the rain on the roof. 'I think we could use a couple of hours' rest and recuperation,' he said. 'If I can persuade the car to start, why don't we drive to Chelsea and see if we can get into *Secret Wounds?*'

'No. No, I'd rather not.'

He squeezed me, laughing. 'You mean you're insatiable and neither of us will walk for a week?'

'No. I just don't want to see *Secret Wounds.*'

'It's had rave reviews. The photography is supposed to be spectacular. And they say Kim Kinsale is brilliant.'

'It's just not my sort of film.'

'Funny, I'd have thought you'd have liked Alex Power. Didn't you see *Desert Flowers?* I couldn't speak afterwards. Kim Kinsale was in that too, playing the schizophrenic librarian –'

'She's in all his films.'

'Well, isn't he married to her, lucky man? You know, beautiful Dee, you remind me of her a bit – small and blonde with wicked eyes.'

I turned my head away. 'I don't want to see *Secret Wounds,* Mel. I'll go to any other movie you like, I just don't want to see *Secret Wounds.*'

He was still for a moment. Then he put up a hand and stroked my hair. 'OK, Deirdre of the Sorrows. We'll go to any other movie.'

'Gosh,' said Chrissie, narrowly saving her gin and tonic from Mabel's tail, 'what's happened to your painting?'

I glanced at the empty easel. Mel had been complimentary, not to say flattering, about most of my work. But, surveying the Madrid trio, he had fallen silent for a moment before muttering, 'Funny how second thoughts

175

kill,' and wandering off to look at something else. It now stood in its old position, face inwards against the mantelpiece. The hardboard, at least, would come in useful for some other project.

'It wasn't working out,' I said. 'Anyway, I've been a bit busy.'

'I'll say,' said Chrissie. 'I don't seem to have seen you for weeks.'

'Only a fortnight.'

She eyed me thoughtfully. 'I suppose what's keeping you busy wouldn't have anything to do with the battered Mitsubishi jeep that keeps pinching my parking space?'

'It might,' I said.

'Mmmm,' she said, tickling Mabel's ears conspiratorially. 'I bumped into him on the stairs the other day. He held the front door for me. Tall? Curly hair? Nice smile, sensitive face?'

'Sounds like the one,' I said.

'He looks lovely.'

'Well,' I said, 'I suppose he's all right.'

'Only all right? Looking at you, I'd have said he represented a serious threat to anti-wrinkle creme.'

'Oh, he's good in bed. Imaginative. You know how most of them seem to have read the same book –'

'Then you don't get on?'

'We get on brilliantly. We enjoy the same things, we laugh a lot. He's an artist too, and he lives in this crazy converted church, and he likes strong coffee and *bleu* steak, loathes football, loves cats.'

'Sounds perfection, doesn't he, Mabel? Then what's the problem?'

'Well, for a start, he's at least seven years younger.'

'Is that a problem?'

'I'm getting cross-eyed holding my stomach in. And then' – I rose to replenish her glass – 'then there's this other thing.'

176

'Oh no.' Chrissie's brow furrowed sympathetically. 'Of course. I should have realized. He's married.'

I paused, half-way to the ice bucket. 'That's just it. He's not.'

'Not married?'

'Not even divorced. Not even a girl-friend.'

'But, Dee, that's fantastic. Incredible. Wonderful.'

'Is it?'

'Well, of course.'

I busied myself ladling chunks of ice for a moment. 'But have you considered, Chrissie – I mean, think seriously about this one – what's wrong with him?'

She laughed. 'Does there have to be something wrong?'

'He's not gay, he doesn't even seem to be bisexual. He doesn't want to make love in a hood or have jam doughnuts thrown at his dinkle. All his moving parts are sound. Why doesn't he have a woman?'

'Perhaps he was waiting for you to come along.'

'Come off it, Chrissie. There's got to be something peculiar. Something very peculiar indeed.'

'Well, does he seem odd? Does he behave strangely?'

'No. He phones when he says he will, he wants to spend time with me, he seems, on the face of it, quite improbably straightforward. That's what I can't work out. I can't see what game he's playing.'

'Supposing he's not.'

'He's got to be. All men play games.' I lit a cigarette, took a large gulp of gin. 'Do you know, last night he said he was in love with me.'

Chrissie gazed at me, quite misty-eyed. 'Oh, but Dee, that's wonderful.'

'Men usually say that when they want to put one over on you. It's a well-known ploy. I've used it myself.'

Chrissie stroked Mabel reflectively. Mabel, in ecstasy, flexed her claws upon Chrissie's knees.

'Do you love him, Dee?'

'I want to. But how can I? I can't afford to believe in fairy stories. How can I let myself be taken in?'

Chrissie sighed, rather sadly I thought. 'Well, what do you think, Mabel? Is he as lovely as he sounds?'

'Oh, Mabel's besotted, but you know what an old tart she is. No, I've got to talk to Ambrose, Chrissie. Ambrose knows him, Ambrose will know what the catch is. But Ambrose, blast him, has been booked solid for the last ten days.'

We had discussed the rent review and the latest batch of details from the estate agents. We had demolished a bottle of the Groucho Club's Sancerre. Ambrose had told me, several times, infuriatingly, how cheerful I was looking, but whenever I thought I saw my moment the conversation had run off into other channels. Now, as he debated with the waiter whether to have cream or ice-cream on his strawberries, finally deciding on both, I took advantage of the pause.

'By the way,' I said, with studied off-handedness, 'I bumped into a friend of yours last week. Mel Jago. Art director. Zig uses him quite a bit.'

'Mmmm-mm,' said Ambrose, between strawberries. 'Talented boy. Remember that chair in our hall, looks like a praying mantis whose mother was frightened by Salvador Dali – that's Mel.'

'He said Sergei had invited him to your Tapas evening.'

'Oh, he and Sergei were in long socks together. I think poor dear Sergei was smitten with youthful passion. Unrequited, of course. The divine Mel always had at least three adoring females in tow.'

'Ah,' I said, hopeful, yet unsure how to continue. 'He seems very pleasant.'

'He's a nice boy. A positive darling when Sergei had his argument with the transit van – always ferrying me to the hospital in that dreadful boneshaker of his. Where did you meet him?'

178

'Oh – just at a party.'

'Pity, we haven't seen much of him recently. I think you'd find him amusing. Do you know, I've just had a splendid idea!' Ambrose, who had been scraping his plate with the concentration of a neurologist performing micro-surgery, suddenly cast aside his spoon as if he had received a vision.

'What?' I said.

'He's a bit younger than you, of course, darling Deirdre, although you sensibly lie about your age. But he's straight, and a joy to look at, and he's been on his own since – oh dear me, why didn't it occur to me before? As you won't have Sergei's bank manager, notwithstanding the golf-club subscription, why don't we invite you and young Jago to dinner? Who knows, you might just hit it off.'

I stared into my wine glass, flushing uncomfortably. 'No, Ambrose, I really –'

'Darling girl, Sergei adores playing matchmaker – there's nothing he likes better than interfering in other people's lives. And besides I'll get a night's reprieve from my ghastly diet. Dim lights, sweet music, a decent amount to eat – who knows but romance may burgeon. I'll instruct Sergei to organize it at once.'

'No, Ambrose. Please, I'd much rather you didn't.'

I had combed Streatham for traces of previous female occupancy, but had found nothing. There were no half-finished tubes of depilatory in the bathroom cabinet, no chi-chi ornaments suggestive of female present-giving, I found nothing amongst the saucepans and kitchen gadgetry that wasn't severely practical – no chicken bricks or Casa Pupo spice urns or pottery mugs decorated with engaging green frogs. In the random collage of snapshots above Mel's drawing-board women featured, it was true, but I saw no face that appeared consistently, and although one rather large black and white portrait of a dark girl

179

with a wine glass turning in mock horror from the camera had originally excited my suspicions, the style of her hair and clothes suggested it had been taken some years ago.

I lay in Mel's vast iron coffin of a bath, up to my chin in water, sipping the Campari and soda he had brought me, while he, draped in his kimono, sat on the lid of the wooden lavatory seat, smoking a cigarette. I stared at the taps. I took a deep breath.

'Why aren't you?' I said, not looking at him.

'Why aren't I what?'

'Married?'

'Well, why aren't you?'

I had not anticipated this turn in the conversation. 'Oh – you know – Fate.'

He grinned. 'There you are. Same for me too.'

'And you like living here on your own? You've never fancied living with anyone?'

The grin broadened. 'Darling Dee, we've been together five nights of the seven this week. I seem, give or take a door key, to be living with you.'

I sighed. 'You're impossible, Melvin Gene. You'd make a Trappist seem communicative.'

'That's choice, Devious Deirdre, coming from you.'

'I'm not secretive,' I protested, sniffing.

'No, my love. Of course you aren't.'

'Well, I'm not!'

He was smiling at me with that maddening, sideways, half-lidded look. 'Anyway, I'd have thought you'd have rooted out Ambrose and Sergei by now and got yourself well briefed on my murky past.'

'Oh Mel. I wouldn't pry into your secrets behind your back.'

'I haven't any secrets. Nothing that wouldn't have come out quite naturally when the time was right. I just didn't want you to –' He paused, suddenly serious, reaching for another cigarette. 'OK. But don't take from

180

this something that isn't there. I did live with someone, for eight years. Until three years ago.'

'And you left her? She left you?'

'No. She died.'

'Oh Mel.' I looked up at him, looked away, ashamed. 'Oh, I'm sorry. You don't have to talk about it. You don't have to say any more.'

'But I'd like to. It's not difficult – not any longer. It's something that happened.'

I met his eyes again. We remained looking at each other very directly. 'All right,' I said. 'What was she like?'

'Her name was Louise. She was dark and a bit taller than you, with a tilt to her nose and eyes that crinkled up when she laughed. I saw you gazing intently at a photograph of her the other day.'

'The black-and-white shot?'

'She was twenty-nine and she was a continuity girl and she was on her way back from a shoot in Spain. The first assistant was driving her and the props man and the hairdresser to Malaga Airport. He misjudged a bend. They were all killed, all four of them.'

There was a pause. 'That's horrible,' I said.

'Yes, it was all of that. I'd gone to Heathrow to meet the flight. At first, I thought they'd just missed it. Then I couldn't understand why there weren't any messages.'

'It must have been – you must have gone crazy.'

'For about a year. I couldn't wrap my brain around it. I couldn't get through my head why she wasn't there. I was wretched. I was angry. I felt guilty that I hadn't treated her better, that I'd been moody, taken her for granted, had a bit on the side now and then. But I was tearingly, savagely angry, most of all. So I did the usual things. I scraped by on the minimum of work. I gave up trivialities like changing my clothes and shaving. I dedi-cated myself to getting systematically slaughtered. I used to crawl home at three in the morning and have that last drink you need like a hole in the head and sit on our bed and scream at her, asking her what the fuck she thought she was playing at.'

'And you decided there could never be anyone else?'

'You're kidding. I screwed everything that moved and a lot more that didn't. I'm the eldest of four brothers, there'd always been a woman around since I'd discovered how to slot the bits together, I'd never in my life been on my own. Sex got to be like sneezing.'

He paused, drew on his cigarette.

'Then one morning I woke from a coma on my studio floor to find a naked redhead doing a line of coke and asking me, quite seriously, why I didn't buy some proper chairs. After I'd got rid of her, I went to the bathroom and threw up a couple of times. Then I made the fatal mistake of looking at my tongue. I remember staring at it, riveted, wondering why this alien creature had chosen my mouth for a graveyard. It came to me that, if this was my tribute to Lou's passing, she wouldn't have been over-impressed. I thought it was probably time I cleaned up my act. Whatever that was. If, indeed, I had one at all.'

'So – what did you do?'

'I decided to find out what it was like to sleep by myself. I sold our house on Wandsworth Common and got rid of nearly everything in it. I found this place. I acquired Boris the Bruiser from the Cats' Protection League. I discovered a whole lot of fascinating things – like, laundry can't walk unaided to the washing-machine and the palate can get a bit jaded after three months of takeaway Chinese.'

'And you got to like living on your own?'

'It was hell on wheels for the first six months. I used to wake up in the dead of night whimpering. But yes – after a while I found I was quite proud of myself. I turned out not to be such rotten company as I'd thought I'd be. I learnt how to mourn Lou as Lou – not some life-support system that had been switched off. And I even began to

182

enjoy being Celibate of Streatham Vale – it's quite pleasant to know who you'll find in bed every morning.' He
bent to the washbasin to extinguish his cigarette. 'So,
Devious Deirdre, that's where I am and how I got there.
My shady past.'

I looked away, making eddies with my toes in the bath
water, studying their movement. Wives caused problems,
but at least they were problems I understood. How could
I compete with a dead woman?

'Poor Mel,' I said, gazing fixedly at the water. 'You
must still miss her terribly.'

'Don't do it, Dee.' I was aware, at the edge of my
vision, of him shifting, leaning forward. 'Please, crazy
person, look at me for a second.'

I looked. He held my eyes steadily. 'Of course I
miss Lou sometimes. And yes, of course I think about
her – you never lose the people you've loved. But she's
trapped, poor much-loved Louie, caught, freeze-frame,
at twenty-nine, still dotty about William Hurt in *Kiss of
the Spiderwoman*, hooked on salt-beef sandwiches, saying
she's going to enrol for a drawing class one of these days.
I've moved on, I've changed. She changed me by dying.
She wouldn't thank me, having paid everything to give
me such a gift, if I just threw it away.'

He rose and leant over the tub to kiss my forehead. 'Do
I look like a person burdened with a secret sorrow?'

'No,' I said. 'No, you don't.'

Taking the Campari glass and kneeling beside the bath,
he kissed me again.

'So,' I said eventually, 'what happened to Celibate of
Streatham Vale? What made you decide it was time you
went back to dazzling us women with your talents?'

'Oh, I didn't decide. I don't decide anything these
days. I just wait and see what happens. So I waited' – his
tongue skimmed mine – 'and see what happened?'

I put up my hands to his face, laughing. Disengaging
them, he examined my fingers. 'Yuk!' he said. 'The

183

woman of my dreams is turning into a prune. I shall go and play Jack the Ripper with the mullet. And, over dinner, perhaps you'll tell me why you react like a vampire to garlic when anyone mentions Alex Power.'

'Oh Mel,' I said. 'Thank God I've got hold of you.'

It was a bad line. His voice crackled through electric fog. 'What's happened, my love? Is Zig casting Loch Ness Monsters? Is Samantha deep in *Das Kapital*?'

'Mel, Sergei's going to phone you and ask you for dinner. Danish food. He's just phoned me. Listen, whatever happens, don't say anything.'

'About what?'

'About us.'

'Really? Why ever not?'

'Because Sergei thinks we don't know each other. I told Ambrose I'd only talked to you once, briefly, at a party.'

'Tell me, Devious Deirdre, why on earth did you say that?'

'Because – well, you know – Oh God, this is embarrassing. And now Ambrose has gone and persuaded Sergei to set up this dinner party. As a sort of blind date.'

Gales of laughter came distantly from the other end of the line. 'So you don't want us to disappoint them? You want us to fuck each other senseless, then go separately to their place where, after four hours' frigid conversation over the gravadlax, we make our way home separately and fuck each other senseless again.'

'Put like that, it does sound a bit weird.'

'Weird? I'm glad you told me you weren't secretive, my darling, otherwise I might not have guessed. Anyway, this is one bizarre game we can't play. I'm afraid I've already blown it.'

'You what?' I said.

'I'd just finished talking to Sergei when you called. He asked me to dinner and I said, love to, may I bring

184

someone? He did, I admit, sound like I'd knocked him for a loop. But when I mentioned it was you he said actually he'd invited you anyway and that was just fine – marvellous, I think he said.'

'Ohmigod!'

'What's the matter?'

'I know Ambrose and Sergei are friends. But they're both the most dreadful gossips. Particularly Ambrose. It'll be all over Soho by now.'

'Well, why not?'

'Why not? People will think we've got a thing going.'

'Oh? So I've been imagining this small blond person in my bed for three and a half weeks?'

'Mel, you understand what I mean.'

There was a pause. Then he said: 'If I didn't know better I'd think you were trying to tell me something. Like you suspect me of belching and farting in public. Or there's a mad Mr Rochester locked up in your West Wing.'

'Oh Mel, I didn't mean . . .'

'You know I love spending every available hour in bed with you. But we can't live in purdah for ever. There are friends I'd like you to meet – Jake and Lizzie, the ones I'm making the chairs for. My brothers. Sid, my lunatic assistant. And I'd like to meet the people you talk about – Gilda, Chrissie.'

'You mean, go out together? As a couple?'

'We are a couple, aren't we? I don't see any reason to hide it.'

This time it was I who fell silent. 'Oh Mel,' I said at last. 'Oh Mel – I do love you.'

'Good,' he said. 'Because I love you too, Dotty Deirdre. I love every missing marble in your beautiful paranoid head.'

When I had put the phone down I gazed at my diary. Though Mel, I had finally discovered, was a Taurus, I had never got round to coding him properly, making do

185

instead with cryptic little Ms. Now I took my pen and with a flourish altered every one to a bold, unambiguous 'Mel'. I giggled to myself. I twirled in my chair. I did a small, mad, sitting-down dance. I was in love. I was totally, wonderfully, absurdly in love with a man called Melvin Gene from Streatham.

NINE

'Of course in past years we've had you round on the actual day,' said Gilda, as Jamie-Beth appeared with my birthday cake. 'But we're glad, darling heart, you could spare us an evening some time this week.'

Jamie-Beth deposited the cake in front of me. Gilda was a *cordon bleu* cook but, as Jamie-Beth's spell of 'resting' had extended, she had taken over the kitchen, where, scornful of ceremony and art direction, she had set about purging the menu of the dual masculine corruptions of carnivorousness and commercialism. Gilda's Armagnac pâté had given way to alfalfa shoots, her Stroganoff to pulses and bean curd. The cake, solid, square and uncompromising, with an unsparing forty-one candles, was, Jamie-Beth announced, a carrot cake, baked by Georgie, who ran the coffee counter at the feminist book shop.

I blew out the candles in several puffs while Gilda applauded and Jamie-Beth took Polaroids.

'This is a lovely evening,' I said. 'You're both very good to me.'

Gilda replenished our glasses with champagne. Jamie-Beth, fetching her pouch from the sideboard, began licking Rizzlas.

187

'We do hope you don't mind us not inviting Mr Single, darling heart. But it just didn't seem – appropriate.'

'He's working late at Pinewood. It wasn't a problem.'

'After holding your hand throughout the long, hard hunt – well, we'd be the last ones to want to cause a rift between you.'

'We do things together. And we do things separately. It's very relaxed. Sort of' – I paused, puzzled by the word that came to me – 'sort of grown-up.'

'Heaven forfend. I thought the point was to have some nice, uncomplicated fun.'

'Oh, we have that too.'

'I'm sure you do, darling heart. I've noted the size of his Oxfords.' She raised her glass. 'Well, here's to you, Dee. Birthday congratulations. And here's to your wonderful new life with Mr Single. Jamie?'

Jamie-Beth, who had not lifted her glass, was applying her Zippo to the joint with heavy concentration. She took a throat-searing drag, then, looking up, observed Gilda's raised eyebrows.

'Oh yeah,' she said, 'here's to you, Dee. Guess I never thought to see you turn into a Barbie doll.'

Gilda lowered her eye-brows menacingly. 'Jamie-Beth!'

'I know what you said, Gil. But I gotta be open, I'm an open person. And frankly, the other night in the restaurant, Dee, when you agreed with him about Post-Structuralism, and then, when he told you he needed an early night and you got up and followed him, meek as your ass – well, I just wanted to up-chuck.'

I laughed. 'He doesn't make me agree with him, Jamie-Beth. He doesn't make me do anything.'

'But you go right along and do it, just the same.'

'We agree because we agree. He's very easy-going. He believes people should suit themselves.'

'Yeah?' said Jamie-Beth, passing the joint to Gilda. 'In my experience, it's those gentle, laid-back guys that are the most into control. They're the ones think they got the Holy Grail in their pants.'

'Enough, child!' said Gilda severely. 'You must forgive the brat, Dee. Remember, Jamie, that Mr Single is a paragon who irons his own shirts and apparently even cleans the bath.'

The conversation moved delicately elsewhere, to whether Zig's producer was having a nervous breakdown, to the pub theatre audition that might have been Jamie-Beth's break, if the director hadn't come on like he wanted her to give him head. At twelve-thirty I said I must be going, and Jamie-Beth rose to phone a mini-cab.

'Of course, darling heart, you must leave in good time,' said Gilda sweetly. 'Mr Single's no doubt calling your answering machine, and we wouldn't want him to think you'd run off somewhere.'

When the cab arrived she held me in the hall for some moments under the pretext of hunting for my umbrella. Jamie-Beth emerged from the study with a flat oblong package, gift-wrapped and beribboned, which she thrust into my hands.

'Surprise,' said Gilda, smiling conspiratorially. 'Birthday surprise.'

'But you've already given me my present,' I said. 'The outrageous hat. I adore it. You know I'm crazy about fake zebra.'

'Aha,' said Gilda. 'But this is something extra. No, don't open it now. Wait till tomorrow when you're in your office.'

I squeezed the parcel, I rattled it. 'It feels like a book – or a tape.'

Gilda and Jamie-Beth exchanged sly glances.

'It is a tape. Hey, come on, you two, what is it?'

'Shall we tell her, Jamie?'

'Oh, I dunno – I guess we could, Gil.'

'Come on,' I said, laughing.

'Well,' said Gilda, 'remember the evening you forced

189

me to drink far too many manhattans and we wrote a casting brief –?'

'Which I made you throw away.'

'Which you *thought* I threw away. But, while you were in the loo, your kind Auntie Gilda, who always has your best interests at heart, retrieved it from the waiter and secreted it in her handbag. And then, one afternoon, when you were at home painting, we held a casting session . . .'

I stared at Gilda. I looked down at the parcel. I stared once again at Gilda. 'So this is –?'

'Fifteen unattached men, forty to forty-five, long shot and close up, full face and profile, with appropriate biographical details.'

'But, Gilda –'

'You'll find a typed sheet inside with our suggested short list. We think you'll like our first choice. Six foot three, fair hair, tanned, deep blue eyes. Quite an Adonis. And a size twelve shoe.'

'But, Gilda –'

'Oh, I know, darling heart,' she said, patting my hand. 'You've already found your Mr Single. But Jamie-Beth and I always said we'd give you a casting session for your birthday, didn't we? And you always thought the idea was a joke, so just consider this tape as the punchline. Of course, you'll need to view it in your office – we wouldn't want Mr You-know-who getting jealous. But just think of the lovely time you'll have, after a good lunch, running through our selection with a glass or two of bubbly and fantasizing about what might have been.'

When I arrived at Fortnum's Annie Smith had already secured a table in the Fountain Restaurant and was sipping lapsang suchong. Her highlights had been daringly accentuated, I noticed, and she had abandoned her glasses.

'Contact lenses,' she said, batting theatrical lashes. 'What do you think, love?'

'Great,' I said. 'Makes you look five years younger. And the new make-up's a triumph.'

'And I adore that suit. So nice to see you in something that isn't black, Dee. You've got good legs, too – I've always said you should show them off more.'

'Mel likes legs. Funny how all men, whatever their generation, seem to have a fetish about stockings and suspenders. Not that I've taken to wearing skirts because of Mel, you understand. I just fancied it.'

'Of course,' said Annie, favouring me with a wicked look from beneath her newly-mauve lids. 'I didn't mean to imply, dear, that you were in any way fragile and yielding.'

'Oh Lord,' I said.

She smiled. 'You know, you're so different from when I first met you. I was quite worried about you that afternoon at the Waldorf. But now – this Mel sounds a thoroughly nice young lad from everything you've mentioned.'

I helped myself to a smoked salmon sandwich. 'You'll be able to judge for yourself in an hour or so. He's coming with us to the movies. I haven't said anything, of course, other than that you're a friend. What you tell him is up to you. But –' I paused. Ridding myself of my Pavlovian tendency towards intrigue was one thing, but there were some secrets that deserved to remain secret. 'I'd be really terribly grateful if you avoided all mention of the ad. You could say – well, would you mind saying you sometimes play bridge with my mother?'

I had remembered the advertisement when I had been prowling my office in search of a suitable hiding place for Gilda's tape. The tape was a present, after all: generous impulses had gone into its making; like the china effigies of Mabel that Mrs Hernandez gave me every Christmas, it could not merely be discarded. In the end I had placed the cassette, unwrapped but unopened, on a shelf where other videotapes had accumulated as a dusty, rarely-consulted library of reference. But, before hitting upon

191

this solution, I had unearthed the file that contained my unanswered *Bright Lights* letters. I had been on the point of consigning them to the waste paper basket when an idea had struck me.

'Speaking of *Bright Lights*,' I said, tentatively, 'you remember, Annie, how you said you sometimes longed for companionship?'

'Oh, I do, love. But I don't think I've got the nerve to advertise like you. Not yet anyway. I'd worry about the explaining. Answering your letter used up all my courage.'

'But supposing – well, supposing you could have a sort of rehearsal. Supposing, without all the effort of placing your own ad, you could answer a few letters and see how things went?'

She glanced up from her tea cup. Her newly revealed eyes were hazel, I noticed, slightly protuberant but large and clear, with surprisingly thick lashes. 'A rehearsal?'

'I only replied to half my letters. And your taste in men seems, well, more conservative than mine. Perhaps you'd find a prize catch I'd missed.'

'You mean – answer your letters? Pretend I'm you?'

'Why not? There's no name in the ad. And we're both blondes.'

'And vivacious.'

'That too.'

She reflected for a moment. Then she began to laugh. 'Hang on a minute, love. Your advert says "petite". I'm five foot eleven.'

'Everyone's economical with the truth in Lonely Hearts columns. Slim appears to mean anything under twenty stone.'

'And then there's my age. You've been very kind about the contact lenses, but even so –'

'The ad says thirty-eight.'

'And I told you I was thirty-eight in my letter. But I'm afraid the horrible truth is I'm forty-five.'

'Am I thirty-eight? What does Oscar Wilde say? "Never trust a woman who tells one her real age – she'd tell one anything".'

'Even so –' Annie stopped laughing, stared gravely into her cup. 'It doesn't seem quite – well, honourable.'

'You look like a woman. You feel like a woman. Only Somerset House begs to differ. And, for one date, all you're trying to establish is that neither of you is King Kong's cousin and that you can hold a conversation without dropping off into your soup.' I unfastened my briefcase. 'It's entirely within the rules of the game. Who knows what murky secrets these men are concealing?'

'Everything's fair in love and war?'

'Exactly.'

Annie took the file and leafed through it, raising her eyebrows from time to time and emitting the occasional giggle.

'Of course the ad was some months ago,' I said. 'They may all be married by now. But I doubt it.'

'I like "I am sorry about the photo, I am having my front teeth capped".'

'Oh, Mr Apologies.'

'And this one here, whose interests run the gamut from historic buildings to hang gliding. When does he find time to sleep, I wonder?'

'Mr Categories? "My ideal life companion should have an appreciation of the disposable tooth-brush market".'

'That's him. "Manly, attractive and economically viable".'

'Well, I have to admit there are a few duds.'

'All the same' – Annie sucked in her lower lip thoughtfully – 'some of them do seem so desperate for a reply.'

'Absolutely. You'd be doing them a kindness.'

'I suppose – if I steeled myself with a couple of sherries – just for a first date – there might be one or two possibilities.'

'Keep the letters, hide them in your bag before Mel comes. And, if you have second thoughts, just put them in the dustbin. After all' – I could not restrain a complacent smile – 'I no longer need them.'

'Oh Dee, oh Mel, I'm s-sorry to be such a n-n-nuisance –' Chrissie's eyes were smudged, her lips raw and bitten. She submitted to being manoeuvred into a chair as if she were beyond protest.

'Kids, the police said. Maybe no older than thirteen. They'll never catch them, probably won't even bother trying. But I'd like to. I'd like to catch the bloody little bastards and kill them.'

Mel came in with a glass of brandy and gently wound her fingers about the rim so that her shaking would not spill it. 'Did they take much?' he asked softly.

All at once she reared up, shouting, drenching her skirt with brandy. 'It's not what they took! I can always buy another hi-fi, another video. I don't even care so much about a couple of gold bracelets. It's not what they took. It's what they smashed. It's what they touched. It's the souvenirs they left behind them. Oh God, they've been through everything, my cupboards, my drawers. It's all contaminated. I don't want to go back there ever again. I don't want even to see it.'

Rescuing the brandy glass, I knelt beside the chair and held her in my arms.

'You see,' she said, gulping for air between sobs, 'the flat's – all I've got. It's my territory – my sanctuary. I feel as if I've been raped!'

After a while her shoulders stopped heaving. She blew her nose on the strip of paper towel Mel had provided. 'I apologize. Oh, I do apologize. At work I'm usually cool in a crisis.'

'Chrissie,' said Mel, 'you're allowed to cry when you're hurt.'

'I'll be all right. I'll pull myself together in a minute.'

194

'Look,' I said, 'you can't go back tonight. Stay here and we'll take care of you.'

She took a gulp from the brandy glass, trying not to gag. 'No. Honestly, Dee. Thank you. The police are coming round again tomorrow morning. And anyway, they said I could clean up, I've got to clean, I've got to –'

With a sound as if she were retching, she buried her face in the kitchen towel.

'Chrissie,' I said, 'you're staying here.'

'No.'

'Please, my dear. It's one o'clock in the morning.'

'No!' She rose up at me, her face contorted, her eyes streaming. 'Don't you see, I can't? I hate that flat now. But if I don't go back tonight, I'll never go back. I'll never, ever be able to face it.'

Mel exchanged glances with me. Then he came and knelt in front of Chrissie's chair and took her hands. 'Dee has your keys. I'll go down and clear up the mess. You stay here with Dee.'

Chrissie protested, but Mel was quietly immovable. In the end, since she insisted it was her mess, she must go too, we all three trooped downstairs.

Chrissie's flat has always been as immaculate and considered and pastel-clean as its owner. Not uncomfortable, exactly. But the kind of flat pictured glossily in furniture catalogues, where the cushions are always ranged in precise colour co-ordination, the ferns never shed brown leaves, and the alignment of *objets* on the coffee table is never disturbed by discarded shoes or half-empty takeaway cartons. At first, when we entered the hall, there seemed little to challenge this homage to good order. A picture or two crooked perhaps, a muddy Doc Marten imprint on the pale blue Wilton. But, as we moved further inside – perhaps it was the unaccustomed savagery of overhead lighting, perhaps it was the stench – I felt what Chrissie felt, a chill, as if something were dead.

195

The sitting room was the worst. A vodka bottle had been hurled with force through the plate glass of the coffee table. The sofa had been slashed, and the colour-co-ordinated cushions. Of Chrissie's cherished Lalique collection, which had taken pride of place on shelves either side of the chimney breast, not one piece appeared to remain intact. To crown their achievements, the intruders had thought fit to defecate in the middle of the rose-patterned Chinese rug, and then to dip in their fingers and smear across one wall 'FUCK YOU COW'.

We stood wordlessly in the doorway, both of us hugging Chrissie. Then Mel fetched buckets and disinfectant and, ushering us out to deal with the rest of the flat, closed the door firmly against us.

By four-thirty, despite a strong smell of Dettol, the sitting-room walls were magnolia once more. The Chinese rug hung over the bath to dry, the slashed cushions were taped to prevent the further escape of feathers, and a cardboard box preserved the pathetic fragments of Lalique for Chrissie's insurance claim.

Mel and I sat at the kitchen table yawning, while Chrissie made tea.

'You're good friends,' she said. 'Such good friends.'

Mel grinned. 'Don't think you've got rid of us yet, my love.'

She rubbed her eyes.

'Since you won't spend the night with us, we'll spend it with you. Dee and I will sleep in your spare room.'

'But – well, what about poor Mabel?'

'Mabel, too, if you like.'

While Mel went to collect Mabel, I tucked Chrissie into bed. In her high-necked Victorian night-gown, she seemed child-like.

'Oh Dee, I'm so sorry.'

'Shush,' I said, drawing the duvet over her. 'If you apologize once more I shall suffocate you with this pillow.'

196

'I know it's wrong to care so much about things. I know you can't build a life out of possessions.'

'Lie back,' I said. 'You'll soon be enjoying your orgies of kippers and muesli again, to the strains of Mahler's Fifth.'

She settled her head on the pillow and closed her eyes. 'I'm glad you've got Mel,' she said.

'You've been buying things,' said my father accusingly.

My mother sighed. 'I suppose you'd better show your father.'

Reluctantly, I tugged the white shoe box from its carrier bag and drew aside the tissue paper. My father snorted. 'What d'you want to spend money on those for?'

My mother had found a new job, another step-up, buyer in a store in Oxford Street. She had purchased a second-hand car on the never-never. She had acquired a radiogram and six long-playing records. And she had bought me the shoes on her staff discount – black high-heeled snake-skin sling-backs. I had travelled up to the West End and met her at work and we had made an occasion of it. And on the way home, collecting my father from the station, we had dropped in at the Rose and Crown.

'In my young day,' said my father, 'girls of Deirdre's age wore sensible walking shoes.'

'They're a present,' said my mother, 'for passing her O levels.'

'In my day,' said my father, 'youngsters didn't need bribes to pass exams.'

'In your day . . .' began my mother: but she tailed off, appearing to think better of it.

She had restyled her hair to cover the scars from the plastic surgery. She scarcely limped at all now, despite the steel pins in her leg. But nevertheless, as if it had drained away with the blood she had lost in the accident, some of the spirit had gone out of her.

'Mind your manners, Deirdre,' said my father, tapping

my arm with his newspaper. 'Don't loll on that bar stool. Grown-ups may want to sit there.'

A red-faced man in a greasy sports jacket bore down upon us from the far end of the bar counter.

'Gerry, you old bugger,' he said, slapping my father's shoulder. 'Damn good show last Saturday. Useful half-century from young Watkins, eh? Looks like we've got ourselves a promising all-rounder.'

'Gussie!' said my father, extending his hand with the jovial smile he reserved for such occasions. 'You know my wife, Kitty, of course. Kitty, you've met Gus Morton.'

'Whajlly'ave?' asked the red-faced man, who looked as if he had already had several.

My father indicated the two of us, his female encumbrances, with a vague apologetic gesture. 'Good of you, Gus, but you're on your own . . .'

'Nonsense,' said the red-faced man, digging out a fiver.

'Mine's just a half then. Kitty would like a bottled Worthington. And a ginger-beer shandy for my daughter.'

'Don't believe,' said the red-faced man, surveying me with Union Jack eyes, 'I've ever had the pleasure.'

Introductions were effected, the red-faced man, to my acute mortification, seizing my hand and implanting moist lips ceremoniously upon it. 'So this is the young lady we've heard so much about. Bet she'll soon be hitting the lads for six, eh? Eh, Gerry?' To me he bent, exhaling yeast confidingly. 'Decent cove, your father. Best secretary the Club's ever had. Salt of the earth, old Gerry. Fancy a game of arrows, Gerry old boy? Best of three, eh? Leave the ladies to their chatter.'

We were installed at a table in the corner, while my father opened up the darts board and scrubbed the slate clean of chalk marks. The red-faced man delivered our drinks, slopping a good deal of my shandy.

My mother surveyed the bottle of beer with unconcealed disgust. ' "Kitty would like a Worthington". Kitty

198

would have liked a stiff gin and It – if anyone had cared to ask her.'

'Why don't you tell him?' I said.

'Doesn't want to burden his friend with a heavy round. Very considerate to his friends, is your father.'

'I'll tell him, if you like.'

'It makes no odds,' she said, with a sigh. She picked up the beer and began to pour it, tilting the glass methodically. 'You wouldn't catch him telling Avril Mayhew she'd like a bottled Worthington.'

The red-faced man, despite a tendency to stagger, was away, already scoring. My father, brow furrowed, tongue protruding, had still to achieve his double. We watched as double nineteen eluded him yet again.

'Why don't you leave him?' I said. 'You've always been saying you're going to.'

She sipped the beer. The froth described an undignified moustache above her lipstick. 'He thinks he's safe now. He thinks no one will want me with these scars.'

'They don't show,' I said automatically.

'He thinks no man will ever look at me now. Perhaps he's pleased the car hit me.'

'But you could still go. You could just go anyway.'

She put down the beer. She stared at her hands. 'Where would I go to?' she said vaguely.

A chorus of shouts announced that my father had at last gained his double. My mother surveyed him thoughtfully as he aimed for the triple twenty. He had a curious throwing stance, rigid as board to the hips and yet with a quirky follow-through in his right leg, like a spasm.

I sipped my shandy. It was not what I had wanted either, and tasted soapy. I thought of the snake-skin sling-backs and longed to go home. I longed to try them on with my short flared skirt and my skinny-rib jumper.

'Don't get married, Dee,' said my mother. 'Marriage is one thing for a man and quite another for a woman.' She pushed aside her beer glass. She sighed heavily. 'Did

199

I ever tell you about the time, early on, when I thought
he was going to kiss me, and instead he grabbed this herring . . .?'

Sometimes the old question would come back; sometimes,
as I sat in Mel's studio, sketching him while he worked, I
would find myself wondering: 'Why me?' Then I would
pause in roughing out the sweep of his profile, in shading
the furrows ploughed by his over-wide smile, and a knot
would gather in my stomach, I would stare dippily into
space like a benign drunk. On nights when we were sep-
arated, I would take his kimono from where it now hung
on my bedroom door, and cocoon myself in it, smelling
his hair, his skin, imagining his fingers exploring the soft
inner flesh of my thighs. In my bathroom, I would drink
in the scent of his shaving foam, linger over his brush,
inexplicably touched by the fine mesh of brown strands
woven round its bristles. Why should a personable, intelligent man like Mel – a man who phoned when he said
he would, a man who did not blow down women's ears,
a man who seemed so perplexingly normal – why should
such a man abandon two years of celibacy for me?

I had come to expect from love sensations not dis-
similar to those produced by shopping: periods of manic
euphoria, succeeded by prolonged spells of lassitude and
self-flagellation. Not so with loving Mel. I seemed possessed, at once, of enormous energy and an uncharacteristic calm. At work, Ambrose and I had almost concluded
negotiations on the premises in Wardour Street and I was
already beginning to interview managers for the new
office. Mel's comments on my paintings had inspired me
to take up portraiture again and I had completed a study
in oils of Ambrose and Sergei which had delighted all
three of us. I slept peacefully and dreamlessly. I ate three
meals a day. I had not been found in possession of carrier
bags, had not even entered a shop with intent, for at least
six weeks.

Like an old lag undergoing rehabilitation, I became gradually used to being part of a couple. I had met two of Mel's brothers, both shorter, sturdier versions of himself – the third was in California doing something impressive for NASA: but I blenched when Mel casually suggested one Sunday that we should drive to Clapham and drop in on his mother. From his references to her, I had somehow typecast Mel's mother as a cheerful Cockney crone, nostalgic for the Blitz, referring constantly to 'my boys' like the progenitrix of a gangland dynasty, and greeting all announcements of doom with indomitable cackling laughter. But were there not, still, so many things about Mel that constantly defied my predictions? What I found was a handsome, dark-haired divorcee in her fifties who designed jewellery and ran a stall in Covent Garden with George (who was not, as I had first assumed, one of Mel's brothers' friends, but her decidedly youthful lover). I was looked over, of course, most thoroughly, but the inspection seemed free from the anticipated disapproval. Only one thing bothered me: if I had met Mel's mother there was an unspoken assumption that I must at some point introduce him to mine; and here my rehabilitation seemed to falter.

One sharp morning in early November, when the tourists had briefly migrated and the first Christmas trees were sprouting in shop windows, Mel and I sat breakfasting in the Patisserie Valerie.

'I'm going to murder Mabel,' I said. 'She's been tap dancing on my answering machine and deleting all the messages.'

'Poor Mabel. She gets lonely the nights you're not there. She probably phones a mate for a chat.'

'Poor Boris, too. He was starving when we got to Streatham this morning. He must have been ravenous to eat that garbage bag.'

'He's sulking. Eating garbage bags is his favourite method of protest.'

'Poor Boris,' I said.

'Poor Mabel,' he said. 'We're rearing a pair of delin-quents.'

He sipped his coffee thoughtfully. The couple who had been sharing our table broke off their earnest conversation about the British Film Institute and rose to leave. He waited till they had struggled into their coats and scarves, then replaced his cup carefully in its saucer.

'You know, we should do something about it.'

'Boris and Mabel? What do you suggest. Hypnosis? A cat counsellor? I'm not sure Mabel has the brain for it.'

'Maybe they should live together.'

'Boris and Mabel?'

'Us too, of course. We're the ones who wield the tin openers.'

'But they may loathe each other on sight, they may . . .' I suddenly ceased buttering my croissant, I put down my knife very slowly. 'Sorry, Mel. What did you say?'

'I said I thought we should live together.'

I stared at him. He fixed my eyes with his usual clear, unwavering look. 'It seems a good alternative to the 6.30 a.m. cat food run.'

'But we – where would we live? My flat's no use – there's no room for you to work.'

'And you don't fancy living in Streatham. We'll buy somewhere. A warehouse or something. A place where we can both work.'

'Buy somewhere – together?'

'It's a thought.'

'But – but we've only known each other three months.'

He laughed. 'Do we have to clock up a statutory number of hours? When was the last time we spent a night apart, anyway?'

I gulped. 'Oh Mel – I mean, it's just sinking in. I mean – it's a shock. It's a commitment.'

He touched my hand. 'Then think about it. There's

no tearing rush. All I know is, it's what I'd like in the long run.'

I continued to stare at him. 'You want – to live – with me – in the long run?'

'I'd like to marry you, really. I'd ask you if I didn't think I was pushing my luck.'

I opened my mouth, closed it again, opened it. 'Melvin Gene, are you proposing to me?'

'For Boris and Mabel's sake, you understand. To keep them from mugging little old ladies.'

'Oh, Mel! Oh Mel . . .' I stopped suddenly, looked down at my plate. 'I – oh God, it's no good. There's something I haven't told you.'

'You mean there's a mad Mr Rochester after all, behind the heaps of clothes in your wardrobe?'

I played with the croissant flakes on my plate. His hands, too, were working, twisting the metallic wrapping from his butter. I sighed. 'You're a lot younger than I am.'

'I'm thirty-six.'

I looked up. 'But, according to my maths –'

'Your maths, Delectable Deirdre, isn't the most brilliant thing about you.'

'Even so – I told you I was thirty-eight . . .'

He was smiling the smile that was too big for his face. I watched the smile broaden. 'You knew all along?'

'Like I said, maths isn't your strongest suit. How come you were already into O levels when Kennedy was assassinated?'

'But don't you see –?' I returned to the crumbs on my plate. 'I'm too old to have children.'

'Plenty of women nowadays have babies in their forties.'

'Supposing I can't?'

'We'll live with whatever happens.'

I looked up. He was still smiling.

'You've thought about this, haven't you, Melvin Gene? You've been quietly thinking it through.'

203

'Yes, Dotty Deirdre, I've thought about it.'

He had twisted the butter wrappers into a crinkly gold band. He held it up to one eye. He squinted at me through it.

'Oh, Mel!' I scraped back my chair. I flung my arms around his neck, sending my coffee cup flying. 'Oh, Mel. Oh, Melvin Gene!'

CHAPTER

TEN

'But that's wonderful!' Chrissie had said. 'Why keep
it a secret? I'd want to tell everyone – traffic wardens,
pigeons, people on buses.'

I could not explain why, precisely. Partly it was a
difficulty with the word 'engaged', a vision it conjured of
casserole dishes and onyx bathroom accessories, of con-
gratulatory speeches seamed with coy innuendo, which
plunged me back into adolescence, stripped of all dignity, laid out naked for public scrutiny. I had managed to
persuade Mel that there was no point in making a song
and dance about anything until we had sorted out where
we were going to live. Thumbing through a fresh set of
specifications from the estate agents, I told myself this
could take months. By the time we had agreed on the
perfect converted warehouse in the ideal location, had
jumped all the hurdles of surveys and solicitors' searches,
had arranged mortgages and remade our wills, I should
feel happily adjusted to my altered state.

Certainly there was no point in telling Mrs Hernandez,
no point yet in burdening her with the job insecurity
that talk of my moving would induce. She had seemed,
in any case, slightly flustered this morning. Usually she

seized upon my unheralded appearances with enthusiasm, relishing the opportunity for one of her rococo monologues. But this morning, coming upon me slumped over a newspaper in the kitchen, she had appeared taken aback, put out almost. Only for an instant, however. Soon she was established opposite me, equipped with coffee and a cigarette, and in full spate.

Her friend Irma, I gathered, had recently visited a clairvoyant – a palmist in Wimbledon (or, perhaps Irma lived in Wimbledon and the palmist had been an acquaintance of Rita's sister in Barcelona, the one whose husband had died after being bitten by a parrot – or was it the parrot that had died?). Nodding, smiling as the words flowed over me, I found myself thinking absently of Mrs Hernandez's four fine sons and her thirty years' marriage to Xavier, the angel. I studied her smooth, consoling surfaces, the creaseless cheeks, the pillowy bosom, the wedding and engagement bands dimpling cushioned flesh. Her eyes were clear, her hair luxuriant. In her overstuffed angora sweater, ripe and downy as fruit nurtured in slow heat, she glowed, comfortable, complacent, cherished. Thirty years of marriage. Thirty years of serenity and peace. It was, after all, possible. Here was the evidence sitting opposite me, palpable and reassuring.

'Don't get me wrong,' she was saying, flashing her rings, shaking her glossy hair. 'Some of them is cockypop, some of them they give you a load of old dribble. But this Madam Yasmin – she don't say nothing, she just look at the cards, then she look at Irma. Then she tell Irma everything, her daughter that had the miscarriages, Reginald's blood pressure, Irma's trouble with her hip. It bring Irma out in goose bumps, I can tell you.'

'It would,' I said.

'Then she say Irma go on a journey in the New Year, meet a stranger initial S, wealthy, smart dresser, a real dishy fella.'

206

'Her chance to boogie?'

'This Mr S boogie the night away, so Madam Yasmin reckon. Irma, she get all excited, rush home and there's Reginald, says – what you think? – the golf is good in Tenerife and why don't she fix them up a package in January? Irma, she laugh all the way to the travel agent's. She counting the days now, I can tell you.'

'What about poor Reginald?'

'He got his golf. He don't notice nothing.'

'But, even so –'

Mrs Hernandez waved my objection aside, brandishing her cigarette excitedly. 'Irma, she so pleased and delighted she think maybe Madam Yasmin should read my cards too. "You got to get out of yourself, Rita," she say, "go where the grass is longer, get new blood in your veins." So next thing I know she fix me an appointment, Monday 4 p.m. What you think?'

I stared at her, shocked. 'But you don't need a Mr S,' I said. 'You've got Xavier.'

Mrs Hernandez examined the depths of her coffee mug. She looked up. She smiled. 'Don't get me wrong, Dee –' she said. But as I hung anxiously upon her words the phone rang. I hovered reluctantly for a moment before being forced into the study to answer it.

A snuffle greeted me from the other end. Then a thick voice said: 'Dee?'

'Hullo? Who is that?'

'Dee, it's Laura.'

'Laura? You poor thing, have you got flu?'

'Do I sound strange? It must be the valium.'

'My God, Laura! What's the matter? What's happened?'

More snuffling. A silence. Then an audible sob. 'Oh Dee, it's Charlie. It's Charlie, Charlie . . .' Her voice tailed away into a gurgle.

'Is Charlie ill? Has he had an accident?'

'An accident?' The gurgle burgeoned into a snort and then into sudden manic laughter. 'I suppose you could call it that. "I was just passing this woman, m'lud, when I slipped and found myself on top of her. Silly little accident, sort of thing that could happen to anyone . . ." '

'Laura,' I said, waiting for the noises to subside, changing tack. 'Laura, where are you?'

'I'm at Mummy's. I've left Charlie, Dee, and I'm staying with Mummy.'

'Left Charlie? But why? How? What about the children?'

'The children are here with me. Do you think I'd abandon them to that dishonest, immoral, unfeeling shit? Do you think I'd expose them to his corrupt influence one second longer? Dear God, poor Titus is barely two years old!'

'Laura, what has Charlie done?'

'Not what, who. Who, Dee, who!' Again I waited for the gurgles to subside. 'He's been screwing his secretary, that's what. He's been screwing that snotty, suburban, squint-eyed slut of a secretary of his. All the time I've been keeping his dinner warm, and worrying he'll get executive burn-out, and telling the children, "Don't bounce on Daddy, he needs his sleep", he's been jumping on a little tart called Janis who goes to "functions" and the "toilet" and thinks Satie is something you eat on a skewer. Two years it's been going on. Two years she's been answering the phone and saying, "How are you, Laura? How are your lovely children? Charlie's told me ever so much about them." Everyone in the office knew. Everyone in the universe knew but me!'

'How did you find out?'

'I was going through his trousers for the dry cleaners, and I pulled out these theatre-ticket stubs. He'd never mentioned the theatre, he'd told me he'd been working late that night. Of course he tried to lie his way out of it, mumbled something about a client from Japan, said it had slipped his mind. But then I remembered other things – the lipstick I found under the front seat

208

of the car, the way his handkerchiefs keep disappearing mysteriously and coming back freshly laundered – Janis likes a good cry apparently, especially in restaurants and other public places. Two years of lies, Dee, two years of Machiavellian deceit. And I believed him! I believed every lame excuse, every devious phone call. Dear God, I swallowed stories that would make Baron Munchausen blush. Well, it's all over now. It's well and truly over. We're getting a divorce.'

'You mean Charlie wants to marry this – this Janis?'

'No, he wants me to take him back, would you believe? He wants me to forgive him. He says it was a mistake, a bad habit he'd got into, like picking his nose. He says it would never have happened except for this party at the office two Christmases ago, and he'd always cherished a secret ambition to have it away on the boardroom table. Can you imagine, Dee? A grown man with three children, a man with a Master's degree, a man who's read *Finnegans Wake* and even understood parts of it – and the height of his ambition, the acme of his achievement, is to bonk some bird-brained bimbo on the boardroom table! Oh my God, hold on a minute, I need another valium!'

'But Laura –'

'And now he keeps phoning me here, crying down the telephone, begging, pleading with me, saying it'll never happen again, saying he doesn't know what came over him, it was just that Janis was there, available – as if the little slut were a late-night supermarket or a dial-a-pizza service. Well, he's dead right, the miserable, conniving, lecherous shit! It'll never happen again. I've already talked to Mummy's solicitor.'

'But Laura, you love Charlie. You always said he wasn't just a husband, he was a friend –'

'Dee, you're my friend. Would you do this to me? Would you lie to me, betray me, make me look a fool in front of the whole world?'

209

'No, but –'

'The Charlie I loved had integrity. The Charlie I loved was decent and honourable and didn't know how to lie. And do you know the sick thing, Dee, the sickest thing of all? I invented that Charlie. He doesn't exist. He's probably . . . never . . . existed!'

Once again I waited until I could hear her trumpeting into her handkerchief. 'But – divorce, Laura? It seems so drastic. After all, there are the children to consider –'

'Did he consider them, Dee? Did he for one minute – fumbling with Janis's one-size panty hose in the front of our car, with poor Titus's kiddie seat in the back, and Cassie's ballet slippers – did he for one second spare them a thought? My God, if he's betrayed me, think what he's done to them. They'll never believe in anyone again, they'll be permanently scarred. Already I can see the signs – Dom wants blond streaks in his hair and Titus peed in Mummy's knitting bag this morning.'

'But all the same –'

'I won't take him back, Dee, I won't. Don't you see, it's not the infidelity, it's not grubby little Janis that really matters. It's that he's lied to me, time and again, without batting an eyelid. He's admitted he's lied for two years. But what about before? Perhaps he's been lying for the whole of our marriage. And if I forgave him, Dee, what then? How could I ever believe a word he said? You can't love without trust, Dee. And I can never trust Charlie, never ever again.'

When I eventually put down the phone I sat for a while, numbed. Yes, in my previous existence I had hated the lonely weekends, the midnight hunts for Y-fronts under the bed: but there had been the excitement too, the restaurants, the hotel rooms, the heightened importance of every snatched meeting. Now a new scenario unfolded itself, a succession of drab evenings on which, imprisoned by squalling children, I grilled fish fingers and listened anxiously for the growl of the car. I saw myself taking the phone calls with background pub SFX, saw myself counting handkerchiefs, frisking the dry cleaning. I shivered.

I recollected Mrs Hernandez and the clairvoyant and the dishy fella, initial S. But surely Rita, adored for thirty years by Xavier the angel, must have been joking?

She was in the sitting room dusting the mantelpiece, with Mabel, ever mindful of the cat treats, lingering close to her heels. She was humming brightly – I made out snatches of 'Some Enchanted Evening'.

'Rita –' I said.

And was interrupted by the buzz of the answerphone.

We both jumped.

'I get it,' she said.

'It's OK, Rita.'

'No, Dee. You don't bother. I get it, I get it.'

Despite her insistence, I was closer to the front door. Strange, no one knew I was at home this morning. Probably the postman, or truanting boys offering a car wash.

'Hullo?' I said into the answerphone.

There was an embarrassed silence, a cough. 'It's Tom, love.'

'Tom?'

'Tom, the window cleaner, love.'

'Oh sorry, Tom. I wasn't expecting you. I thought Rita said you came last week.'

I was aware of Mrs Hernandez breathing hotly upon my neck. 'Stupid fella!' she hissed. 'Here, I send him away with his ears between his tail.' Grabbing the answerphone, she commanded him peremptorily to stay where he was. Then she bustled off down the stairs.

She was gone for almost ten minutes. 'Funny,' I said, hearing her footsteps at last, looking up from the newspaper, 'he's never got confused before. He usually comes regular as clockwork first Friday of the month. And today's the second Wednesday . . .'

Mrs Hernandez appeared in the kitchen doorway. Her angora bosom was heaving, several strands of her lac-quered film-star hair were out of place. I stared at her. I remembered suddenly how put out she had been to find me unexpectedly at home. Enlightenment struck me, communicating itself to Mrs Hernandez before I could banish it from my face.

She shifted in the doorway. Her creaseless, peach-furred cheeks bloomed a vibrant red. 'Xavier don't boogie so much no more, neither. Mostly he sleep in front of the telly. Don't get me wrong, Dee, but after thirty years – marriage is not so exciting.'

'My God,' my father had said. 'What do you look like?'

My first term at university. Sitting alone in my college bedsitter, feeding shillings to the gas fire, contemplating the sellotape-scarred wallpaper, the television-interference carpet, the bedspread striped like an angry wasp, I had thought almost nostalgically of home, had fashioned a softer, gauzier picture of it, with glowing coals and hot-buttered toast and my mother laughing. But even as I paused before the front gate the house had looked smaller, sad-eyed. My father had opened the door. He had studied my long black hair and my boots and my black Dr Zhivago coat. Then he had said: 'What do you look like?' and taken my suitcase without another word. We had eaten supper on our laps in front of the televi-sion, lamb chops and frozen peas and potatoes cooked to flour the way my father liked them. And now we were watching *The Man from UNCLE*. My first term at university. It was as if I had just popped out for a packet of cigarettes.

'Do we have to?' I said.

My father did not stir, but lay slumped in his armchair, the newspaper clutched like a life belt to his chest.

212

My mother looked up from reading a magazine. 'Do we have to what?' she said.

'It's my first night home. Couldn't we turn off the goggle box for once?'

'It'll be the news in a minute,' said my mother.

'But he's not even watching. He's fast asleep.'

My mother rolled up her magazine and, leaning forward, jabbed my father in the ribs with it. 'Gerald, you're snoring again!'

We watched as my father see-sawed upwards, then crashed abruptly downwards again, cracking his neck on the back of the chair. 'Was'n' snoring,' he mumbled, as once more he plunged into sleep.

My mother sighed, unrolling her magazine and hunting for her place.

'He hasn't said a word to me,' I protested. 'He hasn't even asked about university. I could join the Angry Brigade or run away to an ashram, he wouldn't care.'

'He's very proud of you, Deedee. He's always boasting about you to his cronies.'

'He doesn't say a thing to me.'

'Well – I suppose he doesn't want you to get big-headed. You know what he's like.'

My mother returned to her magazine. My father continued to snore. In the grate, dying embers of anthracite stirred and sighed. I rose from my chair, walked over to the television and switched it off.

My father lurched forward, snorting and shaking his head like an elderly spaniel. 'Whajawannerdothatfor?'

'I thought we could try a little civilized conversation.'

'In this house?' said my mother.

'Switch it on again, Deirdre. I'll miss the news.'

'Hard cheese.'

'Deirdre, don't take that tone with your father.'

'Oh, let him watch his precious news,' my mother said.

My father and I stared at each other.

213

'Switch it on, Deirdre. Don't play silly devils with your poor old father.'

'For heaven's sake, let him watch the news,' said my mother, 'or we'll never hear the end of it.'

My father gave his infuriating little laugh. Then, still clutching his newspaper as if it were umbilically attached, he rose and switched on the television. I waited till he had regained his chair, then I switched it off again. 'Fuck the news,' I said.

'Fine language to use to your father! Is that what they teach you at university?'

'How would you know?'

'No daughter of mine uses language like that in this house. No daughter of mine tells me when I should watch my own television.'

'*My* television,' said my mother.

'As long as you're in my house, young lady, you'll show some respect.'

'If you think I want to be in your crummy house —'

'In my day, youngsters were grateful to their parents.'

'In your day, people were pickled in formaldehyde at birth!'

'If you two are going to have a row,' said my mother, gathering up her magazine and reading glasses, 'I'm going to bed.'

'Here, steady on, Kitty,' said my father, as my mother made her exit, jerking the door shut smartly behind her. We listened to her footsteps retreating up the stairs.

'Now look what you've done,' he said. 'You've upset your mother.'

A spark of white heat flashed in my brain, flared up and burst like a Roman candle. 'You upset me!' I screamed.

My father surveyed me for a moment. Then, fixing his lips into The Smirk, he spread his newspaper, adjusted the pages and disappeared behind them.

I felt myself begin to shake. 'You don't care, do you? You don't give a damn.'

Silence.

'All you care about is your boring old cricket and your rotten news.'

Still silence.

' "My God, what do you look like?" What happened to "Hullo, how are you? I'm pleased to see you, Dee, I love you". . .?'

The newsprint wall rustled as my father turned a page.

I took three steps towards the armchair, extended my arm and tore the paper from my father's grasp. He lay, blinking up at me, prone and pasty and curiously exposed, like a crab wrenched from its shell. A tatter of newsprint still adhered between the thumb and index finger of his right hand. He screwed it up. He gave his dismissive little laugh.

I ripped the newspaper in two. Straining my wrists, tearing my fingernails, I began savagely to reduce it to shreds.

My father watched the snowfall of newsprint as it drifted across the carpet, settled in the hearth, whitened the anthracite in the aluminium bucket – the Obituaries, and the Court Pages and the photographs of Wilson and Lyndon Johnson.

'Very clever,' he said. 'I suppose they teach you that at university, too?'

I continued ripping and straining. Tears of rage coursed down my cheeks. 'Couldn't you have said something nice when you opened the door? Couldn't you have just said something nice?'

'When I see my daughter looking like a hippie or a yippie –?'

'Couldn't you even pretend?'

'My own daughter? I don't hold with all this permissiveness and pop music and drugs.'

'Your own daughter! Your house, your television,

215

your bloody coal bucket! I'm just a thing to you, aren't I? A thing without feelings. "Stand aside, Deirdre, don't sit there, Deirdre, give up your stool to that lady, Deirdre." I'm just a thing. And it's all fine so long as I'm not in anyone's way.'

'I've tried to bring up my daughter to have manners, to show some respect for her elders.'

'Fuck respect! Fuck, fuck, fuck, fuck respect!'

My father looked up at me. His lips curled. He looked away.

'That's right, smile. It doesn't touch you, does it? It doesn't mean a thing to you that I'm standing here screaming and crying. You've never paid any attention to Mother and you care about me even less. You'd care about me more if I was one of your mates up The Rose and Crown, or Fred Trueman or – or even a cricket bat! When Mother had her accident and nearly died, all you worried about was that I shouldn't get in the way –'

'Have a heart, Deirdre.'

'Have you got one, Father? Did you ever have one? Or were they an optional extra in your day?'

'Deirdre –'

'You think, because you don't have any feelings, nobody else should have them either. "You should respect your father." Why? Why? Just tell me what on earth there is about you to respect?'

My father's lips had vanished and his face was the colour of distemper. Quite suddenly he clenched his fist and brought it thundering down on the arm of his chair. The chair shuddered, the coal shovel dislodged itself from the bucket and crashed into the hearth.

'You and your mother,' he said, 'you have no compassion!'

His image wavered as my tears blinded me. Mucus trickled gummily from my nose into my mouth. I slid to my knees amongst the shredded newspaper, pressing my forehead into the carpet, feeling the prickle of anthracite

216

dust on my skin. 'Why can't you ever say anything nice? Why can't you ever praise us or tell us we look pretty? Why can't you cuddle us or say you love us – just show some feeling, something, anything . . .?'

My father's voice seemed to come from a long way away. 'It's not what I'm like, Deirdre. It's not how I was brought up to be.'

A PSYCHIATRIST SPEAKS

DEAR VICTIM: I am scarcely surprised you are experiencing anxiety at the thought of committing yourself to a permanent relationship.

I really cannot advise you as to whether the object of your current fixation will take to bonking on boardroom tables – that is surely the province of a clairvoyant (Madam Yasmin of Wimbledon is spoken of highly by many of my patients).

In my opinion, however, your retarded libidinal development suggests a negative prognosis. While you continue to act out your infantile fantasies you will remain the victim of a behavioural pattern that frustrates your capacity as a differentiated individual to achieve mature co-operative relationships with differentiated objects. In layman's language, so long as you strive unconsciously to capture your father's approval and to supplant your mother (and the *Daily Telegraph*) in his affections, you are dished. You will only be happy as long as you are the wrong side of The Eternal Triangle, always the mistress, never the wife.

Your problem requires a thorough spring-cleaning of your psychodynamics. And that's what we psychiatrists are here for, aren't we? However, you may consider suicide a less expensive and time-consuming alternative. Only please, do think the project through properly. Remember overdoses rarely work, the average kitchen knife is too blunt to sever the carotid artery and jumping in front of tube trains is profoundly inconsiderate to your

217

fellow commuters. Besides, the unlikelihood of your attending your own funeral will diminish your enjoyment of the overall effect . . .

Mel idled in my bedroom while I crammed clothes into a suitcase. We were catching an afternoon flight to Copenhagen to spend a week with his friend Leif. Cat sitters had been arranged and Mel, who had work to clear up in the morning, would collect me from The Casting Couch for the drive to Heathrow.

'You know,' he said, toying with the bottles on my dressing table, 'you never cease to amaze me.'

For the third time I turfed a plaintive Mabel out of my suitcase. I began searching for clean tights. 'I do?' I said.

'If I had any preconceived ideas about women, you've shattered them all by now.'

'How so?' I said.

'Mitsouko, Poison, Chloe, Ysatis . . . I always thought women chose one perfume and stuck to it. Like a call sign you could identify them by.'

'Are you criticizing me, Mel?'

'Not at all. I love having sixty-four different women for the price of one. I love watching you rummaging through the department store in your wardrobe and coming up with a new persona. One morning The Wicked Queen, the next The Little Match Girl. And yesterday you looked like a pixie in that crazy fake zebra hat.'

'I do not look like a pixie.'

'Well, an elf then.'

'I do not look like a pixie.'

'Better a pixie than a gnome.'

'I do not look like a fucking pixie!'

He turned from the dressing table, mildly surprised. 'OK, OK. You look nothing like a pixie. In fact, right now you're more of a hobgoblin – or a troll.'

I flung my hairbrush with force into my suitcase.

218

'You're a fine person to criticize me. You're vain enough yourself.'

'My love, I'm not criticizing you.'

'Yes you are, and I'm sick of it.'

'Dotty Deirdre –'

'Don't call me that!'

He moved towards me. To escape his touch I stepped back smartly, treading on Mabel's tail, which she had omitted to tuck in when she had retired under the bed to sulk. 'Now look what you've made me do. Poor Mabel. She hates me going away.'

He surveyed me, seeming genuinely puzzled. 'Dee, are we having a row?'

'You ought to know. You started it.'

He came and put his hands on my shoulders. 'Dee, we're not seriously having a row about whether or not you look like a pixie?'

'It's not about pixies – or piskies, come to that. It's about your attitude. The way you patronize me. The way you're always sending me up and criticizing everything I do.'

He remained with his hands on my shoulders, as if hoping to quell me with that Mr Honest look of his. 'Dee, all I said was –'

I turned away. 'I heard what you said.'

'It was a joke, my love. J–O–K–E.'

'If I'm so God-awful ugly why did you go to bed with me in the first place?'

'Oh, for Christ's sake. I've said I love the way you look – in all your incarnations. I love you when you're just you, all scrubbed and sleepy without make-up in the mornings. I'd probably love you if you had two heads.'

'You're saying I look as if I've got two heads without my make-up?'

'I'm saying I really like you without make-up.'

'You mean you hate my make-up. You think I look horrible with my make-up on?'

'Jesus, Dee!'

I thrust my head into the bottom of the wardrobe, scrabbling amongst a pile of shoes. 'You don't seem to care how much you hurt me. If you can't say something nice, don't say anything at all.'

There was a pause.

'Dee, what's the matter? What's the real reason for this?'

'You're the one who knows. If you don't, I'm sure I don't.'

I heard him sigh. The springs creaked as he settled on the bed. 'Look, my love, stop rushing around. Sit down. Take a deep breath, mainline some valium or something. If you've finished with this suitcase would you like me to sit on it for you? I have to be at Maestro Movies by ten.'

I rose, clutching a pair of boots. I felt close to tears. 'Don't bother about the bag. Perhaps I don't want to come to Copenhagen after all.'

He stared at me. 'Oh Dee, for Christ's sake –'

'I don't want to come to Copenhagen if you're going to behave like a patronizing bastard. I don't want to come if we're going to spend the whole week rowing.'

He continued to study me for a moment. His expression changed. 'Right,' he said. 'I hope I'm beginning to understand what this is about. But if you didn't want to go to Denmark, why didn't you just say?'

'I did want to go. I wanted to meet your friend Leif and watch his production put together. I wanted to drink aquavit and eat herrings and see the Christiansborg Palace and the tattooists in the canal square. It sounded wonderful. But' – my chin was trembling – 'but now you've made me feel it would be a complete disaster.'

'OK,' he said evenly. 'Then don't go.'

I looked at him. I cast the boots into a chair. 'I see,' I said. 'You don't want me to go with you.'

'Jesus wept!'

'You never wanted me to go, you just asked me because you felt you ought to. You'd rather have a good time on your own with Leif and his actor mates, getting as soused as the herrings, steaming in saunas with all those well-built Scandinavian blondes. Why bring draggy old Dee along, with her funny disguises and her pixie hats? Little Match Girl, isn't that what you said? It'd be like taking a brownie pack to an orgy.'

'Christ, Dee!'

'And you said you loved me.'

'God help us, the woman has gone barking mad.'

'I love you and I thought you loved me. Now you don't even want to take me to Copenhagen.'

'Dee, just stop it, will you.'

'Do you still love me, Mel?'

He seemed to pause. 'Would it amaze you to learn that you're not in one of your most lovable modes at the moment?'

I collapsed against the chair, burying my face in the leather of my boots. 'So that stuff about us living together and getting married – it was all garbage.'

He did not reply. A long silence fell. Eventually, hearing the bed springs creak again, I glanced up. He was on his feet with his hands in his pockets, turning towards the door. 'Listen, Demented Deirdre' – he spoke very slowly and distinctly, as if I were hard of hearing – 'I want you to come to Copenhagen if you want to. And I don't want you to if you don't. There's no need to decide this minute. You've got the whole morning to think about it. But right now I'd like to stop playing this game. I don't know the rules and I've got zero interest in learning them. And anyway, I'll miss my meeting with Zig if I don't leave for Soho. If you'd like a lift, fine. If not, we'll talk on the phone later.'

He was almost at the door now, looking back at me over his shoulder. I returned his look steadily, coldly. He took his hands out of his pockets. He smiled. 'Come on, crazy person,' he said softly.

'Don't smile at me,' I said. 'Don't give me that patronizing, supercilious smile. I'm sorry I'm crazy. I'm sorry I tend to object when you hurt me. I'm altogether sorry there's so much about me to find fault with. I'm sure the late lamented Louise was eminently sane and consistent, always wore the same perfume, never looked like a pixie. But then I can't match up to her – I'm afraid I'm not perfect. It's a whole lot easier to be perfect when you're dead.'

Mel's smile vanished. An expression appeared on his face I had never seen before. 'OK,' he said. 'If you don't want to go to Copenhagen, that seems like a great idea to me.'

Next day I dragged myself into The Casting Couch to discover the heating had failed. To my surprise, Samantha, assuming I was in Denmark, had, on her own initiative, telephoned our landlord and an engineer was imminently expected. Nevertheless, you could see your breath in the hallway, and a dismal muttering arose from the twenty or so body builders assembled by Gilda to flex their musculature before Zig in time to the Supremes singing 'Baby Love': a few bravely sported their posing pouches, twitching goose-pimpled biceps, but most huddled in anoraks and scarves, beating a discontented tattoo with their boots or striving to warm bloodless fingers in the vicinity of the coffee machine. Samantha, too, sat shivering in her mackintosh, her body temperature further reduced by an alarming physical transformation: gone were the ornately-rolled girl-next-door tresses, razored to within a quarter inch of her scalp in a suedehead crop that would not have shamed an army recruit. The skin at the nape of her neck showed bluish-white, her ears, newly thrust into prominence, seemed brutally, almost lewdly naked. Yet she bared her

222

chattering teeth in a smile apparently intended to radiate calm efficiency, forbore to ask tactless questions about my unscheduled appearance and even solicitously fetched me a cup of coffee. On her desk lay a leather Personal Organizer, conspicuously new, and a copy of *The Power of Positive Thinking*.

Huddled in my office, gloved hands clasped for warmth around my polystyrene cup, I resisted another useless call to Mel's answering machine. I had not, of course, intended that he should fly to Denmark by himself. I had meant him to telephone The Casting Couch at lunchtime and, finding I was still at home, rush to Battersea, plead with me to go with him, tell me how much he loved me, how much he longed to spend the rest of his life with me. Only at around the time his plane was touching down at Copenhagen airport, when I was surprised lying gloomily in the dark by Chrissie, who had come to feed Mabel, did I realize I was waiting in vain. But then shouldn't I have remembered Mel meant it when he said he didn't play games? And besides, it was Leif's technical run-through tomorrow, Mel hated to let people down – wasn't that one of the things I loved about him?

As I stubbed out my cigarette, reaching automatically for another, Gilda burst in, attired in riding boots, ear muffs, and yards of artistically-draped designer knitting. 'I'm seeking refuge, darling heart. God preserve me, at this time of the morning, from all those pumping veins and arteries, those acres of rippling masculine flesh.' She paused to survey me. 'What are you doing here, anyway? I thought you were in the land of Hans Christian Andersen, taking snaps of Mr Single in front of the Little Mermaid.'

I sighed.

'Have we, perchance, had a lovers' tiff?'

'Oh shut up, Gilda!'

She paused, cocked her head to one side. Perching

herself on the corner of my desk, she assumed a commiserating air. 'So it's serious, then?'

I buried my face in my hands. 'It's all my fault. I've behaved like a complete and utter cow. And now I can't even say I'm sorry.'

'Well, why don't you jump in a cab to Heathrow and get yourself transferred onto the next available flight?'

'Mel's got my ticket.'

'Surely your trusty credit card won't implode in an emergency.'

'It's not just the ticket. I don't know his friend Leif's address or telephone number, or the number where they're rehearsing. I can't even remember the name of the theatre – in fact I'm not sure I was ever told it.'

'Someone must know where he is.'

'I called Mel's assistant first thing this morning. Sid says he's never had Leif's number. Mel always calls in.'

'Well, darling heart, maybe he will.'

'He hasn't yet.'

Gilda was silent, drawing a yashmak of Italian knitting over her face, emerging eventually for a thoughtful drag upon her cigarette. 'It seems odd,' she said. 'What was this row of yours about?'

I had the grace to blush. 'That doesn't matter. What matters is that I started it, that it's all my fault. I don't know what got into me.'

'Hmmmm,' said Gilda, musing. 'It takes two to make a row, you know.'

'Not this one. It was a hundred per cent my own work. I was inexcusably, unforgivably vile.'

'Come, come, darling heart. You can't have been that frightful. Are you sure this isn't the classic male ploy of transferring blame – the oppressor exploiting feelings of inadequacy and guilt in the oppressed? My ex, the awful Arnold, specialized in it. He'd provoke me and then make me feel I was a close relative of Lucrezia Borgia. Are you sure Mr Single isn't up to the same tricks?'

224

'Yes. And, for God's sake, Gilda, his name is Mel.'

'Even so, it all seems very curious . . .'

I sighed. 'What seems curious?'

'Oh . . . oh, nothing.'

'What seems curious, Gilda?'

'Well . . . that he's gone off suddenly, darling heart, and you don't know where he is. That he never thought to tell you so much as his friend's phone number.'

'I never asked. As long as I was going with him, there was no need.'

'But isn't it strange that his assistant doesn't know it?'

'Perhaps Sid was just being tactful when I called him – not wanting to get involved.'

'All the same, darling heart . . .'

I glanced up at Gilda. Her eyes were carefully averted, fixed studiously upon the toes of her riding boots.

'Gilda, what are you suggesting?'

'I'm not suggesting anything, anything at all. It's just that . . . well, he does visit Copenhagen pretty regularly, doesn't he? How many times did you say he's been this year? He must be quite devoted to this friend of his, this Leif.'

I stared at her. She had retired once more behind her knitted yashmak.

'Are you saying Mel's not staying with Leif at all?'

'I've told you, darling heart, I'm not saying anything.'

'Are you saying that Leif's just a cover for –? But that's impossible, I was going with him.'

Gilda could not suppress a smile. 'Until you had the row.'

'No. That's ridiculous. Mel's not like that.'

'You did say you found it hard to believe he'd been celibate for two years.'

'Gilda, he invited me to Copenhagen. I didn't suggest it, he asked me to go.'

'Perhaps he felt obliged to, under the circumstances. And then, when things started to look complicated, when he foresaw he'd be caught out in a tissue of lies –'

'I realize you don't like Mel, Gilda, but that's because you don't know him. He doesn't tell lies.'

'No. No, of course not, darling heart.' Gilda drew herself up, casting swags of knitting over one shoulder, favouring me again with her commiserating look. 'Pay no attention to your poor Auntie Gilda and her over-active imagination. Mr Single is the very model of human virtue, that rare and exquisite creature, the man you can trust.'

'He wanted me to go to Copenhagen.'

'Of course he did, dear.'

'At least I thought he did – till yesterday . . .'

The body builders had departed, the heating had been restored. Nevertheless, I sat huddled in my office filling my second ashtray, immobilized by the silent phone. Images kept flickering before my eyes like four frame clips edited subliminally, shots of a faceless girl with interminable legs and a swaying curtain of ash-blond hair. I rewound the footage, slowed the Steinbeck till it paused on each frame, saw Mel smiling his over-wide smile, saw him touching her lips, her neck, her heavy breasts, saw, slow motion, their limbs move together, her golden skin merge stealthily with his. It was nonsense, of course. Mel would disdain the kind of byzantine plot outlined by Gilda, and I was still almost certain I had begun the row. But supposing there were some element of truth in Gilda's speculations? Supposing there had been a girl – a girl he had not bothered to tell me about since he had intended to give her up and since she was in any case far away in another country? And supposing, by my unreasonable behaviour, I had forced him back into her bed . . .?

I closed my eyes, buried my face in my coat sleeves. But the images still flashed before me like a trailer for a movie I had no desire to see. When, just after four, the phone at last broke its silence, I reached for the receiver without hope, and was not surprised to hear Gilda's voice on the other end of the line.

'Great news!' she carolled.

'You mean – you've spoken to him?'

'Not your Mel, darling heart. Good heavens, aren't we just the teeniest bit obsessed? Why on earth would Mr Single phone me?'

'No, of course not.' I endeavoured to pull myself together. 'Sorry, Gilda.'

'My! What have you been doing since I left you? Reading *Sixty New Ways to Enjoy a Nervous Breakdown*? Never mind. Here's your kind Auntie Gilda to the rescue. What are you doing the evening after next?'

'Well, I –'

'Go on, darling heart, I know you had the whole week booked out for your excursion to the land of The Marinated Herring. So you must be free.'

'Yes, but –'

'Then guess what extra special treat your caring Auntie Gilda's lined up for you.'

'Gilda, I –'

'Carson Cheevers. Car-son *Cheevers!*'

'What?'

'Not what, dear. Who.'

'Gilda, I'm sorry but I –'

'Our Number One selection on your birthday casting tape. Six foot three, superlative head of hair, teeth to inspire spontaneous applause at a dentists' convention – really, darling heart, don't say you can't remember –'

My eye strayed guiltily to the unplayed tape gathering dust amongst its fellows on the shelf by the door. 'Yes. Yes, of course, Gilda. Carson Cheevers.'

'Zig used him in the Rapier aftershave commercial – you must have seen it. You've got to admit, he's quite a find.'

227

'Yes Gilda, but –'

'Handsome, charming, urbane, civilized. Positive perfection if you go for that sort of thing – which, alas, despite all my attempts to show you the error of your ways, you do.'

'Yes, but –'

'Well, how's this for a *coup* by your brilliant Auntie Gilda? Carson Cheevers wants to take you out to dinner the day after tomorrow.'

'Oh, Gilda.'

'There now. Hasn't that perked you up?'

'But I –'

'Never say your friends don't pull out all the stops for you.'

'Gilda, I can't go.'

'But, darling heart, you've seen the casting tape. And remember, he takes a –'

'Size twelve shoe. I know, Gilda. But I can't go.'

There was a small pause. 'Why ever not?'

'I love Mel.'

'But, darling heart, this is the twentieth century and you are – forgive me – a woman of mature years. Besides, no one's asking you to participate in a Bacchanalian orgy. All you're required to do is have dinner with the man. You can sit with your legs crossed the whole evening, you needn't take off so much as a glove.'

'I'm sorry, Gilda. It wouldn't be right.'

A huffy silence fell upon the other end of the line. 'Very well,' she said eventually. 'Forget I ever mentioned it.'

'I'm sorry, Gilda, truly I am.'

'Don't give it a second thought. It's nothing six more hours on the telephone won't fix. I'll simply cancel the whole thing.'

'Oh Gilda, I know you've gone to a lot of trouble on my behalf.'

'Trouble? I frequently drop all my work, call off my

228

lunch, disorganize my whole life to help out a friend – I do it every day. Though I must say the next time I find you weeping tears of Dostoyevskian gloom into your coffee cup I may be tempted to pass by on the other side.'

'Gilda, I wouldn't upset you for the world.'

'You haven't upset me, darling heart. You know my feelings about your unseemly obsession with The Paltry Priapus. You haven't upset *me*. Poor Carson will be very disappointed, of course. But I'm sure he'll live.'

'You mean – you mean this Carson person actually wanted to take me out to dinner?'

'He was highly excited about it. I described you in glowing detail, of course, even took the liberty of biking his agent some polaroids – remember that flattering one of you at your birthday party trying on the zebra hat? He said you seemed just the sort of woman he was dying to meet – attractive, witty, sophisticated. But – there you go.'

'At least he's been spared the appalling anticlimax of meeting me in the flesh.'

'You do yourself an injustice, darling heart. You can be a sparkling dinner companion, when you're on form.'

I paused. 'Oh, Gilda – is it going to be horrendously difficult to cancel him?'

'A trifle embarrassing, dear. But your brave Auntie Gilda can cope.'

'I – I suppose . . .'

'Yes, dear?'

'Well, it's true I'm not actually doing anything that night . . .'

'And it *is* only dinner.'

'That's right. Only dinner. Where's the harm in that?'

'I'm sure your Mr Single wouldn't expect you to retire

229

into total seclusion while he's disporting himself in Denmark. This friend he's staying with doesn't sound like a Franciscan Friar.'

The film clip flashed before me, unbidden, again. 'All right,' I said. 'I can't see how one innocent little dinner can hurt.'

CHAPTER

ELEVEN

Carson Cheevers, 40, 6'3", boyish fair hair, deep tan. Even on fast forward, I should have picked him out as Gilda's recommendation, unaided by her annotated casting schedule. Although it was interesting to observe the selection of shapes and sizes in which the forty-plus male form came, the variety of additional design features (including one or two bald heads and beer guts, which had somehow infiltrated Gilda's net), it was curious, too, how they were all wiped instantly from memory the moment the tape was ejected. Only Carson Cheevers retained impact, inclining his head to camera as he gave his ident and agent's name, assured, yet with just the right air of modesty about his wry smile. Yes, he was single – well, divorced, actually – and, he confessed, an osteopath by profession: the acting and modelling had come about by sheer fluke and now (well, he guessed he'd been lucky) things were really taking off. He mentioned a couple of TV series, casually listed a string of commercials. 'You'll probably remember the Kastel lager film. I got' – and here he seemed genuinely astonished – 'a whole load of fan mail from that. And I've just finished shooting Rapier Aftershave with Zig – I mean, thanks,

Gilda, to you casting me, of course. Gosh, that was off the wall! I mean, he's a truly inspired director, Zig. And what a character!' A gust of boyish laughter showed off his perfect teeth to advantage. There was a faint twang – Australian, South African? – to his otherwise classless intercontinental drawl. 'Yeah, a truly terrific character, Zig. I mean, truly left of field.'

I recalled the Rapier commercial now – since the countdown to Christmas had started it had been hard to avoid, repeated endlessly for maximum exposure in peak viewing time. A solitary voyager wakes in his Jacques Cousteau mini-submarine at the bottom of the ocean, looks out of his porthole at the fish swimming past, begins to shave. He splashes Rapier on his manly jaw and – bingo, the fish have turned into mermaids. The final shot shows a female hand lingering enigmatically over a Rapier pack on the ocean bed, while a title reads: 'A Rapier Man Ventures . . .' Despite Zig's moody lighting and avant-garde camera angles, Carson Cheevers acquits himself well enough, fondling his clean-shaven chin and flexing his glossy pectorals, fixing the lens with a vivid blue look in which there is the correct admixture of intimacy and arousal. It was this look he was projecting now into the Casting Couch video camera, extreme close up, turning from profile to full face, widening his lips a fraction, lowering his jaw. Carson Cheevers, Mr Superlative Single.

Despite his evident qualifications for the role I was not sure, studying him freeze frame, that I could have described his features in any particular, except for that startling blue gaze. He reminded me suddenly of the illustrations in the Boys' Own Adventure Stories my cousin Patrick had devoured at thirteen, where hard-muscled heroes in safari suits had beaten off crocodiles and columns of man-eating ants, their brows noble, their physiognomy Aryan, their faces resolutely blank. And who, outside a Hollywood soap opera, had a name like

Carson Cheevers? Nevertheless as I flicked the tape onto rewind, I did not doubt he would be receiving further cartloads of fan letters along with his Christmas mail.

I had made a pact with Mel in his absence, that were he to phone me, just once, I should abandon this dinner date, even if it meant terminally offending Gilda. But a day and a night had passed in silence. This morning two dozen red roses had arrived at The Casting Couch, with a card announcing that Carson would call for me at my flat at 7.30 p.m. And now here I was, with the clock registering seven and my ears still pricked vainly for the telephone, dancing around in my usual state of agitation about what to wear.

Selecting at last a black bat-wing top, a skin-tight old-gold-and-black brocade skirt and black high-heeled ankle boots (more Wicked Queen than Little Match Girl, I reflected sourly), I settled at the dressing table to apply my make-up. My mirror-image glared back at me, every crow's foot, every pouch and sagging muscle etched with dismay. I did not want dinner with Carson Cheevers. I did not want to spend four hours making polite conversation to a total stranger, an antipodean osteopath who should be out in the jungle making war on man-eating ants. I wanted Mel. I wanted to curl up beside him and listen to his heart beating and drift asleep, comforted by his warm, familiar smell. My eyes filled with tears and I reached hurriedly for Kleenex to save my mascara. 7.25. If he would just phone, if he would just, damn him, phone!

I blew my nose and the tears disappeared. I focused savagely upon my reflection until, muscle by muscle, it tightened into a mask of disdain. Slowly, deliberately, like a gladiator dressing for combat, I clipped on earrings, slotted my wrists through bracelets. I picked up my lip pencil and began to carve out the contours of my mouth as if it were a wound.

At 7.35 the answerphone buzzer sounded and a voice

233

breathed: 'It's Carson.' I stood in the hall, raising my chin, stiffening my face into a bright little smile. Damn Mel! Damn him and his Scandinavian sex object. What did it matter if I went out and had a good time with Mr Rapier Aftershave? What did it matter if I gave him a blow job underneath the restaurant table or ravished him on top of the wardrobe, who the hell cared . . .?

My bell rang. I opened the door.

'Dee?' said Carson Cheevers. 'I want to say what a pleasure this is, how very glad I am to meet you.' And he extended his hand.

He was as tall as Gilda had promised, and still deeply tanned, but fleshier somehow than he had appeared on the tape. He wore a long, navy Pierre Cardin overcoat and black pig-skin driving gloves, the macho sort with key-hole backs. His teeth gleamed, his hair was neatly brushed; and, though beneath the arpeggios of cologne that heralded his approach into my hallway (not Rapier, mercifully, but Dior's Fahrenheit) I thought I detected faint low notes of Scotch, his manner was faultless. With a smile that was friendly yet respectful, he thrust a small gift-wrapped box into my hands. Bendicks chocolates, with my name laid out in gold on the lid. I found myself blushing.

'Thank you, Carson. How thoughtful. And thank you, too, for the beautiful roses. Would you – can I offer you a drink?'

'Thanks, but if you're ready, Dee – I mean, I don't want to rush you – I thought before dinner we might stop off for cocktails at Harry's Bar.'

'Oh, right. Well, how did you get here? Shall I call a cab?'

He smiled his impeccable smile. 'No need. The Ferrari's just outside.'

Crouching in a cubicle of Luard's Powder Room, giddy from three champagne cocktails and the further bottle we had consumed with our hors d'oeuvres, I found myself giggling. At first, when Carson, returning himself from a somewhat prolonged spell in the lavatory, had thrust his hand under the table, I had assumed that he was trying to grope my knee. But then my fingers had found the small paper packet in his palm. Fumbling for my credit card, rolling up a ten pound note, I unfolded the paper carefully, tipped a portion of its contents onto the closed lavatory seat, cut two neat lines and sniffed. It seemed forever since I had last done coke.

Sniffing, giggling, I reflected how conventionally domestic my life had become. What price a few hours of wickedness and excitement? True, I should not myself have chosen Luard's: though still described in the tabloids as 'exclusive haunt of the rich and famous', it was now full of suburban celebrity-spotters scanning one another anxiously for signs of stardom. (I thought Carson was piqued, on making his entrance, not to be recognized, although he recovered himself pretty well.) But what did it matter? Did it matter that Carson's Ferrari was the model you buy when you can't afford a Ferrari, with four seats and the trim peeling round the passenger door, or that his aquamarine gaze, on closer scrutiny, turned out to result from two-tone Cadillac-windscreen-tinted contact lenses? Did it matter that, beyond the initial numbing of throat and gums, I did not much care for coke? There was an exhilaration in this conspiratorial fumbling in lavatories, a naughtiness, like sneaking an Embassy tipped in the changing rooms at school.

Besides, Carson seemed amiable enough. Conversation had been lubricated by the champagne. We talked a little about me and then a little about Carson. In fact, since we rapidly discovered we had few common interests, we talked quite a lot about Carson. He had been born in Rhodesia (hence the twang) and had pursued various careers, as an army officer, a deep sea diver, a sheep farmer in Australia, a tennis coach in Canada, a life guard in Los Angeles, before ending up in London as a qualified osteopath (his patients seemed mainly to be adoring middle-aged women who invited him for country weekends and sent him cases of wine). He had fallen into modelling quite by accident – a friend had suggested him for a magazine spread on male jewellery. And then, well (once again he dismissed his success with a self-deprecating shrug), people just seemed to like the way he looked. Of course (though he wouldn't say this to a casting director) it was all a game to him really, it wasn't his main source of income, sort of a hobby. Through lack of an Equity card his roles had been, well – actually as a non-speaking extra. But now they'd changed the rules about models acting in commercials, he was constantly in demand, forced to turn jobs down. The next thing (though it wasn't important to him really) was to increase his visibility, maybe try a little personal PR, see if he couldn't break into features – I mean, quite often nowadays big-time stars came up through commercials - what did I think?

His vanity seemed harmless. Besides, it was restful to listen, to widen my eyes, incline my head flirtatiously, and let his monologue wash over me like the bubbles of a foam bath. What did it matter that nature, as with Mabel, had endowed him with more beauty than brain? There was a guilessness in his wry smile, a boyish innocence in the way the Cadillac-windscreen lenses seemed genuinely to seek my approval. Every quarter of an hour, as if reminded by some ultra-sonic bleep on his Rolex, he would pause in his paean to Carson to compliment me on my clothes or my eyes or my readiness to understand him. He did this now as I returned from the lavatory and slipped him the paper packet discreetly under the table.

'You know, you're not like most of the women I meet, Dee. It's a real privilege to have dinner with someone as beautiful and intelligent and sophisticated as you.'

Damn Mel! If he was permitted his extra-curricular

Scandinavian, then wasn't I also allowed the odd disposable wickedness when it was on offer?

I could not have pin-pointed the exact moment Carson's
gentlemanly veneer began to peel. I was aware after the
fleurie of his clicking his fingers at the waiter, remembered noticing how the first double brandy brought
beads of moisture to his upper lip. But I, too, was
succumbing to the wine and the liqueurs and the contents
of Carson's little packet, viewing him mistily through fil-
ters, unconscious of the growing loudness of our voices
or of the restaurant emptying.

I could remember him talking a great deal about Gilda,
what a wonderful person she was. It appeared Gilda had
a casting brief from Zig to find an actor to represent
a multi-national men's toiletries company – the rugged
individualist who would precisely personify Slik Shaving
Foam. The job would give whoever was cast maximum exposure, with commercials broadcast throughout
Europe, maybe even world wide. Had Gilda mentioned
anything about it, had she let drop when the first casting
sessions would be?

I could remember, too, his suddenly leaning closer
and saying, almost confidentially: 'Gilda tells me you
know Alex Power, the director. She says you know him
really well.'

I had managed to deflect this without effort the first
time, scarcely considering its implications. But when he
had come by a circuitous route upon the question again
ten minutes later, a needle of irritation had pierced my
alcoholic haze. I was aware suddenly of the deserted
tables, the hovering waiters. I felt a stiffening in my neck,
the beginnings of a headache, or the onset of boredom.
And now he had broached the subject a third time, his
tone, magnified by the emptiness of the restaurant, no
longer deferential or confiding but downright pushy.

I lowered my brandy glass, experiencing a sour taste

upon my tongue. 'Carson, it's been a wonderful evening, but I think it's time I went home.'

'C'mon, Dee, baby. The night is young. What d'you say we go on to Tramp, dance a little, sweat off the booze.'

'Thank you, Carson. But I really am very tired.'

His eyes took on an injured puppy-dog look. His boyish hair, I noticed, now clung damply to his forehead, flesh sagged beneath his jaw. Glancing at his Rolex, he pulled himself up as if realizing he had just dropped a cue.

'Y'know, you're terrific to talk to, Dee. Truly terrific. I feel I can talk to you as an equal, on a one-to-one basis. Not like my ex-wife, for instance – she just couldn't grow with me, she resented my success –'

'That's sweet of you, Carson. But, all the same, I'd better get a cab.'

'Why take a cab? I'll run you home in the Ferrari.'

I hesitated. 'Do you think – ? I mean, we've both had quite a bit to drink.'

'Are you crazy? This is Carson you're with, Dee. Yeah, I've had a couple of drinks. But I can handle it.'

Admittedly I had been forced to close my eyes and breath deeply once or twice, but we had reached Prince of Wales Drive without mishap, were no more than a block away from my flat. The cyclist came bursting out of the side road without warning. Perhaps, even sober, Carson could not have avoided him. Very slowly and inevitably, it seemed, the bicycle hit the rear passenger side of the Ferrari and bounced away to the left. Looking over my shoulder I saw a dark heap in the road and heard myself screaming 'Stop!' An age appeared to pass before Carson reacted, slamming on the brakes and hurling me towards the dashboard. Unbuckling my seat belt, I struggled out onto the road and began running towards the heap. As I ran, miraculously it stirred. By the time I drew level, it

238

had resolved itself into a stringy-haired boy in parka and jeans. 'Are you all right?' I shouted breathlessly. 'My flat's just down the road. I'll phone for an ambulance if you're hurt.'

The boy was already disentangling himself from the bicycle. He glanced round at me, his ashen face at once shocked and furtive. 'No damage done, miss. Don't need no ambulance. Straight up, miss. Honest.'

A white car had drawn to a halt on the opposite side of the road, a taxi was slowing, in the mansion block above lights had flashed on, a pensioner in a nightdress was craning over her balcony. The boy kicked the bicycle savagely, freeing its jammed rear wheel. 'No bones broken, mate!' he shouted to the world in general. Then he swung himself into the saddle and, wobbling a little, made off with all the speed he could muster.

The white car revved its engine, the taxi, swerving to avoid me, continued towards the lights, the old woman reluctantly drew away from her balcony railings. I stared after the retreating bicycle, still hearing the faint, angry rasp of its chain. I felt all at once icily sober. I turned back to look for Carson.

He was standing in the road, surveying the rear passenger side of the Ferrari. 'Christ!' he said, as I approached. 'What a disaster!'

'It could have been worse. He wasn't hurt – just a cut on his forehead and a tear in his parka. It could have been a bloody sight worse.'

Carson appeared not to hear me. My eyes followed his to the scar in the Ferrari's crimson paintwork. I turned on him in fury. 'The boy could have been killed, Carson. Or badly injured. You're lucky it's late and there's not much traffic about. You're lucky the kid was up to no good, looking for drunks to mug or car radios to pinch. It's only by amazing good fortune you're not banged up in Lavender Hill nick, donating blood and urine and rehearsing for a starring role at Knightsbridge Crown

239

Court. "I've had a couple of drinks but I can handle it."
God, you make me sick!'

He gave me his dumb animal look again, as if not
comprehending. 'But what am I going to say to Colin?
He'll give me hell –'

'You mean the car's not yours?'

'I borrowed it for the evening. I wanted to make a
good impression, women go for that sort of thing.'

'Jesus Christ!' I drew in breath, suddenly reminded
that I had let him drive with scarcely a protest.
He stood shoulders slumped, mouth disconsolate, a
six-foot-three child whose Dinky toy has been caught
in the lawnmower. After all, it was not his fault that
his body weight, like a dinosaur's, was disproportionate
to his brain. I reached into the car for my cigarettes. As
he fumbled with my lighter I saw that his hands were
shaking.

'Look,' I said, 'you've had a shock. Park the car and
come up to my flat for some coffee. Then I'll call you a
cab and you can collect the Ferrari tomorrow morning.'

Rather to my surprise he accepted the suggestion,
trailing after me meekly. Once installed in my kitchen, he
said he would prefer brandy to coffee and, since he was
no longer driving, I poured him a measure. Downing it
in one medicinal gulp, he seemed to shed his hang-dog
air, to draw up his shoulders with something of his previous swagger. I refilled his glass and went into the studio
to 'call the mini-cab company.

On the threshold I paused. The red light was flashing
on my answering machine. I felt a lightness in my stomach, knowing at once, with absolute certainty, that my
caller had been Mel. Blast Carson! I needed privacy to
replay the tape. I picked up the phone and began to dial
the mini-cab number.

And then, suddenly, I was assailed by the stench of
brandy. A hand came down, wrenching the receiver from
my grasp and slamming it into its cradle, another hand

seized me unceremoniously by the waist. I struggled free, swung round. The hands grabbed me by the shoulders, and slobbery lips were clamped on mine.

I twisted my head aside. 'No, Carson. I'm calling you a cab.'

'Oh come on, Dee baby. Let's have some fun first.'

'It's cab time, Carson.'

'Haven't you heard the slogan, baby? "A Rapier man ventures . . ." '

I took a pace backwards, wiping my mouth on my hand. 'Not with me, he doesn't,' I said, giving a little laugh and reaching once more for the phone.

This time the struggle for possession of the receiver lasted some moments. Letting go suddenly, I ducked under his arm and ran into the hall.

'Stop it, Carson. Pull yourself together.'

'But you invited me up for coffee.'

'I offered you coffee to prevent you decimating Battersea's burglar population with that ridiculous borrowed penis-substitute of yours.'

'You offered me coffee because you were hot for me.'

'No, Carson.'

'Don't give me that! You've been begging for it all evening.'

'I'm afraid, contrary to popular myth, no means precisely that. Non, nein, nej, nyet! Now will you please let me past so I can call you a cab.'

He lunged at me. I darted sideways and into the sitting room. He came on after me. I dodged behind the sofa. This was ridiculous, this could not be happening to me.

'Stop it, Carson. Leave me alone or I shall scream.'

'You knew what you were doing when you invited me up here, baby. You knew what you were doing when you had dinner with me. What d'y'think I am, for fuck's sake? Some limp-wristed fucking arse bandit? D'you think I'm going to fork out for cocktails at Harry's

241

Bar and a three-course dinner at Luard's, and not expect to get my rocks off in return?'

My mouth was suddenly dry. This could not, could not be happening. I was cornered behind the sofa, he stood between me and the door. My only hope lay in his drunkenness. If I could outwit him somehow, move faster, I might dodge past him into the hall.

He lumbered across the carpet towards me. I let him advance, waiting until he reached the sofa. Stretching across it he seized me by one arm. I tore myself free, hearing my sleeve rip, racing for the door. Halfway across the sitting room he was upon me, jerking my legs from under me in a flying rugger tackle. We fell together prone upon the hearth rug, I face down, he with the weight of his body on top of me, pressing his pelvis hard against mine. I kicked, I screamed. He thrust my face into the rug and, pinioning me with his chest, ripped the crotch of my tights. I wrested my head aside, gagging on fluff and carpet dust, felt his weight shift as he unzipped his fly, managed to free my right arm, thought if I could stretch as far as the coffee table I might grab some hard object (an inventory of the coffee table recalled only two magazines, a china ashtray, a half-eaten biscuit and a small potted palm, but perhaps I could knock him unconscious with the plant pot, or at least bewilder him with earth and leaves). But no, he had both hands available now, was crushing my wrists against the carpet, trying to force my legs apart with his knee. I wrenched my mouth clear again, filled my lungs and screamed. My screams seemed to take on an independent dream-like quality, as if I had abstracted myself and some other person was kicking and bucking on the rug. As if from an infinite distance, too, I heard the front door slam open and running feet in the hall. Someone flung himself upon Carson, jerking him upwards violently by the scruff of his neck. His weight was hauled off me, there was heavy breathing,

242

scuffling, then a crash, followed by the splintering of glass.

Gingerly I raised myself on all fours and turned my head. My limited edition Hockney print was sliding very slowly down the wall, and with it, in a shower of glass fragments, slithered Carson, buckling at the knees. At a distance of about three feet from the skirting board the two parted company, the picture continuing noisily downwards while Carson seemed to hang suspended by his shoulders, dazedly contemplating the palm Mel was thrusting, pot uppermost, towards his jaw.

Mel took a decisive step backwards, smashing the plant pot against the mantelpiece. Carson goggled at the jagged terracotta. 'Not my face!' he whimpered, putting his arms up protectively. 'Please. Whatever you do, not my face.' Then he slithered down to join the picture with a thud and a tinkle of glass.

I stared at Carson cowering with his knees beneath his chin, and at Mel poised to strike, wielding the palm by its stem, obliviously dripping earth and water. I opened my mouth and unleashed a nervous giggle.

The sound seemed to startle them. They fixed their eyes upon me, Mel as if he were only now seeing me, Carson with a sudden glimmer of daring.

'I wouldn't screw you,' Carson said, 'if you were the last woman in the fucking universe. Open your legs, bats would fly out.'

'Right!' bellowed Mel, lunging at him in a hail of earth.

'No!' yelped Carson, half-crawling, half-scuttling towards the door. 'No! Please. This nose job cost four grand!'

'Out!' snarled Mel, grabbing him by the collar and propelling him into the hall. There were more thuds, a howl, the crash of a chair overturning, then sounds of a struggle receding towards the front door and out into the common hallway.

I tried to rise to my feet, only to fall back, hobbled

243

at the knee by my tights. Slowly, painfully, I removed my boots and stripped off the tattered lycra. Far away at ground level the heavy wooden entrance door slammed, then tired footsteps came up the stairs and in at my front door.

Mel was no longer clutching the palm. There was earth on his jacket and a substance that looked like vomit on the toecap of his left shoe. He surveyed me for a moment. His face was grey and his eyes were curiously blank.

'Are you all right?' he said.

'Oh, Mel!' I moved towards him, pausing in surprise as he stepped away. 'Oh Mel, when did you get back? I've missed you so much.'

'I couldn't stand this pointless row of ours. After Leif's dress rehearsal I caught the first plane I could. I called you from Heathrow and several times from home. Then I thought I'd come over and let myself in to wait till you got back. I thought I'd surprise you.' His lips twisted into something that was not a smile. 'And so, it seems, I did.'

I saw myself suddenly as he saw me, bare-legged, smear-faced, still clutching the remains of my tights.

'Oh, Mel,' I said, beginning to cry, 'it wasn't the way it looks. Please believe me. He only came up for coffee . . .'

'Ah yes. Coffee.'

'Coffee, Mel. Brown stuff, comes in cups. God, you're as bad as Rapier Man. And anyway, what's this double standard? It seems you can grind whole sacksful of Arabica beans in Denmark, but I'm not even permitted a sniff at the percolator –'

His face stiffened. 'What did you say?'

'I said, I don't see why I'm not allowed near the percolator, when you –'

'Je-sus!' The flat of his hand smashed against the wall, this time dislodging a small Edward Gorey cartoon, which narrowly missed a lamp in its descent. The crash and the pain in his hand seemed to pull him up. He flexed his wrist carefully. Then, not looking at me, inspecting the glass for damage, he replaced the cartoon upon its hook.

Still avoiding my eyes, speaking softly, but with deliberation, he moved towards the hall. 'Sorry about the Hockney. And the rest of the mess. Matey was last seen treating the privet to a spot of unscheduled manure. His next move is probably a kip by the dustbins. But, just in case, before you go to bed put the chain on the door.'

My father died on the top deck of a 185 bus *en route* from the Oval to Victoria. He had just seen Boycott hit Lillee for a century in the Sixth Test against Australia, he must have been borne out of the ground on a tide of euphoria, anticipating a triumph to cap Headingly and Edgbaston, knowing England had won The Ashes whatever the outcome. He had jostled his way onto the bus, climbed the stairs; and by the time the conductor had appeared to collect his fare he was dead.

The police had given us the contents of his pockets, a life reduced into a transparent polythene bag and carefully sealed, the bag not even half full – his watch, a pen knife, the driving licence he never used, keys, wallet, a few loose coins, a box of Swan Vestas and a crushed packet containing six unsmoked Senior Service – oh, and his Test Match programme, of course (there would have been the inevitable newspaper, too, an *Evening Standard* probably, but no one would have thought to pick it up and it must have travelled on without him to the depot, its pages unread, sports reports, local news, world events all compelled now to muddle out their course in limbo, summarily bereft of his help).

Seeing him after the post-mortem in the hospital chapel of rest, my attention divided between viewing the remains of my father and confronting this singular novelty, death, I wondered what I should feel. I thought he looked happy. His half-open eyes held a glint and his mouth, to which the dentures had been tactfully restored, was parted in what looked like a smile, although it may have been merely the effect of rigor mortis. I could not feel sorry for him. He had died, without prolonged suffering, doing what he enjoyed most, pursuing his one exclusive passion. And anyway he was an old man, he'd had a good innings, as Gus Morton might have said – his heart had just worn out, according to the doctors. I fingered his cheek gingerly and felt, beneath the softer epidermis, a chill, deep, impenetrable heaviness, like the solidity of frozen chicken in a supermarket cabinet.

Two days before the funeral, escaping my mother's distress at my failure to cry, I went home to Alex. He had grilled me fillet steak with mushrooms and tomatoes, which I could not eat. In the end, he gathered me up and carried me to the bathroom, where he undressed me and, lifting me into the tub, began silently, methodically to bathe me.

I held out my arm, watching without sensation the sponge glide over my skin, darkening the hairs on my forearm, trailing tiny bubbles in its glistening wake. I sighed. 'I don't know what to do, Alex. I don't know how to be.'

He rinsed my arm carefully, then sat down for a moment on the side of the bath. 'Trust in your producer's skills to get you through the funeral. You've fixed the location, booked the crew – the only thing you can't predict is how many extras there'll be on the set.'

'But I don't know what to feel. I don't feel anything.'

He rose and, gently inclining me forward, began soaping my back.

'You will, my darling. You will.'

'But how can I feel sad for him? He had Geoffrey Boycott's one hundred and thirty-seven runs and that's all he ever cared about. And if I can't feel sad for

him, how can I feel anything? How can I feel anything at all?'

Two days. Mel had not phoned, Sid, Ambrose – no one
had seen him. I spent Friday in bed, rising only to make
futile calls to his answering machine and to feed Mabel.
Most of Saturday, too, was spent staring at the cracks in
my bedroom ceiling, although later I trudged out for cat
food, before slumping in my dressing-gown in front of
the television. A succession of savagely hot baths had not
served to purge my contamination, and purple bruises
were flowering profusely on my thighs and upper arms.
Occasional fits of anger outvoiced the dull monotone of
shame: why had I not been allowed to explain myself,
who was Mel to judge me? Yet I was pathetically grateful
when at last, on Sunday afternoon as I was lethargically
brushing up the remains of the palm, he called to ask if he
could come round. He'd been at Jake's and Lizzie's place
in Suffolk, he said. He'd needed to think. His voice was
flat, carefully devoid of expression, conceding nothing.
But at least he was anxious to see me, at least he would
be here, with me, in half an hour.
   I dressed carefully in French knickers and suspenders
and a cream wool dress he had often said he liked,
masking any visible bruises with foundation and powder.
Examining my reflection, I was pleased with the effect –
demure yet sophisticated, neither Wicked Queen nor Little Match Girl, but Grace Kelly, perhaps, in *Rear Window*.
He would be angry with me for a while, but we should
talk it through, talk until we had talked ourselves into
bed; and when we woke the next morning we should find
Carson Cheevers edited out of our lives, a momentary
aberration on the part of an over-inventive scriptwriter.
Brushing a few stray clods of earth out of sight into the
fireplace, I arranged myself on the sofa with a cigarette
and a book.
   His face, when he arrived, still wore its strained,

bleak look and he did not kiss me. Fussing brightly in the kitchen, making mugs of tea, I found that my hands were shaking. I noticed that he, too, moved cautiously, carrying his mug to the table nursed in both palms.

He raised the tea to his lips, then put it down again, untasted. He stared at it for some moments as if he detected a foreign body floating in it. At last, he lifted his eyes to my face. 'Dee,' he said, 'I'm afraid I think we shouldn't go on with this.'

A quavering in my stomach made me reach abruptly for a chair. 'What?' I said. 'Go on with what?'

'Us. I think we should stop now. Before we begin to destroy each other.'

'You mean, because of Mr Rapier Aftershave? Because of something you haven't even let me explain? You can't be serious about this? You can't seriously believe I'd volunteer to be violated by an alcoholic osteopath with a borrowed Ferrari and marginally fewer brain cells than an amoeba –'

I elaborated at length on how Carson had come to rugger tackle me on my hearth rug, mentioning Gilda's role in the affair (though prudently omitting any reference to the casting tape). He listened in silence, still studying the untasted liquid in his mug.

'So you see,' I said, 'I was only doing a friend a favour.'

'Gilda's a bitch,' he said, without emphasis. 'But anyway, it's not that. I could cheerfully have hanged, drawn and quartered both you and Matey at the time. But it's not that.'

'And besides, who are you to talk? You're not exactly a suitable candidate for canonization yourself, are you, Melvin Gene? What about your blonde in Copenhagen?'

He glanced up and I watched his disbelief gradually transmute itself into a dismal look, as if I had offered him confirmation of an unfavourable diagnosis. 'Oh, Dotty Deirdre,' he sighed, shaking his head.

I was suddenly breathless with panic. 'Mel, this is

248

lunatic. You and I love each other. OK, I was wrong about your reasons for going to Denmark – just as you were wrong about Mr Aftershave. But in any case, does infidelity matter, is it really such a big deal? Every person you go to bed with is different, a different body, a different sensation. If, God help me, I'd wanted sex with Carson Cheevers, it wouldn't have been anything like making love to you. It wouldn't have been important, so it couldn't have been a betrayal. Oh Mel, if we love each other shouldn't that be bigger than everything, shouldn't we be able to forgive each other something that, when you come down to it, isn't much more than a nervous reflex?'

He continued to ponder the surface of his tea, on which a brown scum was forming. 'Maybe in theory I agree with you, although in practice the thought makes me sick. But I'm trying to explain – I'm trying to explain that Matey isn't the problem.'

'Then what? What's the problem? For God's sake, Mel, what?'

He paused, licked his lips. Then he levelled his eyes with mine. 'It's just that however much I care about you, Dee – and I do care, a lot – I can see now that things won't work out.'

'What won't work? What things?'

Again he licked his lips. He held my eyes with deliberation, as if he were watching himself hammer in a nail. 'It's not what I want, Dee. I don't want to spend the rest of my life cast as the enemy. I can't cope with the pain.'

I stared at him, feeling sick and sweaty. 'The enemy? But I don't understand. I love you, Mel, help me, I don't understand what you're saying. I know I shouldn't have agreed to have dinner with Rapier Man, but it was only because I thought you were up to no good in Denmark. And I know that was wrong, I know I should have trusted you. But it's only because of a habit of mind I've

249

got into, a psychological pattern. And you can help me break the pattern, Mel, I want you to help me. I only behave like this because I'm so used to being hurt.'

He did not look up. I expanded upon the mental conditioning acquired from prolonged exposure to married men, I told him my theory about my father, about how I'd spent all those years acting out my childhood need to win my father's love. Mel did not interrupt, but merely glanced up at me once or twice, his eyes still bleak, his face frozen. I heard my voice rising in despair. 'Oh Mel, it's just that I need time to adapt. I'm so used to being second best, so used to ending up a victim.'

There was a pause. 'I don't think you're a victim, Dee,' he said.

'But I've explained to you –'

'You're funny and sexy and terrific to be with in so many ways. But deep down, you're after scalps.'

I gaped. 'I – I don't understand.'

'Your view of life's rather like a western, Dee. Easy to follow, but pretty one-dimensional. The women wear the white hats and the men wear the black hats. And I don't think I can live with it. I don't want to be stuck forever playing a cardboard cut-out baddie.'

I continued to gape. 'But what are you saying, Mel? Are you saying you've fallen out of love with me? Or are you just telling me you've gone off the idea of us getting married? Perhaps we rushed into things, perhaps neither of us is ready for commitment. But that doesn't mean we have to throw everything away. We could go back to where we were, couldn't we? We could pretend we never had breakfast in the Patisserie Valerie that morning.'

He sighed. 'No, Dee, I don't think we can go backwards.'

He was staring at the mug again, apparently preoccupied by the dark brown ring it had imprinted upon the table. I watched his fingers trace the circumference of the stain, thin fingers, square-nailed, widening to knots at the joints, familiar yet suddenly belonging to a hostile stranger. I wanted to shout and throw things. 'You say I'm not a victim, Mel. You seem to imply I'm causing you pain. Well, from where I sit, I'm the one who's hurting, I'm the one who's being dumped on and discarded as usual.'

'Oh don't, Dee. Please.' He rose abruptly, catching the mug with his sleeve. We watched the puddle of tea spread, dripping from the edge of the table.

'I'll find a cloth,' he said.

'Just go!' I screamed. 'Go, since that's what you're so anxious to do. Get out. I don't want you here. Get out!'

I rushed past him, across the hall and into my bedroom, tearing at a pile of discarded clothes, unearthing my handbag. When I ran back into the hall he was standing between the kitchen and the front door as though he were hesitating. I raised my arm and hurled his keys at him, aiming for his head. He did not flinch as the keys struck him above the third shirt button. As they fell jangling to the carpet he did not move to pick them up. He merely stood there, white-faced, looking at me.

'I don't want my things, you can throw them away. And I'll pack yours up and send them over in a cab this evening. I don't want to see you again, Mel. I don't ever want to see you or hear from you again!'

He bent then, slowly as if his back ached, and took up the key ring. 'If you'll trust me with your door key till tomorrow, I'll bring your stuff over and collect mine while you're at work. We needn't meet. But it would be a bit more civilized.'

'I don't care what you do. I just don't want to see you or even think about you.'

We stood for a moment, studying each other in silence.

'You said you loved me, Mel.'

'I do love you, Dee. I love you a lot. But somehow I'm going to have to learn not to.'

251

The keys chattered in his palm as he transferred them to his pocket. He turned towards the door.

'I don't understand,' I whispered. 'Oh Mel, I don't understand.'

He turned back to look at me and I watched with amazement as tears welled up in his eyes.

'Goodbye, Deirdre of the Sorrows,' he said.

CHAPTER

TWELVE

'I've discovered a startling new conversation opener,' said Gilda, perching on my desk, swinging an oversized rope of pearls like a speakeasy flapper. 'Just utter one word – one teeny word, darling heart – and you'll be an instant success with the female guests at any party.'

I stared at her dumbly.

'But what, I hear you asking, is this open sesame, this password to social acclaim? Is it sex? Is it money? Is it childbearing, or creativity, or crochet? What is this one magic word that will bring women of all ages flocking to you, desperate to share their experiences, compare notes on their suffering, unburden the most intimate details of their private lives?'

She paused for effect, allowing the pearls to describe one last dramatic parabola before they declined upon the embroidered folds of her Ballet Russe shirt. Avoiding her glance, I switched my eyes firmly to the sheaf of bills on my desk.

'Piles,' she said.

I did not look up.

'Piles, darling heart. Haemorrhoids. Everyone's got them, nobody talks about them. But – forgive me – we're all itching to. Inside every sophisticated career woman is a martyr to piles trying to break out.'

She paused again, making a moustache of the pearls, peering at me with raised eyebrows. 'Did you know, darling heart, that St Fiacre was the patron saint of piles?'

'Oh, for God's sake, Gilda! I'm trying to get on with some work.'

'Nonsense, dear. I observe you have been staring at that interesting pink catering invoice for the last twenty minutes as if it contained the meaning of life, but you don't fool your perceptive Auntie Gilda. Besides, I want to know why you've been failing to return my calls, why I'm obliged to corner you in your office to find out how things went with darling Carson.'

I pushed the stack of invoices aside. 'Gilda, did you promise darling Carson you would cast him as Mr Multinational Shaving Foam if he took me out to dinner?'

'Would I do that, dearest? Would I stoop to anything so utterly unprofessional?'

'And did you tell him I could introduce him to Alex Power?'

'Darling heart, you surely don't mean to suggest –'

'I do, Gilda. I am suggesting it.'

She nibbled the pearls. 'Well . . . I may unintentionally have hinted . . . dear Carson may have over-interpreted a casual reference . . . but anyway, darling heart, as you and I know only too well, there's no such thing as a free fuck.'

I buried my head in my hands.

'So it didn't go too brilliantly? I feared as much from your ominous silence. Still, I think it's a little unfair to blame your poor Auntie Gilda. All she did was throw the ingredients together. You can't shoot the chef just because there's a caterpillar in the salad. Anyway, you must have got your Mr Single back from foreign parts by now.'

'His name is Mel, Gilda. And I haven't got him back.'

254

'You mean he went off with his bit on the side?'

'He hasn't got a bit on the side. He hasn't . . . he doesn't . . .'

'Darling heart, don't cry. You can't cry here. What if Samantha were to burst in, what if the boys in the studio should see you? We steely independent women are supposed to have our tear ducts extracted along with our first face lift. Come on, dearest, deep breath, stiff upper lip. Mustn't let the side down, mustn't undermine the credibility of the sisterhood, must we?'

Slithering from my desk, she went to the door and ostentatiously locked it. Then she lit a cigarette, which she proffered to me, together with my cup of cold coffee. I delved in my handbag for a tissue and blew my nose.

'That's better, dear. Can't have everyone thinking you're coming down with a nasty attack of PMT. Besides, maybe it's all for the best. Frankly, from what Jamie-Beth and I have seen of Mr Single, he simply wasn't worthy of you.'

'Mel, Gilda. His name is Mel. And he's the nicest, gentlest, most honest person I've ever met – I don't give a stuff what you and Jamie-Beth think.'

'Then why has he left you, darling heart? If he's so gentle and honest? Why has he cast you aside like last year's designer watch strap?'

'I don't know. He said – Oh God, I don't know. He said it wasn't what he wanted.'

'There you are. Typically male. Makes an all-singing, all-dancing production out of what he wants. But what about you? You get a non-speaking part in the chorus.'

'Mel isn't typically male, Gilda. Mel isn't typical of anything.'

'So you say, darling heart. But don't we all have a tendency to recreate the person we love in our own image. To you he's Sir Galahad on roller skates. But to us impartial observers he might come over as a trifle bossy, not to say domineering.'

255

'Mel is not bossy!'

'No, dearest, of course not. Telling you when to leave the dinner table isn't bossy. Or telling you who to be friends with. Or how to think, when to breath.'

'You don't know anything about him, Gilda.'

'What about your painting, for instance? He even had the nerve to interfere with that. Remember that study you put so much work into – the mysterious trio on the park bench? Jamie-Beth said she'd never seen a more accurate depiction of the isolated female psyche, drawn to and yet struggling to reject the conformity of gender stereotypes. But when Mel came along and said he didn't like it you abandoned it instantly – just threw it away, one of the best things you've ever done.'

'I valued his criticism.'

'You let him trample you underfoot. And then, when he'd finished making porridge of your identity, he got bored and went away.'

'That isn't why he went. It was because I – because – Oh, I don't understand why. I just don't understand him . . .'

I gave up any attempt not to cry, turning my head aside, dripping steadily and unashamedly over the invoices.

'But what is there to understand, darling heart?' said Gilda. 'He left because he's a man. Men like to screw, but they hate to be screwed down. In case you hadn't noticed, they have this serious allergy to commitment.'

'Mel wanted commitment. We were – we were going to get married.'

'Well, there you are, dear. He cut and ran before his feet got frostbite.' She placed a consoling hand upon my shoulder. 'Never mind. A few days of ritual mourning and you'll wake up realizing how lucky you are to have been spared a lifetime bolstering The Wilting Willy. Your Auntie Gilda's been married, darling heart, you take her word for it. He may clean the bath

256

now, but the moment he's ringed you like a barnacle goose –'

I shook off her hand. 'Shut up, Gilda,' I said. 'Just shut up!'

'Darling, I'm only speaking to you as your dearest, possibly your closest friend –'

'Just go away. Go and fall upon one of your own Charles Jourdan stilettos. Or better still, throttle yourself with those preposterous pearls!'

She slid abruptly from my desk, snatching up her coat and bag. At the door she paused, breathing huffily. 'I despair of the sisterhood sometimes, I truly do. What price friendship, what price solidarity, if all it takes to burst the bubble is one small prick?'

I had scorched my way from Soho across Covent Garden like a flash fire, devouring the shops in my path, until I could recall only dimly acquiring my first carrier bag and was, in any case, already bored with its contents. Long Acre and the Piazza were crammed with Christmas shoppers, noisy, ill-disciplined dilettantes who hovered in shop doorways and cluttered up sales counters, indecisive as Sunday drivers. I swooped down Garrick Street, across St Martin's Lane and into the relative calm of Charing Cross Road. My bags burdened me, the handles constricting the blood in my fingers; with the onset of pins and needles came the inevitable first twinges of guilt.

Mel would not like the wide bookmaker's-check trousers with their severe, short-waisted jacket, nor would he care for the cream-and-black polka-dot culottes (any more, on second thoughts, than I did). But he would approve of the velvet-collared redingote, the black leather jodhpurs, the clinging lycra cat-suit and the wader boots. And he would be bound to admire the tiny pearl-grey jersey dress with its low neck and ruched skirt, particularly if he saw it with the matching suede stilettos. I wondered what he would think of the cocktail hat.

I did not, strictly speaking, have much occasion to wear a cocktail hat. But they had been there when, exasperated beyond measure by the Sunday drivers, I had dived for escape into that hitherto unexplored shop off Neal Street: hats like chocolate éclairs, hats in the shape of Valentine hearts or liquorice allsorts, a cloud of a hat on which tiny putti gambolled, a pillbox where a sequinned mackerel swam in a river of veiling. They had been there, a whole wall of them, like a challenge; and, catching the mackerel's beaded eye, I saw at once how it would lift the grey jersey dress, elevate it from the interesting to the dramatic. The price tag made me flinch – but, after all, here was not so much a hat as art work. I knew if I tried it on I should be lost. My hand reached out as if through some involuntary spasm. I surveyed my reflection, tilting my head, peering coyly through the veiling. Discreet pearl ear studs, grey gloves, perhaps, with my rings worn over them? I reached for my credit card, felt the adrenalin coursing as my trophy was carefully wrapped in tissue paper. Would Mel think it was over the top, yet another of my disguises? But Mel would not see it. Even as I signed the Visa slip, my excitement faltered, I felt the drab, toothachey pain take over. Mel would not see the leather jodhpurs or the cat suit or the wader boots. I was entirely free to wear a mackerel cocktail hat, or laddered tights, or a polythene garbage bag, Mel would not see or even know about it.

I was warmed by a comforting spark of anger. Who did he think he was, anyway, to approve or disapprove? Perhaps I had been a little harsh with Gilda. Hadn't I simply been blinded by his gentleness, coaxed into ignoring the desire for control beneath it? Oh, he had pretended to be easy-going, to respect my space, to view me as a separate and equal individual. But hadn't he, all the same, been just as bossy as she had said he was, criticizing me, manipulating me, insisting that I should take account of what he wanted? The painting of the Madrid trio, for instance – wasn't that proof? I had hauled it from the mantelpiece and studied it in the light of Jamie-Beth's comments; and yes, though it needed a great deal more work, I thought I could see how I could save it. Wasn't she right about the female figures, the plump, spider greed of the stereotype wife and the exquisite loneliness of the waif-like girl, valiantly asserting her independence? Wasn't it in the male figure that the flaw was located? Beside the two women, he seemed insubstantial, bereft of identity and purpose. If I could somehow bring his stilted lines to life, rescue him from the one-dimensional, endow him with motive . . . I seized a brush, dipped it in paint and began to redraw the outline of his shoulder and the angle of his head. But no, it required more thought. Still, now that I was free, no longer inhibited or criticized, I should have plenty of time to bestow on it.

Oh yes, there were virtues in being my own person again. No one stole my shampoo or left soggy flannels in the soap dish, I need no longer lay in stocks of tuna fish and bananas. I could forage for chocolate digestives at four in the morning, festoon the bathroom with any amount of dirty underwear, slum around all day in a T-shirt and ski socks if I wanted to. I had regained possession of my side of the bed and Mabel was once again permitted access, curling oppressively in the crook of my neck or making wild forays beneath the sheets where, dribbling, purring, she would nibble my toes or rub herself passionately against my buttocks like an importunate tea cosy.

Yet – tactless Mabel – she did not seem satisfied with the resumption of her bedtime routine. She would keep looking for Mel, squatting disconsolately on his chair in the sitting room, sniffing vainly under cupboards and tables. Sometimes she would sit for hours beside her ping-pong ball as if waiting forlornly for him to throw it. On other occasions she would occupy the hall, her eyes glowering, her stance obstinate, and set up a drawn-out banshee wailing, till I felt like crouching down and howling with her. It did not matter how many times I rehearsed Gilda's view that I had enjoyed a lucky escape: the pain was there, a pain impervious to alcohol or aspirin.

My friends, too, had proved on the whole unsympathetic. Gilda, though I had apologized, was still distant and huffy. Chrissie had treated the news of Mel's departure as though it were her own personal tragedy and Ambrose had refused to be drawn, remarking only on the continued availability of Sergei's anarchist bank manager. I did not know whether Ambrose and Sergei had seen or talked to Mel. Certainly he had vanished from the pubs and restaurants where I might have anticipated bumping into him. Oh, I would imagine I saw him sometimes, feel my legs shaking as I crossed a street or entered a crowded bar; but it was always some other tall man with tangled hair and a long black overcoat, turning an unfamiliar face to mock my raw stomach.

Trudging down Broadwick Street with my carrier bags, taking a circuitous route to avoid Old Compton Street and the Patisserie Valerie, I felt once again the desire to sit down, just where I was, and yowl like Mabel. A fine drizzle had begun to fall, blotching my mascara and gluing my fringe to my forehead. Glancing into plate glass to check the extent of my disintegration, I observed that a new shop had opened. 'Evening Dresses for Sale or Hire.' The window seemed promising. There was no harm in going in – just to look round.

The carrier bags occupied two-thirds of the sofa. Seated at my desk, sipping stewed coffee, I tried to add up exactly how much I had spent. It would, of course, have been the work of moments to perform this task with my calculator. But somehow the trial and error of mental

260

arithmetic, the struggle, the false starts, the sudden painful recollection of bills not yet accounted for seemed more appropriate to the occasion, both a recognition of my guilt and a fitting penance.

It was true that I had not needed a new evening dress. I had only one black tie invitation this Christmas, the Maestro Movies party, for which I had firmly intended to recycle last year's frock. But, well – net bubble skirts already looked so terribly dated; and besides, once I had tried on the strapless sheath in petrol lurex with its clinging skirt swirling into a 1950s' fish tail – well, it was meant to be, or why else should the only one in the shop be precisely my size? It was true, also, that I need not have bought the matching long-sleeved bolero jacket, but then if I was spending the money (and it was really not so much for a one-off evening dress), wasn't it a false economy to skimp? The long black gloves, of course, had been a must (very Jean Harlow) and when I had seen the shoes – oh, I knew I had nine pairs of black heels in my shoe cupboard, but none in suede as high as these or so entirely perfect. The evening bag, the earrings and the cascade of silver bracelets had followed as a natural consequence of my final trek back to D'Arblay Street. But then detail was important – precisely the right size and weight of earring, the correct balance of heel height with hem. Detail made you feel confident. And Mel had, without doubt, been invited to Maestro Movies. Mel would see me, composed, elegant, roots attended to, lipstick in place. Mel would watch me laughing, flirting, apparently oblivious to his existence. And he would be sorry.

Arriving at a more-or-less accurate total and receiving a sudden vision of my Visa statement, I buried my head in my hands. I felt a profound need to telephone someone. Laura was back in London (Charlie having done the decent thing and moved out to an hotel); it would do me good to talk about the treachery of men to a fellow sufferer, and besides I had not heard from her for a fortnight.

261

The phone rang for some while before Laura at last picked it up. 'Hullo, darling,' she squealed.

'Laura, it's Dee. How are you feeling?'

'Oh, Dee – oh – could you hold on a moment?'

I held on for several moments. 'Sorry about that,' said Laura eventually. 'I'm just showing Mrs Croxley how to make garlic mayonnaise.'

'You sound a bit better. Are you beginning to cope? Are you off the valium yet? Who's Mrs Croxley?'

'My new nanny. She's divine.'

'Oh Laura, I'm so pleased, I think that's really sensible. After all, you've got to regain your self-respect, re-establish your identity. Friends help when you're on your own. But there's nothing like a job to –'

'A job, Dee? Why would I want one of those?'

'Well, now you've got Mrs Croxley to look after the children –'

'Mrs Croxley isn't here so I can become a wage-slave. Mrs Croxley is here so that Charlie and I can have a civilized dinner à deux, like this evening for instance.'

'You mean you're meeting Charlie tonight to discuss the divorce?'

'Divorce? Oh gosh – oh, Dee, I'm sorry, I would have called you, except that so much has happened, first Venice, then I've been rushing around interviewing nannies –'

'So you've decided against a divorce?'

'Why would I divorce someone as wonderful as Charlie? We've been blissfully happy together for over fifteen years?'

'But – but what about squint-eyed suburban Janis?'

'A trivial incident. I was wrong to go overboard about it. Mummy had the children and while Charlie and I were away in Venice we talked the whole thing through. I must say we had the most amazing week – a real second honeymoon. And isn't it splendid how the Grand Canal

262

looks just like a Guardi or a Canaletto, as if life really were imitating art –'

'But what about the treachery, the handkerchiefs, the bonking on boardroom tables?'

'We agreed there were faults on both sides. I have rather let myself go recently, and I've tended to be pre-occupied with the children at Charlie's expense. So now I'm taking aerobics classes and hormone replacement therapy, I've been to Vidal Sassoon for a light perm, Charlie's given me the run of his American Express Card to buy a complete new wardrobe. And then, of course, there's the divine Mrs Croxley –'

'But – well, I mean, don't you worry? After – what happened. Having another woman in the house?'

'Mrs Croxley isn't another woman. She's at least fifty-eight, with a Neville Chamberlain moustache and those sensible shoes with built-in bunions. She's an absolute jewel – got Titus completely potty trained already, if you don't count yesterday's little slip with the weeping fig. But even if she were Kim Bassinger, I know I could trust Charlie.'

I took a deep breath. 'Laura, you told me you could never trust Charlie again.'

'Did I? Well, I expect I was a little overheated at the time. Of course I trust Charlie, Dee. He's not just my husband, he's my best friend.'

Annie Smith had already arrived at the Hyde Park Hotel and was settled by the window, looking out at the premature December dusk. She sported oversized hoop earrings, a lovat jersey tunic and – a daring new development – black, clinging matador pants. Though I liked Annie, I approached the table with a sinking heart. I was not in the mood for another of her disquisitions on the duty of yielding femininity to massage the male ego.

We exchanged pleasantries as we ordered jasmine tea

263

and the full English clotted-cream menu. She appeared unusually perky, batting her eyelids at the waiter, smiling and jangling her silver hoops. I slouched in my chair, heavy with misgiving.

'Well,' I said eventually, 'how did *Bright Lights* go? Did you ever reply to any of the letters?'

She bit into a muffin, tonguing honey indulgently from her fingers. 'Oh, it was interesting, love. Very interesting.'

'I'm afraid I probably lumbered you with a job lot of non-starters – nose pickers and nail biters, every one of them.'

'Oh no, Dee. I learnt quite a bit, I can tell you.'

I eyed her reluctantly. 'You mean you managed to pluck something from the swamp? Your old-fashioned gentleman, your knight in well-cut tweed?'

'Well, yes. And then again, no.'

I raised my eyebrows. 'You remember the one who made disposable toothbrushes?'

'Mr Categories? "Manly yet economically viable." But didn't he bore for Europe, as well as being a practising megalomaniac? And how did he manage to fit you in with all those hobbies?'

'He isn't as bad as he sounds on paper. He's rather helpless really. And as for hang gliding and karate – well, he's a bit stretched by a quick game of tiddlywinks. His name's Cedric.'

'And you and Cedric had a thing together?'

'He's very chivalrous in an old-school-tie, cavalry-corset sort of way.'

'Always punctual, opens doors, treats you like a priceless porcelain figurine?'

'That sort of thing. The first date went quite well, and over three weeks it got so we were seeing each other almost every other day.'

'Very nice for you, Annie,' I said, fixing my scone with a lugubrious eye.

She leant across and put her hand on mine. 'Oh, Dee, love, I must admit I owe you an apology.'

'Do you?' I said, astonished.

'Oh, it was terrible, love. Bloody appalling. He seemed to believe I had cotton wool for brains. I really think if a bill came before Parliament rescinding votes for women, Cedric would be in favour of it. After three weeks of him being patronizing about my job and calling me "petal" and telling me not to bother my little head about anything more weighty than the price of peas – well, I just snapped.'

'Good Lord,' I said.

'Things came to a head when his car upped and died in the middle of nowhere on the M4. I could tell right off it was the alternator. But would he listen? No, Cedric would rather flap around with oily rags, and peer under the bonnet as if he expected to find the secret of the universe there, and order me back in the car in case I messed up my pretty frock. I was tired, I was cold, I was hungry. So in the end I let him have it. I told him if I could come to grips with the avionics of the Jaguar and the Harrier Jump Jet, I could probably diagnose what was wrong with his geriatric Rover.'

'You told him about Andrew?'

'I told him I'd had a sex-change, not a full-frontal lobotomy.'

'And so that was the end of the big romance.'

She sipped her tea, then smiled. 'Well, not altogether. A few days later he wrote saying he'd like to go on seeing me, provided I never breathed word to a living soul about my dark secret. He said he'd fallen in love with me. He said I was the most feminine woman he'd ever met.'

'So you were reconciled, amidst hearts and flowers?'

She chuckled. 'I've learnt my lesson now, Dee love.'

'And you've decided to give up men as a thoroughly bad lot.'

'Well . . .'

She lowered her eyes and I saw with amazement that she was blushing. 'There's this lad in the flat upstairs. We're good friends, he knows all about me. It started with us cooking each other the odd supper – I mean there's not much point cooking for one, is there, going to all that effort? And then – well, you know how it is – he likes fell walking and so do I . . .'

She glanced down at her buttered tea cake with an enigmatic little smile. 'Anyway, enough about me. You haven't told me yet how your lovely Mel is.'

CHAPTER

THIRTEEN

'Gosh,' said the girl with frizzy brown hair, 'it's enough
to put you off the canapes, isn't it?'

The Jasper Garmisch Gallery was combining its
Christmas celebrations with the private view of a North-
ern artist much preoccupied with a concept he called
'Technochasm'. It seemed the realization of Technochasm
involved taking everyday objects – a tea bag, a hamburger,
a dead mouse – photostating them with geometrical
bands of masking tape applied to the glass so as to dissect
and distort the image, and then transmitting them by fax
on a series of disparate time scales to an equally disparate
series of destinations. The work that confronted us, as,
squeezed like toothpaste from the seething epicentre of
the gallery, the frizzy-haired girl and I burst out coin-
cidentally into the calm of the perimeter, juxtaposed a
hand-coloured A2 xerox blow-up of the artist's private
parts with a monochrome A4 fax of the same. A scrawled
legend announced that the elapse of time between the
making of the original stat and the arrival of the fax in
Middlesborough had been a mere five minutes. 'Quick
Dick', the whole was entitled.

'Thing is,' said the frizzy-haired girl, biting emphatically into an asparagus roll, 'you can't really see it, can you, hanging over the mantelpiece in your front room, above the clock and the postcards and the souvenir jug your Auntie Eileen brought back from Harrogate? Or am I missing some essential significance?'

'It says in his résumé that the artist is exploring the dynamic tensions between the objectivity of late-twentieth-century communications systems and the iconography of subjective reality, thus exposing the central human dilemma of the negation of individuation by technological imperialism.'

'Oh,' said the girl, giggling. 'The existential meaning of life? The conflict between being and non-being?'

'Absolutely,' I said.

A bearded man clutching two Kir Royales arrived at her elbow. He looked vaguely familiar – I remembered I had met him once in a pub with The Virgin, seemed to recall he was an art director at The Virgin's agency. The girl grinned as he drew her back into the crush. 'By the way,' she said, over her shoulder, 'I love your hat.'

'Salmon?' asked a male voice to my right. 'Or is it trout?'

Turning, I found a medium-sized, medium-aged man in a brown leather jacket eyeing my veiling.

'Or whiting perhaps, or perch?' His glance moved down to the cleavage revealed by my new pearl-grey dress. 'Or maybe it's a sprat. Out to catch a mackerel.'

'It's a mackerel,' I said, applying my spiky party smile. 'But it's not out to catch a sprat.'

'Oh, good! Very good! Now tell me, are you one of Jasper's starving artists? Or, as the hat suggests, do you put your art into your life?'

With effort, I galvanized myself into vivacity. Mel had not made an appearance at the Maestro Movies party. And now there were a mere seven days until Christmas and everyone but me seemed to have plans. Gilda and Jamie-Beth had been invited to a house party in the country, Laura and Charlie were celebrating the inviolability of the nuclear family, even Annie Smith was sharing a turkey with the man upstairs. I remembered how Mel and I had discussed flying somewhere distant and romantic – Istanbul, Tangiers, Bangkok. Now I supposed I should do the decent thing and join my mother on her trail of neighbourhood sherry parties. In the supermarket I observed with a jaundiced eye couples choosing puddings and crackers together. I had sighted The Scorpion briefly on my arrival at the party and, while we had cut each other stone dead, as was entirely appropriate, this had not served to lighten my depression. Even the sudden reminder of The Virgin had given me a melancholy frisson.

The medium sort of man was called Jonathan and ran an interior design company with his wife. Although he lacked the height that was my usual preference, he had interesting lazy-lidded eyes and a mouth fuller in the lower lip than the upper and slightly unstrung at the corners, which indicated, I thought, a generous sensuality. I could not fail to be aware that he had been talking to me now far longer than party convention required; when he had offered to find us more drinks he had actually returned with them – and in the space of five minutes. I watched myself go through the motions, listening intently, smiling, laughing, taking care to hold his eyes. It seemed only inevitable when he suggested we had seen the best of the party and might perhaps escape for a spot of dinner. I accepted gracefully, enquired after his star sign, and a few moments later excused myself to visit the cloakroom.

The cloakroom was in the basement, through the office and, as I reached it, the frizzy-haired girl was just emerging from the lavatory. We exchanged smiles as she held the door for me. Struggling with my diaphragm, which, as was its wont when I had consumed alcohol, had taken on a rebellious, reptilian life of its own, I felt my mood lighten, succumbed to an irresistible

269

urge to giggle. True, this Jonathan person was married and I had foresworn married men. But hadn't I simply been deceiving myself? Didn't I crave the intrigue, the tensions, the sex in imaginative locations? Didn't I, even now, crouching in this cold lavatory, giggling silently to myself, feel a delicious sizzle of adrenalin, as if I were anticipating an afternoon's shopping? Others might long for the predictable, warts-and-all security of a steady relationship. I was born to be a mistress. It was what I was good at.

I tidied myself, straightened my face and unlocked the lavatory door. The girl with the frizzy hair was still outside, touching up her mascara in the mirror above the washbasin. Absently, I watched her as she wiped away a smear or two from beneath her lower lids. She looked younger than me, probably by a good five or six years and, while she was not pretty exactly – too broad in the cheeks, too snub of the nose – there was an attractive sparkle about her, an air of cheerful mischief. Though she stood aside politely to let me check the tilt of the mackerel, her reflection still hovered at my left shoulder; I was aware of her bright eyes inspecting me with disquieting interest.

'That really is a brilliant hat,' she said at length. 'You aren't by any chance an actress?'

'Thank you,' I said. 'But no, I'm afraid I'm not.'

'Sorry,' she said. 'I thought – you know, what with the hat and everything – I thought if you were an actress I might ask you a favour.'

'Oh?' I said.

'You see, I'm not supposed to be here at all. I'm supposed to be in Birmingham, as a matter of fact, doing a course on psychometrics.'

'Ah,' I said.

'And the thing is – well, my husband's a very jealous man. And he's got this mania about the telephone. Whenever we're apart, even if it's only for an hour or two, he phones me. He phones at least three times a day at work, he phones me at my sister's, at the hairdresser's – he once even called my evening class. Phone, phone, phone – it's like an extension of his left ear. I wish Bell had never invented the bloody thing, really.'

'I can see it's a problem,' I said.

'No kidding. Of course if I'm away for a whole night he goes completely bananas.'

'So he's even now calling your hotel in Birmingham and discovering they've never heard of you?'

'Good grief, no. I've had years of experience. I told him the course was at the university and I'd be staying on campus where there were only pay phones, so he'd never get through to me.'

'Then you're home and dry.'

'Not really. You see, the thing is, if he can't phone me he insists I phone him.' Observing my raised eyebrows, she gave a self-deprecating grin. 'Oh, it seems feeble, I know. But if I don't humour him I bring down The Spanish Inquisition. It got so bad I threw him out for a couple of months last year – but, well, I'm fond of the paranoid idiot. And anyway, now I feel guilty. Daft old thing – if he hadn't kept on about other men, then I might not have wondered what I was missing.'

I recalled the bearded art director, thought of my medium-attractive married man, sipping his Kir Royale, deciding upon a suitable trysting place. I felt a sudden comradeship with the frizzy-haired girl, the bond between fellow conspirators. 'So what was this favour you were going to ask me – if I'd been an actress?'

'I wondered if you'd pretend to be the long-distance operator putting me through on a reversed charge call. You know – just to add authenticity.'

I laughed. 'But won't your husband smell a nest of rodents when he gets the telephone bill?'

She, too, was laughing. 'He never even sees the phone bill. If I left it to him the gas, the electricity, everything would be cut off. He's great on the ozone layer and Third

271

World Debt. But try him on something complicated like boiling a kettle and he goes to pieces.'

'I used to know a guy like that. Some days even his fly buttons presented a heavy-duty problem.'

'Sounds like a dead ringer for my old man.' She smiled at me coaxingly. 'Will you do it then, if I give you the number? Just tell him it's his wife calling from Birmingham.'

I paused for a few moments to think myself into the role. Then I gave her my Samantha impersonation with a nasal overlay of Brummegen.

She skipped up and down delightedly. 'Fantastic! Oh, he'll go overboard for it. We can use one of those phones outside, I'm sure no one will mind. Oh, just looking at you I knew you'd be brilliant.'

We waited, giggling, in the office while two departing guests retrieved their coats. Then I took the slip of paper on which she had written her home number, composed myself and dialled.

After three rings, a man's voice, breathless and slightly agitated, stuttered: 'H-hullo?' I paused. There was something unaccountably familiar about both the voice and the agitation. But the frizzy-haired girl was raising her eyebrows anxiously. I pressed on.

'Hull-o-o, caller. Are you 233–5478? I have your wife on the line, calling long distance and asking to reverse the charges. Will you accept the call?'

'Oh. Oh, right. Yes. Put her on. Right.'

This time, there was no doubt about the voice. I turned to stare in bewilderment at the frizzy-haired girl, who was making questioning gestures. I managed to nod, to mutter: 'Putting you through now, caller', before numbly handing her the receiver. I watched as she settled beside the telephone, assuming an expression of breezy innocence.

'Hullo darling, it's Rosemary. How are you? How's The Dog? . . . Oh dear, has he? . . . Well, you shouldn't have let him, you know sausages bring on his eczema . . .'

272

I wondered how I could have been so slow. Telephone mania, the ozone layer, fly buttons – even the obvious clue of the bearded art director. I heard The Virgin saying: 'I'd better phone Rosemary. I've given Rosemary your home number so she can call me. You don't understand, my wife's a very jealous woman.' Watching the frizzy-haired girl chattering happily, laughing, twining the telephone flex in her fingers, I tried to reconcile the image with my mind's-eye Rosemary, the vengeful harridan wielding the upholstery mallet. I itched to interrogate her, about the mallet and the Tummy Trainer and Visionary Video, and about the time she had thrown him out, the time he had told me he'd left her. I felt my head crackle with an electric storm of unaskable questions. Yet it all seemed so obvious now. How could I have heard only what I wanted to hear? How could I have listened to The Virgin all those months and taken every word literally, never once read the sub-text?

In a daze, I drifted towards the stairs. As I reached the door I turned to look back at her. She waved at me brightly. Up in the gallery the noise and heat hit me like a blast from a blow torch. I paused, reeling, blinking about me stupidly. Here, too, it was as if a new director had arrived on the set and changed all the camera angles. Faces seemed subtly transformed, their contours redrawn, their expressions alien. Chance snatches of conversation were all at once fraught with new layers of meaning. Even the gallery itself seemed smaller, seedier, frowzy with smoke and sweat and over-turned glasses.

My medium married man was still standing near 'Quick Dick', waiting for me. As if wading through water, I progressed slowly towards him. I focused upon him care-fully. He, too, looked changed, unfamiliar, as if we had never indulged in our half-hour's flirtation.

He smiled at me.

I made to smile back. But, instead, I heard my voice

273

saying: 'I'm afraid I've got to go home, I can't make dinner.'

It stayed with me somehow, nagging at me like physical discomfort. Oh, of course I tried to dismiss the whole episode as yet another instance of male dishonesty, The Virgin telling me lies to string me along and protect his ego. But all the same, how could I have so misinterpreted things, how could I not have perceived that there might be two sides to the story? I found myself looking about me warily, distrusting my own understanding. I was reminded of a picture in a puzzle book: at first sight it looks like the face of an old crone, her nose curving towards her chin; but take a second look and the image magically changes into the head of a young woman, her hair piled high, her neck turning so that only the contour of her cheekbone is visible. Once you perceive the second image it is nearly impossible to recover the first.

I thought of Mel, often and with pain. Wandering aimlessly into the studio I stood before the easel and heard him say: 'Funny how second thoughts kill.' I saw the Madrid painting clearly now, saw it as he saw it – the female figures stiff with overwork, the male figure an unconvincing shadow, the whole concept crippled at birth and now entombed beneath crusts of paint like geological strata. 'You're after scalps,' he'd said. I saw his face as he'd mumbled goodbye, saw Alex, grey and sick, when at last I'd made him hit me, saw my father thumping the armchair with his fist, muttering: 'Have you no compassion?' I saw my father's teeth bared in the little protective smirk.

The phone rang and a tremor of false hope set my legs shaking. But it was only my mother, calling to finalize the Christmas arrangements. We talked purposelessly for a while. Then a thought occurred to me. 'How's Bill?' I said. 'You haven't mentioned him recently.'

'Who, dear?'

'Bill. Your Don Giovanni from the Gas Board.'

'I gave him the push, Dee, weeks ago.'

'Good for you.'

'He turned out to have a nasty problem with sweaty feet. And besides, he wasn't a patch on your father.'

I paused, uncertain I had heard her correctly. 'Mother, you couldn't stand Father.'

'I was sometimes a bit hard on him, Deedee. He was a decent man and he did his best for us.'

'All he cared about was his rotten cricket.'

'He loved you, Deedee. He loved us both.'

'Mother, this is ridiculous. You were always about to leave him.'

'You only remember the bad parts, dear. Think of the good times. Remember those lovely holidays we had in the Lake District.'

'You quarrelled constantly about how to light the primus stove.'

'You were always a child for taking things too seriously. All marriages have their ups and downs. Your father's heart was in the right place. It's just that – well, like most men of that generation, he didn't know how to show his feelings. But he was a good husband and a good father, he loved us both in his way.'

I paused again, speechless. 'But Mother, you told me . . . What about the herring?'

'What herring?' my mother said.

'Good heavens, Dee,' said Chrissie, 'am I interrupting you in the act of murder?'

I set the axe aside on the hall table. 'I've been down to the dustbins. I was chopping something up.'

She drifted towards the studio while I went to fetch the gin bottle. I found her standing in front of the empty easel.

'I know it wasn't one of your best paintings. But taking an axe to it – I mean, aren't you carrying self-criticism a little far?'

275

'I just wanted to get rid of it. I couldn't stand looking at it an instant longer.'

We exchanged gift-wrapped parcels and discussed the hazards of parental Christmases. Mabel appeared from the airing cupboard to show her appreciation of Chrissie's present to her, a furry spider on an elastic string. We watched her chase it, wash it, tear off several of its legs and finally lose it behind a pile of canvases.

Chrissie straightened her shoulders, drew herself up as if she had something of great moment to communicate. Then she hesitated. Setting her lips together, she transferred her glance once more to Mabel, who was now rolling over with her legs in the air, pretending to be carpet fluff.

'What?' I said.

'I saw Mel yesterday.'

I paused in the act of lifting my glass, lowering it carefully into my lap with both hands. 'Oh?' I said, indifferently.

'I went out for dinner and he was there in the restaurant.'

'Oh.' I kept my glass where it was. 'Who was he with?'

'Another man. And a blond girl.'

'A blonde? Was she – I suppose she was nice looking?'

Chrissie described Mel's dinner companions. I took a grateful gulp of my gin. 'That's only Zig Zigeuner and his PA, Julie.'

'It was great to see him – Mel, that is. He came over and talked to me for about ten minutes, asked me about the flat and my insurance claim and what I was doing for the holidays. And when he was leaving he came over again to say goodbye. And – he said would I wish you Happy Christmas.'

She was looking at me expectantly.

'That's nice,' I said.

'Oh, Dee –'

'Well, what do you want me to say? Did he ask after me, did he express any interest in how I was doing?'

'Not exactly, but –'

'Did he say he was missing me, that he couldn't live without me, that he regretted going?'

'No, Dee. But –'

'No. He just wished me the season's greetings as if I were the dustmen or the paper boy. And you expect me to get excited.'

Chrissie's eyes returned to her gin. She sighed. 'Oh Dee, he looked so sad. He said: "Wish Dee Happy Christmas for me, will you?" and he looked so sad when he said it.'

I, too, glanced away.

'Couldn't you call him? Couldn't you just call him?'

'No.'

'You could ring him up to wish him Happy Christmas back. You could try, and see what happens –'

'No. No, Chrissie, I can't.' Bending to stroke Mabel, who was weaving herself about my legs, I moved my hand blindly, fought to steady my voice. 'You don't understand. He was right to go. I thought I loved him, but it turns out I didn't know how to. I never have. Not properly, not ever.'

After she had gone, Mabel jumped on my lap, as she always does when I cry, purring beseechingly and shoving her nose into my face. 'Poor Mabel,' I said, pushing against the thrust of her head so that her ears were flattened and her eyes showed their whites squintily. 'Poor Mabel. It really is just you and I against the world. Poor old Mabel.'

It's easy to love Mabel. All that's required is that I open the cat food tins on time and pet her occasionally and look to make sure she's not shut in the airing cupboard. She doesn't require sensitivity or unselfishness or generosity of feeling to earn her kneading, ecstatic paws. Cuddling her vibrating body as she squeezed her nose under my arm, settling there, head invisible, a furry rump, I wondered if Mabel were all I ever could love. It seemed to me that there was only one human being more dangerous than the

277

person who is perpetually on guard against pain; and that was the person blind to her own power to inflict pain on others. Perhaps, all things considered, I had better restrict myself to Mabel.

RADIO DJ: Hi there, and a great big welcome to our weekly personal problems phone-in, The Agony and the Empathy. For the next three hours you emotional cripples listening at home will be able to call our panel of experts here in the studio and bore them senseless with your trivial hang-ups. And today's experts are – everyone's favourite Agony Auntie, the delicious Angela, of Angela Advises –

ANGELA: Hullo there, lovies.

DJ: And an eminent psychiatrist.

PSYCHIATRIST: Good evening.

DJ: And our first caller – do we have our first caller? – yes, we do, it's Dee of Battersea.

ANGELA: Oh Jesus!

PSYCHIATRIST: This is all we needed.

DJ: Hi, Dee babes, what's your problem?

CALLER: My problem is –

ANGELA: Lovey, haven't you been in touch with me before?

PSYCHIATRIST: And me too. I think you have written a large number of letters.

CALLER: My problem is –

ANGELA: Your problem is, you don't listen, lovey. I've told you all men are bastards.

PSYCHIATRIST: I've told you that you have defective libidinal development and dry rot in your super-ego.

278

ANGELA:	I've advised her to take up Bargello.
PSYCHIATRIST:	I've advised her to kill herself.
ANGELA:	I've recommended Flamenco Dancing.
PSYCHIATRIST:	I've suggested Prussic acid.
ANGELA:	Or she could try Tai Chi.
PSYCHIATRIST:	Or hara-kiri.
ANGELA:	Or breeding goldfish for companion-ship.
PSYCHIATRIST:	Or Black Widow spiders.
ANGELA:	You've got to get out there and make the best of things, lovey. So you're an ugly, unlovable, self-obsessed bore? Send for my pamphlet 'It Takes One to Know One', which will help you meet people with whom you've got lots in common. Put yourself about, introduce yourself to your neigh-bours –
PSYCHIATRIST:	Or your local Mad Strangler.
ANGELA:	Take long healthy walks –
PSYCHIATRIST:	In the fast lane of the M25.
ANGELA:	Or, if all else fails, I've told you before, build a relationship with the one who truly loves you. Masturbate, lovey. Don't be embarrassed or inhib-ited. Go ahead, masturbate.
CALLER:	But you don't understand. My prob-lem is –
DJ:	Now, Dee babes, let the experts get a word in edgeways.
PSYCHIATRIST:	This caller's problem is that she does-n't comprehend the organization and self-discipline it takes to commit felo de se. Do you realize most suicides give it less forethought than killing the weeds on their lawn.
ANGELA:	This caller's problem is she doesn't

	know when she's well off. If she's got no further use for this hunky ex-boy-friend of hers, perhaps she could send me his phone number. My own social life's on a bit of a downer at the moment, and maybe he and I could –
CALLER:	I –
DJ:	Quickly, Dee baby, we're running out of time.
CALLER:	My problem is I let you into my head in the first place. My problem is I swallowed all your quick-fix theories and your simple folk remedies for avoiding pain. Oh, I loved your handy cop-outs and your painting-by-numbers vision of the universe. My problem is you're such easy listening –
DJ:	Dee, babes, I think you've had your say –
CALLER:	And you've had yours, lovies. Because I'm switching you off. I'm switching you off and tuning in to another wavelength. I'm switching you off right n . . .

CHAPTER

FOURTEEN

As I trudged towards D'Arblay Street through a murky drizzle, London wore the dismantled air that always descends the last working day before Christmas. The shoppers have gone, and the office girls in their party glitter; those who can are truanting, contemplating motorway jams as they bus fractious children to chilly cottages in Gloucestershire or Suffolk; those who remain are hunched in their offices, nursing their hangovers and thinking about drinking, or drinking already, needing the kick start to get through to lunchtime – even supposing there is anyone left to lunch with: so that, through the streets of Soho, in deserted shops, over piled plastic bags containing tinsel and cards already put out for the dustmen, a dismal silence prevails, as if someone had just announced the end of the world.

At The Casting Couch Bert Goldoni was interviewing Marilyn Monroe lookalikes. Plump Marilyns from her early *Asphalt Jungle* period nibbled their finger nails, sequinned *Some Like It Hot* Marilyns pouted into hand-bag mirrors, *Seven Year Itch* Marilyns in circular skirts hovered lamely, waiting for the transforming gust from an air vent. A scream of perfume rose above the soothing base–notes of smoke and stewed coffee; a whimper of panic quivered beneath the feverish comradely chatter; eyes widened, smeared lips trembled, fingers drifted self-consciously to imperfectly-disguised pimples. In this raw sea of femininity, Samantha gleamed like a jagged iceberg. Her suede hair now dyed a fierce red, her mouth a gash, her peachy-sweet girl-next-door make-up exchanged for aggressive pallor, she rose from behind her immaculately tidy desk, glinting with efficiency.

'Good morning, Dee,' she breezed. 'I thought since this is our last booking before the holidays we ought to throw a little party. I've invited the whole gang from here, of course, and a couple of casting directors and the crowd from Maestro Movies. Ambrose is coming, need I say, with Sergei. And Bert'll join us when he's finished with the Norma Jeans. 11.30 a.m., mulled wine and mince pies. If that's all right by you. It's under control, I've organized everything.'

Grunting my assent, I fetched a coffee and retreated to my office, resolutely closing the door. I unpacked my cigarettes and my fountain pen. I found sheets of clean white paper and shuffled them into a neat block on my desk. I sat down. I took the phone off the hook. I removed the cap of my pen and, bracing myself before the top sheet of paper, scrawled the words: 'Dearest Mel . . .'

I paused. I sipped my coffee, stared at the paper, laid my cigarette in the ashtray. Closing my eyes, I lowered my head slowly until it was buried in my arms.

A knock at the door jerked me upright again. Samantha entered, clutching in one scarlet-taloned hand a white envelope. Retrieving my cigarette, I hastily covered my pad with my handbag.

'If it's about the party again, Samantha, I've said it's OK.'

She seemed to lose confidence, as though reverting for a moment to her old persona. 'No, er, Dee – it's not the party.'

She lowered her eyes, fiddling with the zip of her new biker's jacket. I searched for something to say to break the silence. 'I suppose you'll be looking forward to Christmas. I expect you have a big get-together, don't you, with all your relatives?'

'It's a bit of a drag, really. My relatives are pretty seriously boring. But at least it's the last time. I'm getting a flat of my own in the New Year, sharing with Zoë – you know, Rodney Peacock's assistant.'

'Oh. Well, that'll be good. I expect you'll be more central.'

'I mean, if I'm going to strike out, find myself, I can't do it, can I, with my Dad thinking I've got mashed potatoes for brains and my Mum snooping around like a CIA agent?'

'No,' I said. 'I don't suppose you can.'

'I mean, I'm nearly twenty-five, I'll soon be thirty. But you gave me good advice, Dee, I really listened to you and I'm seriously grateful. It's not too late for me to maximize my potential. Which is why' – marching over to my desk, she suddenly thrust the white envelope at me – 'which is why I'm handing in my resignation.'

'Oh,' I said.

'Don't get me wrong, Dee, I've been happy working here, you've been ever so kind to me. But what I need now is more of a challenge, a career opportunity. And Julie, Zig's PA, is leaving in February, so I'm taking her place. I know I'll have to put in some time typing and fetching coffee, but Zig says if I show commitment I'll soon get made up to assistant producer. And after that, well, there's a rumour Zig's producer's leaving because of his nerves, so who knows, if I really work at it . . . Of course, eventually I'd like to start my own company, take on a couple of directors, maybe open up a second office in Los Angeles, expand out of commercials into documentaries and features –'

283

'Hold on,' I said, laughing. 'You're making my head spin.'

'I've got it in me, Dee, I know I've got it in me. I'm taking Accountancy evening classes and I've been on this course of weekend seminars on Women in Business. You opened my eyes, Dee, you really did. If you hadn't said what you said, I'd still be trapped by gender stereotypes, still searching for my own identity. Six years I wasted with that ignorant slob Wayne, can you imagine?'

'You'll find someone else,' I said. 'You'll settle down and be happy.'

'You've got to be joking. I've had men, Dee, up to here. They do nothing but cause you grief and bring you down. They can just forget it – unless they're old and rich with a spot of angina. I'm in it for me now, and no creep in trousers is going to dump on me, I'm travelling first class all the way. And it's thanks to you, Dee, for setting me straight.'

I wanted to tell her to beware. I wanted to explain that revenge was not so sweet nor life so simple, to remind her of her Auntie Sandra and the flat smelling of cat's pee. But, looking at the determined set of her biker's shoulders, I realized it was useless. Instead, I congratulated her and said that, while I was sorry to be losing her, I wished her well.

By noon party guests were mingling with the last of the Norma Jeans and my letter to Mel had reached its eighth draft. I floated, head anchored to my desk, on a tide of crumpled paper and empty coffee cups. I did not know, given the vagaries of the holiday mail, when Mel would receive the letter, whether he were even in London, whether, when at last it reached him, he might not simply discard it unopened. But I knew I must write it, put it in the post, now, today, while I had the strength. Ambrose had already poked his head round my door to grimace at the mulled wine, a drunken gofer from Maestro Movies

284

had burst in with mistletoe and been summarily ejected by Samantha: soon I should be obliged to graft on my party smile and sally out amongst the balloons and end-of-term streamers.

With a sigh, I levered myself upright and fumbled through my crumpled failures. Three had faltered at the second line, one I had cried over, blotching the ink irretrievably, most combined pomposity and grovelling in equal measure. I scanned my eighth and last attempt; it read like a Government Health Warning on a cigarette packet. I hurled it into the waste-paper basket. Then I took a deep breath, closed my eyes and emptied my mind.

Picking up my pen for the ninth time, I wrote the first words that came:
SELF-CENTRED BLONDE IDIOT (41 going on 14) seeks forgiving, infinitely patient man to teach her how to love . . .